TEN DAYS IN MAY

by Maxine Sarr

Ten Days in May

© 2017 Maxine Sarr

Ten Days in May is dedicated to every Manchester United Football Club supporter- past, present and future.

My overwhelming gratitude goes to Bernardo Celis, Kristel Ralston, Irene Garcia Hurtado, Michaela Steinhauser and Jens Wűller for their support throughout the writing of this book and beyond. I wouldn't have been able to write it without you.

Maxine Sarr

The twenty-five dead men, who, I believe, watched three football matches, along with so many, over ten days in May 1999.

Geoff Bent
Roger Byrne
Eddie Colman
Duncan Edwards
Mark Jones
David Pegg
Tommy Taylor
Liam (Billy) Whelan

Walter Crickmer
Tom Curry
Bert Whalley
Willie Satinoff

Sir Matt Busby
Johnny Berry
Jackie Blanchflower
Jimmy Murphy
Dennis Viollet

Alf Clarke
Donny Davies
George Follows
Tom Jackson
Archie Ledbrooke
Henry Rose
Eric Thompson
Frank Swift

The Flowers of Manchester

One cold and bitter Thursday in Munich, Germany,
Eight great football stalwarts conceded victory.
Eight men will never play again who met destruction there.
The flowers of English football, the flowers of Manchester
Matt Busby's boys were flying, returning from Belgrade.
This great United family, all masters of their trade,
The pilot of the aircraft, the skipper Captain Thain,
Three times they tried to take off and twice turned back again.
The third time down the runaway disaster followed close,
There was slush upon that runway and the aircraft never rose.
It ploughed into the marshy ground, it broke, it overturned,
And eight of the team were killed as the blazing wreckage burned.
Roger Byrne and Tommy Taylor who were capped for England's side,
And Ireland's Billy Whelan and England's Geoff Bent died,
Mark Jones and Eddie Colman, and David Pegg also,
They all lost their lives as it ploughed on through the snow.
Big Duncan, he went too, with an injury to his brain,
And Ireland's brave Jack Blanchflower will never play again,
The great Matt Busby lay there, the father of his team
Three long months passed by before he saw his team again.
The trainer, coach and secretary, and a member of the crew,
Also eight sporting journalists who with United flew,
and one of them Big Swifty, who we will ne'er forget,
the finest English 'keeper that ever graced the net.
Oh, England's finest football team its record truly great,
its proud successes mocked by a cruel turn of fate.
Eight men will never play again, who met destruction there,
the flowers of English football, the flowers of Manchester

KEEP THE RED FLAG FLYING HIGH

United's flag is deepest red
It shrouded all our Munich dead
Before their limbs grew stiff and cold
Their heart's blood dyed it's every fold
Then raise United's banner high
Beneath its shade, we'll live and die
So keep the faith and never fear

We'll keep the Red Flag flying here.
We'll never die, we'll never die
We'll never die, we'll never die
We'll keep the Red flag flying high
'Cos Man United will never die

CHAPTER ONE

Up Above on the clouds, all anyone can see up above is a blue difficult to define. Some have described it as Cerulean, others Cobalt blue, regardless of the shade whenever a flash of gold streaked across the sky, a new soul had transitioned. The feeling it evoked followed by the thought– is it somebody I know?

Over the years the Munich twenty-three had split into the Munich twenty and the Munich three. The natural break came within three years of their arrival Up Above; the Munich three found loved ones and settled on different clouds.

Willie Satinoff, although he had family and friends on other clouds chose, as in life, to remain close to the Busby Babes. He spent a great deal of time with them in the beginning, his presence helped them adjust to life Up Above.

The transition for everyone including the journalists, Walter Crickmer, Tom Curry and Bert Whalley was made easier in their company. In the first decade, they spent time together out of shock, later out of a sense of camaraderie. Over the years, as their families joined them, they only saw each other on match days.

Skies were bright, sunnier than days Down Below. The Manchester rain that most had grown to know and love was now a thing of the past. Up Above with billowy clouds, the weather was always the same.

The clouds, before becoming the homes of souls, were not standard. Red Cloud became Red Cloud within seconds; a cloud for those that died that day to acclimatise and *find their feet*. On Red Cloud, wild meadows covered with primroses, yellow buttercups, red poppies, silver lakes, tall flowering trees and so much more

Willie had developed a pre-match tradition different from the one he had practised Down Below. It was something he treasured. Everyone has their own form of match day ritual that, to others, seem strange, but not to the doer.

He took off his tweed suit jacket and carried it on his right shoulder. Willie drew in deep the heady aroma of stargazer lilies then started on a slow ramble through the meadows, eyes alighted on voles and salamanders. Butterflies and moths swooped in and out of the cocksfoot grass and flowers, vying for his attention. Parakeets and macaws delivered a soundtrack that was unobtrusive and, in fact, quite melodic. This part of the walk led to a serene lake, populated by pink flamingos.

Willie sauntered clockwise around the lake, his eyes alert for the second favourite part of his pre-match day tradition; the Red Admiral butterflies came to flutter around his head. Smiling, he sat against a weeping willow with golden yellow foliage the colour of the sun. Willie closed his eyes and listened for the rustle in the fallen leaves behind him. He had only to wait three minutes.

"Well, hello Caspar, hello Tigger; you've left it a bit late." Willie accepted, as an apology, nuzzles to his ribs. Caspar and Tigger, two Caspian tigers, began to nip at his black shoes and pull at his shoelaces.

"Oh, you want to play?"

The tigers began to wrestle each other at his feet; they looked to him in anticipation.

"It'll have to be later. I've got a couple of football matches to watch." Willie stroked their heads, put on his jacket and set off for the valley.

It was Sunday, 16 May 1999. Willie ran up a hill from the lake, his eyes sparkled and excitement flittered in his stomach. At the top he unbuttoned his jacket and threw his arms wide, eyes closed and head back, face pointed upwards. He took deep breaths and his mind went, as it often did on match days, to how supporters Down Below must be feeling. He slowly brought his focus to the here and looked into the valley below, to the pitch.

Two hours before every Manchester United Premiership game Down Below, it had become a tradition to get the Babes together for a four-a-side game. Tom Curry and Walter Crickmer were the managers and Bert Whalley, the referee.

Jimmy Murphy's arrival, in 1989, caused Tom and Walter to get prepared for any attempt by him to perform a take-over. Fortunately, Jimmy no longer had a desire to sit in a dug-out again. The first game after his arrival he sat and revelled in the vision before him. He decided it was his time to sit back and enjoy watching the Babes play.

Willie waved to those milling around the immaculately mown pitch and made his ascent to his seat. In the beginning, he had sat with the journalists but when Johnny Berry arrived they soon found themselves together on the opposite stand. The arrivals of Jackie Blanchflower, Jimmy and Dennis Viollet meant they were increasing in number. Time Down Below was taking its toll.

Dennis, a relatively new arrival Up Above, could not contain his excitement at the prospect of watching his former teammates take to a pitch.

He jumped up and beckoned Willie. "I've kept a seat warm for you. What've you been up to?"

Willie shook Dennis' hand and sat beside him; both heads directed towards the crest of the hill, awaiting the arrival of the teams.

"I've got this routine." He took off his jacket and folded it on the seat in front. "Before watching a United game, you know, I go for a walk, collect my thoughts, that kind of thing. How's everything with you? And more to the point," Willie jerked his chin towards Jackie and Johnny. "What are those two up to?"

Dennis lifted his shoulder in a half-shrug as he stretched his legs in front of him. He concentrated on rotating his ankles as he responded. "Your guess is as good as mine. Do you know, this is my tenth United game here and it's still not sinking in? Do you know what I mean?"

Willie chuckled. "I know exactly what you mean; it was the same for those two." He gestured towards the now silent duo of Jackie and Johnny.

Jackie spun in his seat when he heard Willie's voice. "Sorry, Willie didn't see when you got here." Johnny turned slowly and winked at Willie; his attention returned to the crest of the hill.

Jackie stood and made his way over to Willie and Dennis; he shook Willie's outstretched hand. "We were miles away; jabbering about something or nothing. Been for your pre-match walk?"

"Yeah, I met with Tigger and Caspar underneath a tree." The look of puzzlement on Dennis' face caused Willie to chuckle; he explained. "I've made friends with a couple of Caspian tigers and they've become part of my match day ritual."

"Nice." A wide-eyed Dennis said. "For you, that is, not for me." He shuddered. "I can think of a few more, shall we say, relaxing ways to start a match day."

Tom Curry raised a hand in greeting. "How're things Willie? Come down, have a chat."

Willie descended the stairs and made his way to the green and gold dugout. He shook Tom's hand and waved to Bert and Walter outside the opposite dug-out.

"How are you Tom?" Willie continued without waiting for a response. "I'm excited." He rubbed his hands together. "You can't beat that final championship game of the season feeling, can you?"

"True. I'm not sure the lads are going to put their total concentration on their game today but, we'll give it a go." He bent to lift the kit bag onto the bench, removed the shirts and the never eaten halftime bag of oranges.

Hot dog aromas, mixed with the essence of myrrh, wafted over to other clouds. Fresh cut grass fragrance mingled with nostril-tingling fried onion smells, the sound of sizzling burgers on the grill. The novelty of tasting smells by sticking out the tongue never got old for the inhabitants of any of the clouds.

Today, Red Cloud vibrated in anticipation of the final game of the Premiership season. Energy waves of every shade and hue danced through the trees, the grass, the air; they tickled the hairs on the arms and caressed the faces of everyone.

Willie patted Tom on the back. "Good luck."

He strolled towards Bert and Walter as they looked through an unnecessarily large kit bag. Willie put on a serious face as he put his arms around their shoulders and peered into the bag alongside them.

"What a beautiful day guys, truly beautiful."

Willie had once asked why the need for a kit bag as large as the one Walter had acquired. His response had been, 'you never know'.

His attention distracted, face still in the kitbag, Walter half-acknowledged Willie's presence. "Uh huh; it'd be even better if I could find…"

He pulled his head out of the bag and called over to Tom. "Have you seen the ball, Tom?"

The Red Star Belgrade match ball had been *acquired; h*ow it was acquired was never revealed. It was used at all the match games between the Babes.

Tom looked at Walter; his head cocked to one side, raised an eyebrow and waited for the penny to drop; for Walter to answer his own question. The second the words were out Walter *did* answer his own question.

"Duncan." Walter threw his hands up, in mock despair. One day the match ball would be in its rightful place.

Willie left the managers and the referee to complete their matchday preparations. He climbed the stairs of the stands behind the dugouts to speak to the journalists congregated there.

The journalists had devised, early on, a system of drawing straws to implement a rota. Four journalists would write about the Up Above game and four would write of the game Down Below. It was a fair system.

Newspapers by the Up Above journalists covered every single kick of the game, the image provoking words were a virtual replay for those not in attendance. Red Cloud inhabitants and other interested clouds read of magical moves by Billy, majestic performances by Roger, brave defending by Geoff, clever play by David; evocative words. Friendly competition between the journalists meant substantial superlatives were used in their articles. The four assigned to the game Down Below found their job easier; they were more detached from the players.

Down Below journalism and media had moved on; for George Follows, Tom Jackson and Alf Clarke, not for the better. They considered themselves traditionalists and eschewed new words and new technology. The trio believed pen and notepad were adequate tools of their trade and scoffed at the informal vocabulary that peppered the articles of the *new wave* journalists.

Today, extolling the virtues and brilliance of the Busby Babes game fell to Donny Davies, Henry Rose, Archie Ledbrooke and Tom.

Donny sat with his feet on the bench in front of him, a copy of The Guardian open on his lap. He looked around at his colleagues. "Manchester is buzzing right now. Can you imagine it? Working for a newspaper Down Below when this is unfolding?" His voice exhibited childlike wonderment.

Tom had just finished reading the Manchester Evening News, he slapped it shut and discarded it; he shook his head. "It's a bit sloppy, the internet, or whatever they call, it won't last. People down there are used to the feel and smell of ink on paper, that's how people have gotten their news from when Adam was a lad. Real journalism and journalists will survive it."

Henry and Archie tried not to enter into a discussion with Tom on this subject. They had tried, numerous times, to educate Tom in the marvels of the internet and new technology but gave up their fruitless exercise. Computers, for them, were a beacon of progress. Up Above, they had access to all human events, thoughts, words, emotions and intent ever to have occurred in the past, present or future, but they preferred to revel in the experience of events as and when they occur.

Archie lowered his head. "It's called progress Tom. The world has to move along as developments are made. Anyway," he said as he flexed his fingers. "They'll always need someone on the ground reporting back to the office, so the job of a journalist will be safe."

Tom pursed his lips and remained silent. Today he was amongst the *new wave* and decided to wait until he got to Red Cloud Bar to find *solace* with the *old guard* who shared his passion for pen and ink. He felt confident that time would tell which faction would prove to be correct, and they all had something resembling a lot of time.

***

Willie made his way back over to the stand where Jimmy had now joined Jackie, Johnny and Dennis.

"What's the joke? Hey Jimmy, how are you doing?"

"You know Willie, I'm feeling a little nervous, and I have to say." He rubbed his solar plexus area. "It's like I'm experiencing butterflies. I'm sure it'll be alright on the night, as Dennis Norden says, it's just…"

Willie placed his hand on Jimmy's shoulder, no words necessary to show his empathy, a touch was sufficient.

"Sit yourself down Willie. Is that part of your match day ritual too? Talking to everyone? Are you looking forward to the games?"

Johnny's questions didn't faze Willie. "Not really, not really and yes, I am." He sat sideways on the bench, his leg underneath him. "Tom's not sure the lads will be able to concentrate but I feel it's a good distraction for them."

"They'll be right," Jackie said in a confident manner. "I'm looking forward to it. it will stop me thinking about what's going on Down Below for a bit."

Dennis nodded over to the journalists. "Did they give you the line-up?"

"To be honest, I didn't ask. We'll get the news soon enough, let's just take one game at a time."

***

Bert looked up to see Geoff and Eddie making their way over the hill to the pitch; Eddie talking nine to the dozen. Geoff stopped mid-stride, grabbed onto Eddie's arm and let loose a laugh that emitted from his belly. Following close behind, deep in conversation, were David, Tommy and Mark.

Tommy stopped; his twinkling eyes shot out waves of dancing energy as he ran his fingers through his black curly hair he said. "Today, my friends, is going to be a good day."

Walter covered his mouth with his hand in an attempt to disguise his laughter. The Babes seemed to be wearing a uniform, dark jumper with yellow and gold compass arm patches, jeans and white trainers. He sensed Eddie's influence and laughed out loud; more like a cult than a fashion, he said to himself.

With his hands on his hips, Walter shouted. "Come on lads, where's the rest of you?"

"On their way boss, Roger can't find his boots." Walter knew Eddie knew more about Roger's missing boots than he was saying, he looked skywards and sighed.

Tom threw a practice ball towards Geoff and Tommy. "Start doing some warm-ups until Duncan gets here with the match ball."

The instant they stepped onto the pitch their casual wear transformed into the relevant football strip. He walked backwards; his hands beckoned Tommy to him. Tommy laughed and, as he inched forward, rolled the ball under the studs of his boot and approached the goal Geoff was now defending. He sidestepped, dummied as though to pass to David, spun and took a shot that caressed the post. "These balls go all over the place; I don't know how they do it Down Below," Tommy said.

Geoff retrieved the ball and kicked it back to Tommy. "Practice I suppose. I much prefer the leather. I wonder, if they had the chance to go back to the leather, would they?" He mused.

"In this squad? I don't know." His foot atop the ball, Tommy thought for a second. "I reckon Keano, Denny Irwin, Butt and possibly Scholes; maybe even David Beckham. The rest, I'm not sure, to be honest." He fired the ball into the top right corner of the net Geoff had just vacated.

Tommy stopped the roll of the practice ball, looked up and waved to Duncan, Roger and Billy as they jogged down the hill.

Duncan ran to the edge of the lush green pitch, an impish smile danced across his face. Tommy turned to speak to Tom and Duncan saw an opportunity. He exaggerated creeping forwards and tapped the ball from under Tommy's foot. With grace and balance worthy of a ballet dancer, Duncan spun in a full circle and sliced the ball to Billy.

Tommy stumbled and, as he looked to see who had *fouled* him Duncan held his hands up in mock apology and, in a heartbeat, spun, tackled Billy, kicked the ball up and caught it in his hands. Duncan was in a cheeky mood today.

Eddie flashed his pearly white teeth and danced himself between Duncan and the goal. Duncan dropped the leather and faced Eddie; he fake pawed the ground first with his left foot and then with his right, eyes switching between Eddie and the goal. Eddie shimmied and danced in front of Duncan, he waggled his eyebrows.

Duncan tried but could not contain his laughter. "Is that a new defensive move? Stop me from scoring by mesmerising me with your snake hips?" He stumbled as David kicked the ball from under his foot and put an end to the *dance-off*.

"Oy, it was one on one then," Duncan said.

"I'm bored; I want to get on with the game."

Walter had just finished being interviewed by Archie and Henry. He clapped his hands together three times. "Right, come on, let's get down to business; Roger, David, Mark, Duncan, over here." They danced, jogged and frolicked their way over to the red and white dugout.

After several years of *discussion* between the teams (both wanted to be called Busby Babes), The Omnipotent One had settled the dispute. Newton Babes Football Club, managed by Walter played in red and white shirts and black shorts. Heath Babes Football Club played in white shorts and green and gold shirts were managed by Tom.

Geoff, Tommy, Billy and Eddie sauntered and joked their way to the bench where Tom Curry patiently waited for them.

Over the years team talks had been reduced to mere minutes. In fact, the position of manager was more as a figurehead. They always used the diamond formation and the last man covered both defence and goalkeeping position. In Newton Babes F.C. this dual position fell to Roger and in Heath Babes F.C. to Geoff. At halftime, Billy and Tommy switched positions for the Heath Babes from forward to midfield.

Tom stood with one foot on the bench and clapped his hands. "Okay, same as usual guys. There's not much I can tell you that you don't already know; especially after forty odd years. Have a good game and keep it clean."

Eddie frowned, a finger pressed against his lips. If you didn't know him you would perceive it to be a look of confusion. "Sorry, but remind me again, I'm playing left back then?"

With a glance upwards Tom sighed and said. "Alright if you must insist, yes Eddie, you play left back." Tom looked at Tommy retying his boot laces. "Tommy, forward for the first forty-five, Billy right back first forty-five and Geoff..."

"Goalkeeper and defence, I know." He ran towards his goal, leapt up and swung from the crossbar; he brought his knees to his chest, rotated and dropped to face the pitch.

Tom applauded the move. "Bravo, bravo. Beautiful pirouette Geoff; Nijinsky would be proud."

A blush swept over Geoff's cheeks. "That stuff is difficult to do, don't knock it."

"I get how difficult it is to do Geoff, not sure how it fits into four-a-side, but that's probably just me."

Tom turned. "Eddie? Try and get back a little to help instead of shimmying all the time."

"The world was bright when you loved me. Sweet was the touch of your lips..." Tommy threw an underarm ball and it made contact with the back of Eddie's head which cut short his serenade to Tom.

Eventually, some of the tomfooleries ceased and Tommy and David faced each other over the centre spot. Their gladiator style poses merited a stern look by Tom and Walter. Bert blew the whistle and game one thousand six hundred and fifty-two on Red Cloud began.

David took possession, eyes locked on Geoff. He flicked the ball to Duncan on his left. Duncan advanced towards Billy with a smile on his face, eyes shooting sparks. Billy matched the smile and accelerated, dispossessed Duncan, squared the ball to Eddie who side-kicked it onto the chest of Tommy.

Tommy turned on a sixpence and, seeing Roger off his line, volleyed the ball towards the top left-hand corner. In a catlike move, Roger leapt up and brought the ball to his chest and to continue the mesmerising move, dropped it and played it wide to Duncan. Duncan noticed Geoff off his line and shot a blistering volley towards goal; it was saved by the stretching agility of Geoff.

As he dropped the ball Geoff smirked at Duncan. "You're going to have to do a bit more than that to get past me today."

"I *do* love a challenge."

Geoff took a step forward, maintaining eye contact with Duncan he kicked the ball left to Eddie. Mark knew what was coming and using his hand beckoned Eddie forward. Eddie crossed the halfway line, performing step-overs and pullbacks along the way. He saw Tommy to his right, dummied a pass and wrong-footed Mark. Eddie was around Mark and, using the right side of his right boot slid the ball to where he knew Tommy would be in a fraction of a fraction of a second. Tommy chipped the ball, aiming for the top right-hand corner of the net but Roger, calmness personified, had seen it coming.

"You're a bit off your game today Marilyn," David said to Eddie who, in response gave his best Monroe pouting impression.

"You do know this is a team game and not some football skills training camp? Pass the ball every now and again Eddie." Billy wasn't sure why he wasted time saying it, these days Eddie thought of himself as a striker regardless of the position he played in.

Walter made eye contact with Tom, shrugged and shook his head. The half-time whistle couldn't come soon enough.

***

On the stands, the journalists tried to concentrate on the game.

"I wish I could pop Down Below for the next ten days," Tom said.

Henry, eyes focussed on the pitch, clicked away on his laptop. He paused. "Do you think they've got a chance?"

Archie sighed, "I don't know." He stopped typing; confident he would catch up if he missed anything of significance. "It would be almost too good to be true. You know? There's talk that it's written in the stars and all that kind of stuff."

"Well, we know that's not the case," Henry said.

Donny opened his mouth to say something when Archie brought their attention back to the ongoing match. "Look, guys, we've only got an hour or so here and then we can talk to our heart's content about strange things and stars. For *now,* Walter and Tom will not be happy if we don't give a good account of this match."

On the pitch, David and Eddie were sumo wrestling, Geoff was on the floor holding his ribs, laughter spilling out from behind the fingers of the hand covering his mouth. Bert tried to bring order to a match that had quickly degenerated.

When he did blow the whistle for half-time the Babes ran to their respective benches.

Tom faced his team, hands on hips, feet splayed. "Tommy, you could have scored at least two, what's going on?"

Tommy grimaced as he rolled an orange in his hands. "Sorry, I guess my mind's elsewhere today."

"Well, it shouldn't be." Tom looked around and cast his critical gaze on his players. "Focus on the job you have to do now lads. There's nothing we can do about Down Below." He pointed to the pitch and his voice became strident. "Up here, Up Above, you play your games with the same passion as before. Understand? And I'm not just talking to Tommy; this goes for the rest of you."

Geoff, Eddie and Billy knew their half-hearted, even unfocused display was more show than substance and steeled themselves to perform better in the second half.

"We'll do better next half, sorry." Geoff got to his feet and ran back onto the pitch.

***

Walter had much the same team talk with the Newton Babes.

David felt the weight of Walter's hand on his shoulder, he wasn't sure if the pressure was real or imagined but he knew he couldn't move from the bench. "What's the matter, David? Scared of messing up your hair? You had an opportunity to score and fluffed it."

David blushed, produced a half-smile and, as he used his fingers to comb his hair, let out a slow, low breath. "I just can't concentrate today Walt, sorry."

Duncan, elbows on his thighs and chin in his left palm, came to David's rescue. "It's all of us chief; we're half here and half down there." Mark and Roger nodded in agreement.

Walter sat cross-legged on the ground and faced his players. "I know, I understand but what will happen Down Below will be what happens. You acting like a bunch of girls will only affect our scoreline against Heath F.C. Right now they're winning eight hundred and twenty-eight games to eight hundred and twenty-three. Come on lads, let's get a grip."

Suitably chastised Tommy, Geoff, Eddie and Billy took up their positions on the pitch and focused their collective minds on winning. Walter's words were simple but powerful motivation.

Bert blew the whistle for the second half to get underway. Within seconds David fired a sizzling shot that surprised Geoff and gave Newton F.C. the lead. He celebrated the way Ryan Giggs had celebrated against Arsenal in the FA Cup semi-final replay back in March.

The journalists stood and applauded the goal and the celebration. Henry remarked. "You'll need to grow more hair on your chest but I like it."

The Babes took note of new ways to celebrate and, to the fake dismay of the journalists, feign injury. Acrobatic rolling around the pitch, swan diving over a barely there foot earned *criticism* in the papers but amused the Babes.

Bert blew the whistle and beckoned David towards him as he took the notepad and pencil out of his shirt pocket. David put his shirt back on and received the yellow card with a gentlemanly bow to the stands. Willie, Dennis, Jackie and Johnny gave him a standing ovation and Jimmy shook his head in mock dismay.

"Well celebrated lad, eight out of ten for execution," Jackie said as he took his seat back on the bench.

Scoring early was the downfall of Newton F.C.; they sat back and tried to defend their one-goal lead. Heath F.C. became more aggressive; it was necessary for Bert to blow the whistle several times. Then, five minutes before the final whistle, Tommy scored a header and copied the David Beckham celebration from the Leicester City game at the beginning of the season.

"It was okay but not much to get wrong really." Johnny took ranking the goal celebrations seriously.

"It's good, don't get me wrong but the context is not the same." Jimmy looked around the stand and continued. "It wasn't the ninety-fifth minute, it wasn't the first game of the season, it wasn't the point saver; you know what I mean?"

Dennis agreed. "Beckham's face that day; it was indescribable. After that kerfuffle from the World Cup, so…"

"I'd give it seven out of ten." Jackie looked to the others for their opinion and everyone agreed. Anyway, he thought, it would be difficult to beat taking off your shirt and running around the pitch twirling said shirt around your head.

Bert checked his watch and brought the whistle towards his lips; before he could pucker and blow, Duncan slid past Eddie, sidestepped the ball and chipped it over Geoff, into the back of the net. Duncan flicked the collar of his shirt up, stood still and turned his head slowly to the right, arms down by his sides. The archangel *running* the burger stand let loose a giggle.

Three seconds later Bert blew the whistle. "Good game lads, okay get a quick shower, kick-off is in an hour."

A heated discussion took place as to the best goal celebration.

Willie, his eyes closed, had his hands up in a surrender position. "Jackie, I know what you're saying but you've also got to take into account the impact of the Giggs goal *and* celebration."

Jackie advocated that Duncan's Cantona celebration should get at least eight out of ten. "I don't know how else to say it but, it's Cantona! Johnny, what do you think?"

Johnny tried to hide his smile; he looked to Jackie and Willie and then to Dennis who was laughing uncontrollably and realised they were not much help. Jimmy had his head down inspecting something on the ground. Johnny took a deep breath and knew someone was going to be disappointed. "I have to say, unless Dennis, or Jimmy, wants to chip in."

Jimmy moved his head from side to side, slowly; his lips pursed together to prevent words from escaping. He had learnt the art of sometimes being silent.

Dennis shook his head and rose to leave. "No, no, no, leave me out of this one lad."

"The Giggs celebration it is then. It's not just the energy of the celebration, it's the fact it was scored this season, and it was a goal that will go down in history and so…"

Jackie threw his scorecard to the floor in mock indignation. He got up and took two steps to where Willie sat and held out his hand. "Congratulations, next season it will be different."

Willie took his outstretched hand and shook it. "Come on and let me buy you a commiseration pint."

They all stood and watched as Newton F.C. and Heath F.C. ran to the shower cubicles, full of energy. Laughing, joking; excited. Newton F.C. had won by two goals to one, the gap between them now reduced to four.

***

Walter, Tom and Bert headed to Red Cloud Bar. Through the enormous arched doors, they saw Frank Swift, George Follows, Eric Thompson and Alf Clarke sat on stools at the bar. The twenty-five all had their own bar stools with their physical form carved onto the upper outside back of the stool and their essence moulded into the backrest.

Tom shouted to Frank. "Hey Swifty, what's the starting line-up?"

Swifty spun round in his stool and raised his hand in acknowledgement; he walked towards the door. "Schmeichel's in net, of course. Defence is Gary Neville, Johnsen, May, Irwin." He shook hands and continued. "Midfield of Beckham, Giggs, Keane, Scholes and upfront we've got Sheringham and Yorke. It's a great attacking midfield. Ole, Butt, Cole and Phil Neville are on the bench, oh and Van der Gouw."

George walked towards the door playing with the zip on his black tracksuit jacket as he went. "It's a good strong line-up, don't you think? Who won?"

Tom smirked, "Newton, but you can read about how we were *robbed* in the papers."

Ten minutes later, *showered* and dressed in their casual wear the Babes made their way to the doors of Red Cloud Bar. The stained glass doors were a life-like image of the Manchester United squad and Sir Matt lifting the 1968 European Cup. The image was so life-like that if you touched the glass you could feel the atmosphere from that evening.

David's confident voice contradicted his energy waves. "Spurs haven't won at Old Trafford for ten years. We should win this."

"You're right," Billy said, "but, nerves can take their toll on a team."

"I know; do you want me to sing you a song? You know, to get us in the winning mood." Eddie began to click his fingers and swayed to the music in his head; when he opened his mouth to sing, shouts of *no please don't,* echoed from inside and outside the Bar.

"Your loss my friends, your loss."

"Who's the referee?" Roger asked.

Eric leant against one of the door jambs. "Graham Poll. He's decent, in my opinion; and won't be overawed by the occasion."

"Yeah, he's a good choice. The referees this season have been okay to United, let's hope that continues." Swifty looked around the door frame, to the corner. "It's going to be an incredible ten days, lads. I can't wait." He smiled, rubbed his hands together and returned to the bar. "He'll be here soon."

***

Sir Matt Busby strolled towards the Bar; two great auks waddled in front of him. His *escorts* had adopted him on his first walk to the Bar and now he could not imagine the walk without them. Flora and fauna surrounded him; he took in a deep inhale of the myrrh perfume in the air and brought his attention to Old Trafford, the last game of the Premiership season.

He had declined to watch the Babes play in the pre-match game; he knew his presence distracted them. On his arrival on Red Cloud, the notion he would watch a lost team play again was beyond description. The novelty had not worn off but he was conscious of the effect he had on the lads so only went on the odd occasion.

Sir Matt took the unlit pipe from his mouth and used it to wave towards Willie, as he stood against the mossed wall close to the corner of the Bar.

When he drew close to Willie the great auks made a slow turn and went back to wherever they came from. They shook hands and hugged. "Did you see the pre-match game?" Sir Matt asked.

"Yeah, but the guys had one eye on the game at Old Trafford so not as many goals as we expected." They turned and started towards the corner. "How are you Matt?"

"I'm good thanks Willie, looking forward to the game, like everyone else."

"It's got the lads a bit nervy but I feel this game is in the bag, the F.A. Cup game too if I'm honest. The Bayern Munich game is a different matter."

"You know football is a strange game and anything can happen but I'm more optimistic than not."

The duo turned the corner and as a man, those at the door of Red Cloud Bar turned and greeted them with waves.

Willie grinned when Sir Matt straightened his tie and said. "I guess we're not the only ones wearing suits today."

***

Since Sir Matt's arrival five years ago, the Babes waited at the doors for him to arrive before they entered the Bar. The sight never failed to make him catch his breath and hesitate. It had been a blink of an eye since they had seen the Boss; to Sir Matt, he had missed them for thirty-six years.

They told him the breeze became warmer, the sounds more melodic, an indescribable aroma filled the air. They *knew* he was close when those signs presented themselves.

Sir Matt approached the group, smiled and with a sweep of his head included everyone in his greeting. "Good afternoon lads. How are you all doing?"

The responses came at once but Sir Matt acknowledged each one.

"Great Boss."

"Good thanks."

"We won two one."

"Excited."

"A bit nervous."

The crowd parted to allow Sir Matt to step into the Bar, they followed.

***

Outside, Red Cloud Bar never changed in appearance, inside it morphed. For every away game it became the pub where Manchester United supporters drank before the match. The Babes appreciated it. The feeling they were amongst the supporters before the game meant a lot to them. Talking their talk, feeling their excitement, their nerves, it created a connection that made every match day special.

For home games the interior was modelled on The Bishop Blaize; the layout was the same yet different. The fixtures and fittings and dimensions of Red Cloud Bar were incredible. Never-ending shimmering white walls, a ceiling more expansive than the eye could see; bedecked with every poster, portrait, scarf and shirt dating back to 1878. Every home and away shirt ever worn by a Manchester United player adorned the walls and ceiling of Red Cloud Bar; all, somehow, signed; every piece of silverware was there too. At first, the expansive but cosy dichotomy confused the senses of everyone.

George dashed forward, eager to get the first word from Sir Matt.

"Are you looking forward to the match Mr Busby?" Pen poised, ready to write Sir Matt's response.

"Hello George; yes, I am. It's going to be a thriller, I'm sure." Before George could ask a follow-up question Sir Matt arrived at the point in the Bar with the optimum view. The oval quarter sawn oak bar faced him and, to his right, behind him, was the red damask clad tiered booth where the journalists sat and to his right in front was the booth everyone else sat, including him; the Busby booth. In between the red booths, parallel to where he stood was a see-through *screen;* both booths could see every detail, every movement played out on the pitch. It felt cosy and intimate and large and expansive at the same time.

Sir Matt waved to the archangels behind the bar and noted the extra special gleam in the brass work; he smiled at their giggled greeting. Swifty broke off the conversation he was having with Eric Thompson and Alf Clarke and waved.

"How are you Matt? Excited?"

Sir Matt answered as he walked to the booth. "Aye, Frank. I've just been saying to George…"

The air was filled with a cacophony of sounds, of conversations, all concerned the same subject, Manchester United's game with Spurs.

***

The archangels poured a variety of beverages and lined them up on the bar. Too many pints of Guinness, pints of Boddies, mugs of tea, glasses of wine jockeyed for position with beer mats and ashtrays. There was no need for food or drink Up Above, the smells and visuals were used for connection to the past, memories. A soul could choose to dispense with connected senses but the aroma of a pint of beer, the smell of a cup of tea was too interwoven with a football match to reject.

Walter took his seat in the back row of the Busby booth and unzipped his cardigan. He leant forward. "Good afternoon Boss. Hey, Swifty you forgot to give us the team sheet for Spurs?"

Swifty turned to Walter. "Sorry. Well, Graham's named a decent squad, I suppose." He began to list the Spurs players who had made the trip from north London. "Walker's in goal, of course, Carr, Campbell, Scales, Edinburgh, he's playing because Taricco's suspended, remember?"

"Yeah, go on."

"Okay, Anderton, Freud, Sherwood, Ginola, Ferdinand and Iversen. The substitutes are Dominguez, Young, Sinton, Baardsen and Clemence."

"Thanks Frank."

"Thanks Swifty. I wonder if there's a bookmaker taking bets on how long Darren Anderton lasts before he's injured." Walter laughed at his own joke; Swifty exaggerated a yawn.

"Well, it's nearly time; kick-off in ten minutes." Eric left the bar area and made his way to the journalists' booth, through the screen. The screen, both transparent and *solid*, was not of Down Below dimension, specification, material or ilk.

He took his usual seat between Alf and George. "I can't believe it. Is it really forty-one years?" Just saying the words, *forty-one years* filled him with incredulity. Time had passed in a heartbeat for him, for those Down Below fifteen thousand and seventy-four days had passed.

Alf slowly ran his fingers down his throat and, in a faraway voice. "I know; it seems like yesterday."

"What do you think of the Sheringham and Yorke combination?" said Archie as he plonked himself down in the back row. "You know, Yorke's been looking a bit tired, I would have thought Sheringham and Solskjaer would be a wise choice; but, what do I know?"

Tom Jackson laughed and threw his hands in the air. "Finally, that's what I've been saying for ages. And what exactly *do* you know Archie?"

The Omnipotent One had noted that although the journalists' booth only had eight occupants it was generally the noisiest.

Swifty looked up at Donny. "What was the score earlier?"

"Two goals to one to the Newton Babes; goals by David and Tommy with Duncan scoring a corker of a last-minute goal, it was an okay match. Only four games separate them."

Henry took his seat and asked. "Is Anderton playing?"

George, unable to disguise the smile in his voice, said. "He's in the lineup but who's to say how long he'll last."

Henry had written a paragraph about Darren Anderton substitution in the *nth* minute, how he was dogged by injury problems, how Spurs would miss his tenacity. The art, and the ability, to write good copy before a game had taken place had become competitive between the journalists.

Swifty reflected on the woes of Darren Anderton. "Looking back now, I'm glad he turned down the move to United. Don't get me wrong, he's a great midfielder but he's been plagued by injuries for so long, he would be a hindrance rather than a help."

"He's not a shirker though, is he? I've never seen him pull back from a tackle." George commented.

"No, I'm not saying that. I just think he's unlucky."

Archie admired Anderton. "Some players know it's possible the challenge they make could put an end to their career but they go for it anyway."

Henry joined in. "Whenever I think of injuries to players I think of Bryan Robson. Remember? He broke his leg in 1976 against Spurs, believe it or not, and was back playing two months later."

"Yeah, but he broke it again a few weeks after that, in a game against Stoke," Donny countered. "They patched him up again and then, in a derby four months later, he broke his ankle."

Tom Jackson's gaze took on a faraway look; he cupped his chin and tapped his fingers against his cheek; a look of remembrance. "A challenge with Dennis Tueart."

"Injuries never kept him out for long, that's why they called him Captain Marvel", said Alf. "When he first got injured I looked and thought to myself, this guy has a lot of courage. Time and time again he got injured picked himself up and continued playing."

The nods and sighs from his colleagues were confirmation for Alf that everyone had alighted on visions of Bryan Robson in his thirteen years at Manchester United.

***

Five minutes before kick-off the singing from the Stretford End circulated the Bar. Each soul had the ability to adjust the audio emanating from the Theatre of Dreams. They had the capacity to pause, replay, zoom in or out on a particular player or part of the pitch, so much more was available. However, they had an unspoken agreement to view a match the way those Down Below would view it, in real time.

The Manchester United shirts above their heads, undulated, synchronised in the energy waves of the Bar. Silverware captured and reflected bright sun rays slicing through the stained glass windows; tableaus of past significant matches in clear detail.

Mark made his way to the front row of the Busby booth, between Tommy and David.

"This is gonna be the most difficult out of the three to win, I think."

Tommy nodded. "You're probably right, but they will win it, comfortably. I hope so anyway."

"I'm not so convinced," said David. "The tension running through Old Trafford right now, you know?" He shook his head and crossed the ankles of his outstretched jean-clad legs and continued. "We know Alex Ferguson has won the Premiership before, but he's not actually won it *at* Old Trafford before. It's possible the occasion maybe too much for them."

Bert slid to the edge of his seat and tapped David on his shoulder. "Don't worry lad, they've got a strong line-up and bench; just look at that bench! Most of them would be in the starting line-up for most Premiership teams. Keep the faith lad, keep the faith."

"Aye, you're right Bert, just a bit of pre-match nerves, so to speak. I'm good." David shook himself a little. "Okay." He rubbed his hands together; a blossoming smile brightened his face. "Let's have this shall we?"

Eddie rushed to his seat at the far end of the booth, late as usual, and as he passed in front of Sir Matt he heard. "Eddie, I'm just having a chat here with Willie about Cantona. Do you feel he would have fit in with the Babes?"

Eddie paused mid-stride and gulped, his stance resembled a naughty schoolboy caught by the headmaster, but more reverential. Most of the Babes continued to be awe-struck when Sir Matt spoke directly to them, Eddie in particular.

He coughed, opened his mouth but barely a squeak came out; he tried again. "It's difficult to say now Boss", said Eddie, a slight tremor in his voice. "The game has changed too much to even think about it, but I'm sure that particular type of player is a dying breed."

Billy sat at the very end of the Busby booth on the front row. He turned his head to the left, to the area that displayed the various boots worn by players and every important football kicked. He studied them as if for the first time.

Eddie sat and nudged Billy in the ribs. "I know you're laughing."

In the journalists' booth, Eric flexed his fingers and said, in his best Richard O'Brien voice, "Let the game begin."

CHAPTER TWO

Both teams, eager for action, eyed up the opposition, took mental notes and rocked from one foot to another. They were ready to take part in the final game of the season for Spurs and first in a trio of matches for Manchester United. Graham Poll blew the whistle and Spurs kicked off. Conversations halted, archangels ceased giggling and full attention was directed to the pitch at Old Trafford

Tommy moved his head close to Mark, eyes glued to the screen. "On paper, this should be Manchester United's game. Spurs haven't scored at Old Trafford in their last four visits."

Tom Curry opened his buttons on his dark grey suit jacket and inched forward. "You're not wrong. They've won once in seventeen meetings between the two. It's United's to lose. And yet…" He sat back.

Sir Matt looked behind, directing his comments to Tommy and Tom Curry. "The enormity of the situation they find themselves in could overwhelm them and, it's football; anything could happen. You should know that." Sir Matt laughed and settled back in his seat leant his head towards Willie. "They could bottle it."

"I doubt it Matt, I really do doubt it."

Manchester, Manchester United. A bunch of bouncing Busby Babes, they deserve to be knighted. If ever they are playing in your town, you must get to that football ground. Take a lesson come and see football taught by Matt Busby.

"I tingle when I hear those chants," Roger said. He spoke for them all. They loved to hear their chants reverberate around Old Trafford and away grounds. It made them feel ever present in the action on the pitch.

"When I was down there the feeling made the hairs on the back of my neck stand up, honestly, I tell you. It feels even more surreal hearing and feeling it up here." Dennis marvelled.

"You'll get used to it," said Jimmy.

***

Billy made a steeple of his fingers. "You know, they've only lost one game at Old Trafford this season, against Middlesbrough, back in December. They're not going to lose today. Believe me. Actually, that was the last time they lost a game, never mind just at Old Trafford."

Everyone turned to Billy; they were not used to him speaking out.

Eddie broke the silence. "Be quiet Billy, you're forever butting in," The amusing comments, the mimicking and giggles from the archangels relaxed the souls in the Bar.

"Hey listen. They're singing another one." Roger nudged Geoff. "I can't quite believe it, you know? We were only together for a bit."

Hello, hello, we are the Busby Boys. Hello, hello, we are the Busby Boys. And if you are a City fan surrender or you'll die; we all follow United.

Geoff cast his eyes down and scrutinised the tread of his new Adidas trainers. He looked back at the pitch and the corners of his eyes wrinkled. "I think it has to do with the fact that our potential, at the time, was recognised but that potential was cut short."

Eyes fixed on the pitch Willie stretched over Roger and patted Geoff on the arm. "You've hit the nail on the head there. From the date Matt picked you, to the day it all ended, was what should have been a perfect story. It's a story that should have ended with you achieving the greatest rewards of any footballing team." He gestured to the action at Old Trafford. "They recognise that and so, they will always remember you."

Sir Matt crossed his legs and brushed a piece of lint from his trouser leg, his pipe clutched in his hand.

At Old Trafford, David May and Tim Sherwood battled over a ball travelling down the wing towards a potential Spurs corner. The ball was deemed by Graham Poll to be a Spurs throw-in; however, he had harsh words for Sherwood.

"Sherwood's telling him to *calm down, calm down.*" Eddie held his ribs as he laughed long and loud at his own joke.

A throw-in by Justin Edinburgh found Les Ferdinand just inside Manchester United's eighteen-yard box. He tried to return a pass to Edinburgh but David Beckham intercepted and the ball crossed the line off Edinburgh. Gary Neville's long throw reached the head of Edinburgh but, May was there to prevent progress and he managed to pick out Ryan Giggs as he went to ground.

"David May was determined to play that pass," Duncan said.

David's face lit up. "I really admire that guy. He's such a loyal player. He'd be picked every game if he was at another club."

Willie gesticulated towards the pitch. "Look, that's beautiful; the sight of Ryan Giggs running down the wing. It's an awesome sight to see."

"Aye, but only true if you're a United supporter." Sir Matt put the pipe to the corner of his mouth.

Darren Anderton checked the run of Giggs and the recipient of the ball, Steffen Iversen, was able to hold off Paul Scholes and continue his run into Manchester United's half. Roy Keane deftly tackled the ball from Iversen but a split second later turned to berate Denis Irwin.

Jackie frowned. "What's happening with those two?"

"Keane obviously thinks Irwin should have dealt with it," answered Johnny.

Oh me lads, you should have seen us coming. Fastest team in the League; just to see us running. All the lads and lasses, with smiles upon their faces; walking down the Warwick Road, to see Matt Busby's Aces.

Peter Schmeichel's long kick landed midway into the Spurs half; the result was a mid-air coming together between Sol Campbell and Teddy Sheringham. Campbell was the winner but he could only lay it off as far as Paul Scholes.

Duncan turned to David. "There's a bit of edginess down there; on the pitch I mean, can you *feel* it?"

"They'll be fine, they'll settle down in a bit."

***

Archie scratched the top of his head. "Can you believe this is the first game of what could be history in the making?"

"Incredible, truly incredible." Tom Jackson muttered. He was busy scribbling down his article and quickly averted his eyes away from Archie typing away on a laptop. Tom wondered if he should at least give new technology a go next season.

Swifty appeared to be less bowled over by the event unfolding before him. "It's exciting, but, it's a big ask of the lads. They've played sixty games so far this season and I'm not sure they can take it all the way. It would be nice but, it's a big ask."

Everyone in the booth noted Swifty had spoken softly and ensured his words could not be overheard by those across the room.

Donny shrugged. "They've got to be careful not to make any silly or costly mistakes but it's theirs for the losing, in my opinion."

Suddenly Swifty felt disloyal and added. "Of course, nothing ventured, nothing gained."

***

Ian Walker launched a goal kick and Denis Irwin got a head to it but was unable to finesse the trajectory. Paul Scholes read the situation and stopped Anderton from advancing.

"That was well-read by Scholesy. I love the guy but I hold my breath every time he goes in for a tackle." Jackie had instinctively put his right hand over his heart as if to demonstrate the heart-stopping ability of a Scholes tackle.

Johnny laughed. "He's not shy to throw his body on the line, is he?"

Roger jumped to his feet and clapped his appreciation. "Beautiful play from Scholesy."

Denis Irwin raced forward onto Paul Scholes' insightful pass and found Ryan Giggs. In a heartbeat, with his left foot, Giggs hit the ball to the edge of the six-yard box, into the path of Dwight Yorke.

"They're quick off the mark. Great attempt there, by Yorkie." Henry spoke as he clicked away on his laptop. He liked to write his article and watch the game at the same time. Others marvelled at his ability to embrace new technology; others did not. Henry had developed the art of multitasking.

"Good instinctive save. I get the feeling he's going to be the busiest man on the pitch today." Eric was convinced of United's victory and believed the game would and could only be spoilt by Ian Walker pulling out a world-class performance.

George was not so convinced. "They need to get the game by the scruff of the neck and control things early on."

"I suppose, but the fact that Spurs are eleventh in the table should tell you that if Manchester United *are* going to be serious contenders for the history books then this game needs to be put to bed early." Donny turned. "What do you think Henry?"

Henry opened his mouth to answer; however, Swifty remembered something and spun in his seat. "I nearly forgot! Do you know what I've heard, on the grapevine, some Spurs supporters want Spurs to lose?" He lifted his eyebrows at the incredulous looks of his colleagues. "Yeah; can you believe it?"

Alf's mouth resembled a goldfish; he finally formed the words. "You've got to be kidding?"

"No, seriously; they'd rather lose and hand the title to Manchester United than see Arsenal win it."

Alf waved his hand dismissively. "That's just crazy talk."

Hands held shoulder high, Swifty sat back in the booth and stretched his legs in front of him. "Just what I've heard, don't shoot the messenger."

***

Meanwhile, on the pitch, David Ginola pulled up abruptly and limped off the pitch.

"What happened to him?" Willie asked.

Sir Matt shook his head. "I'm not sure. I didn't notice him go down or anyone tackle him."

"He's come in for a lot of stick from the Spurs fans for praising Manchester United."

"Praising them? What do you mean?"

"Well, sort of, according to the media Down Below. He, Ginola that is, said they, Manchester United, deserve to win trophies and they're good for the game of football."

"He's not after a transfer, is he?" Sir Matt laughed.

"I doubt it. Anyway, it's not the kind of thing you say to the papers just before you play United, is it?"

"It's probably been taken out of context; you know what they're like Down Below these days."

Walter placed both elbows on the back of the booth and ironed down the front of his knitted cardigan. "Aye. It's…"

The Babes chorused, "… *different from our day."* Walter blushed; his face set in a countenance that resembled a sulk.

David looked up at Walter. "Sorry Walter, we couldn't resist it."

"You're alright lads, I get it. I'm a fuddy-duddy but…" Walter shrugged; relaxed in the knowledge he had no interest in some of the *progress* of the world Down Below.

Attention was brought back to the screen as Roy Keane raced along the wing and slid a pass to Dwight Yorke. John Scales nudged the ball from the foot of Yorke for a Manchester United throw-in.

We'll win the football league again, this time in Manchester, this time in Manchester, this time in Manchester. Oh, we'll win the football league again, this time in Manchester, this time in Manchester.

Shirts and scarves in the Bar waved in rhythm. The archangels giggled in time with the chant; a couple had taken to whistling along. The result was melodic.

Gary Neville's throw-in found David May just inside the Spurs half; he delivered a precise pass into Teddy Sheringham who was being tightly marked by Sol Campbell. Campbell's presence meant Sheringham had no time to think and his intention, to head the ball down into the path of Dwight Yorke, was out by a couple of inches.

Ian Walker was grateful to take possession of the ball; scanning the pitch he launched the ball towards what he hoped was a Spurs player.

***

Tommy found himself drifting from the game; he sat up straight and gave himself a little shake. "Is Ginola back on?"

"No, he's still being treated." Mark had not said a word for a while; his thoughts with the chants at Old Trafford.

Tommy gave a wry smile. "So, ten men, for now, they should try and capitalise on that."

"That's not very sportsmanlike, is it chief?" Duncan winked at Tommy.

"Well, the referee has allowed play to continue and, until the ball goes out of play, then play should continue. Play to the whistle lads, play to the whistle."

Forever and ever; we'll follow the boys; of Man United; the Busby Babes; for we made a promise; to defend our faith; In Manchester United; the Busby Babes.

Roger stood up and stretched. "Not much happening here for now. I'll go and get the ballot slips." He checked his arm patches as he walked. "I've already picked mine out."

Every season, at half-time of the final Premiership game, ballot slips were handed out for everyone to vote for Manchester United's first, second and third goal of the season. They also did it for the League Cup, the FA Cup and Champions League if they reached as far as the final. The winning goal was announced at the end of the game.

Geoff grimaced. "It's going to be difficult this season; we've had some real corkers."

"I don't think there's any competition for the goal of the FA Cup season when we vote for that," Eddie replied.

"Really? I'm undecided." Billy smiled as he began to hum along to the chants at Old Trafford

A stray pass by Beckham gifted the ball to Freud. Sherwood received the ball and made his way along the wing into Manchester United's half. Beckham's blushes were spared when Spurs exhibited stage fright and relinquished possession back to Manchester United.

Jimmy rubbed the knuckle of his index finger under his chin. "He's not doing a bad job since that debacle last year in the World Cup."

"It wasn't his fault," Jackie said.

Eric, ears alert, sat bolt upright, his head thrust forward. "No, I know what you mean; the media and the public's reaction to it?" Eric took in a deep breath and said, in a loud voice. "It was pure scapegoattery." He had been waiting for this very conversation to start, he looked around in anticipation.

Every now and again, a new word or phrase was created by one or other of the souls. On Red Cloud, Eric was a regular contributor to neologism.

The archangels behind the bar giggled uncontrollably; some of the lads looked confused, others pretended they hadn't heard him.

Dennis, only Up Above for two months had not read the script. "Is that a real word Eric?"

David put his head in his hands. "And we're off."

Eric cleared his throat. "Well, no, not yet. I made it up a few weeks ago. I'm a neologist now." He paused to answer any questions but when none were forthcoming he quickly added. "When it gets into the Oxford English Dictionary, as it will, it will have David Beckham's face right next to the word."

Eyes were still being rolled when Willie jumped up and shouted. "What's he doing?"

Ian Walker, under no pressure, had taken a goal kick and as it hit Dwight Yorke close to the edge of the eighteen-yard box, it rebounded off him and appeared to be goal-bound. Inexplicably it hit the inside of the post and, not for the first time this season, The Omnipotent One felt obliged to clarify matters.

I never interfere with events Down Below.

Collectively they heard and believed but at times events Down Below played out as though divine intervention orchestrated the performance.

David could only shake his head. "Bizarre."

"I hate it when that happens. It's like some kind of jinx. When you hit the post once, you always hit the post, never the net." In his excitement, Alf thought he was sharing his thoughts with his booth only but his utterances caught the ear of Geoff who sat opposite.

"I suppose you have statistics to prove that?" Geoff knew he sounded defensive but couldn't help himself.

"No, but I've seen it with my own eyes. It's not a good omen."

"There's that never-say-die attitude we love so much about you Alf."

He laughed and loosened his tie. "Mark my words. It's going to be one of those games."

"It's certainly got the crowd in even louder voice. They smell blood."

Roger returned from the bar and handed around the ballot slips. He was aware of the action at Old Trafford from the bar but Eddie felt obliged to update him, just in case. "A weird Walker assist to Yorke was prevented by the goalpost. Ginola's off and Jose Dominguez is coming on. But don't ask me what happened to Ginola."

Billy chipped in. "None of us are sure. He just seemed to pull up short."

"My sources tell me he's got a calf injury. I'm not sure how he's done that, he was only on the pitch for four minutes." Henry quipped. "He didn't take a backward glance, he practically ran off the pitch and down the tunnel."

George shrugged: "He's been great for Spurs this season. Whatever the reason, I'm happy he's not taking any further part in the proceedings."

Duncan gave David a wide smile and fluttered his eyelashes. "I think his hair got a bit messed up."

Tommy laughed. "You could be right there."

David decided to play up to the banter. "It's a David thing, you know." He began to exaggerate combing his hair with his fingers. "The name David equals great footballer and even better hair. Just look at Beckham and Ginola. Both are now famous for their hair as well as their footballing prowess." He pointed to his chest. "I started it."

Duncan draped his arm around David's shoulders. "Can we include David Batty in that illustrious David team?"

"Definitely mate." David held up his left hand and began to count the reasons David Batty should be included in *David Squad*. "He has a lovely head of hair, he played in the Champions League, he was capped for England *and* he was so good Leeds United signed him twice." He finished his sentence by wiggling his fingers in front of Duncan's face.

A glance, raised eyebrows and stifled smiles were exchanged between Sir Matt and Willie.

At The Theatre of Dreams, Beckham picked up a stray ball in midfield, took a second or two to calm proceedings then passed forward to Sheringham. Teddy glanced up and made the decision to bring Roy Keane into the mix. Keane, in his penultimate game of the season, squared the ball out to the wing, to Gary Neville.

Beckham made a run Neville was aware of so possession was returned to him. A cross into the Spurs eighteen-yard box had too much on it for a Manchester United player to reach; Spurs regained possession.

"Good teamwork," Willie noted.

Steffen Freud and Steffen Iversen worked their way up the pitch towards United's eighteen-yard box but a misunderstanding saw Iversen deliver the ball straight to Schmeichel.

In midfield United confidently passed the ball between the team. Keane delivered a ball that released Giggs who happened to be sandwiched in between two Spurs players. Unfazed, Giggs raced into the Spurs' penalty area and squared a ball just outside the six-yard box to Yorke. Carr reached the ball first, to kick it out for a Manchester United corner.

Willie said, "I'm fancying Giggs to score today."

Johnny slowly nodded. "Yeah, I'd probably put a bet on that too if was Down Below."

"They've got every man behind the ball, bar Walker! Incredible; they're only ten minutes into the game." Dennis spoke as though he was the only one who could see what was taking place on the pitch. Spurs eventually got the ball out of their danger area.

"They're way too defensive for so early on, don't you think?" Jimmy asked

"Even Iversen was back defending." Walter sighed. "They're not even trying to take advantage of a possible counterattack."

"It's going to be a boring game if they continue with those tactics." Duncan started to roll the ball between his feet, it was like a metronome. "United will start to pick them off when they go forward *but* they have to go forward for that to happen."

"It will open up in a bit. They're just getting themselves settled." Tom Curry sounded confident.

"Yeah, patience and concentration are what's needed, you're right they'll open it up in a bit."

Bert noted Jose Dominguez's first touch of the ball. "He's a good player, Dominguez but he doesn't have the same flair as Ginola."

Geoff said. "Go on Gary." He applauded Neville's tackle of Dominguez; his appreciation for the oldest Neville brother was evident.

La la la la, la la la la Keano. La la la la, la la la la Keano. La la la la, la la la la Keano. La la la la, la la la la Keano.

Manchester United supporters could feel their team building for an attack, it was obvious. The passing was millimetre perfect; each player appeared to psychically read the next move. Up Above they felt it too; relaxed and confident.

A sloppy pass by Ferdinand and Giggs was happy to take advantage. He brought the ball across the halfway line and squared to Beckham who backheeled it to Keane. He took his time and was deliberate with his movement when he flicked the ball to Irwin on the wing.

Irwin looked up and decided on a chip forwards to Yorke. Campbell rose above Yorke and was able to head the ball away from Yorke but only as far as Giggs. The opportunity was lost so Manchester United made their way back to move forward.

Peter Schmeichel launched the ball and it appeared to hang in the air before it dropped to Sheringham, Campbell hot on his heels. Spurs regained possession and pressed forward using the width of the pitch but team cohesion failed them when Anderton's chip, meant for Carr, was collected by an unperturbed Schmeichel.

Ryan Giggs swerved towards the Spurs penalty box and his subsequent cross towards Beckham was blocked by Freud for a corner. The noise in Old Trafford rose, every supporter inched closer to the edge of their seats as Beckham's corner curved into the Spurs box, to be met by the head of Giggs. A collective *ooh* Up Above was replicated Down Below as the ball was collected by Walker.

His hands still clasped to the sides of his head Tommy slowly eased back onto his seat. "He was a tad unlucky there. I was convinced that one was in."

Mark agreed. "A beautiful header, it just needed more pace."

Tommy leant forward and caught the eye of Willie. "I think you could be right there Willie, you know, Giggs scoring one today. He's looking predatory and close to clinical."

Tommy adjusted the legs of his jeans as he settled himself back into the booth. He resolved to ask Eddie why he insisted they all should be part of this end of season fashion show every year. Modern attire had become an acquired taste over the past two decades.

"He's actually only scored three goals in the League this season."

The fact startled Tommy. "You're kidding me?"

Jimmy beamed as he continued to speak of one of his favourite subjects, Ryan Giggs. "No, honestly; he scored in the five one against Wimbledon at Old Trafford in October and then he scored the only goal against Coventry City three months ago and…" A look of contemplation on his face Jimmy brought his hand to his chin. "I can't remember the other, I think…"

"I'm not surprised you don't remember the goal he scored against Nottingham Forest on Boxing Day. All attention was on Ronny Johnsen that day after he scored. *Twice.*" David said as he brought the goals to mind and replayed them.

His head back, Jimmy let out a loud laugh that startled the archangels behind the bar. "Yeah, you're right; the *Ronny Johnsen must be on drugs* game."

"That was a good game," said Mark.

Sir Matt continued. "It feels like he's scored more because of the impact he makes on the pitch."

Another unusual, clumsy pass by Campbell saw the ball retreat to the subject of conversation Up Above, Ryan Giggs. After noticing the run of Sheringham Giggs switched play to the right.

"That's the first time I've heard the Spurs fans booing Sheringham," Billy remarked.

"Fortunately, there's no real passion in their hatred though." Geoff had watched, in shock and disbelief, the Euro 96 games and had heard England supporters booing the United players playing for England. He pondered how times really had changed in that respect.

Teddy Sheringham kept the ball in play and squared it back to Beckham who crossed it into the Spurs eighteen-yard box. It could only reach the head of a Spurs player and not the head of any of the three Manchester United players gathered in the box.

"That's it lad." Geoff smiled as a diving header by Gary sent the ball back towards the Spurs goal. It fell to Yorke who could only hit it across the face of the goal; no United player there to stick a foot out and score.

In Red Cloud Bar they were mid-action; they settled back into their seats after almost leaping up in celebration. Hands raised, heads clasped and eyes cast towards the ceiling. The force of their combined willingness for the ball to steer off course into the back of the net caused the shirts hanging from the ceiling to oscillate in the air.

Roger moved closer to Geoff. "Gary did well to keep that attack alive."

"Aye, a diving header, you don't see them too often."

"No, you don't. He's always ready to get stuck in."

"The angle was a little off but it's going to happen soon."

"I know. It's brewing, I can feel it."

Eddie piped up. "I'd have put my house on Yorkie scoring."

"He'll get one I think and maybe land the Golden Boot as well." Billy was in awe of the progress Dwight Yorke had made in his first season at Old Trafford.

Hello, hello, we are the Busby Boys. Hello, hello, we are the Busby Boys. And if you are a City fan, surrender or you'll die. We all follow United.

Roy Keane delivered a pass from the halfway line with Yorke's name etched all over it. Yorke chased towards the goal line with Campbell shadowing his every movement; he kept the ball in play, fended off Campbell's attention and passed to a waiting Beckham. A cross was delivered into the box by Beckham and Sheringham, in the middle of two Spurs defenders, used his head to guide the ball down to Scholes.

For a split second, everyone *saw* Paul Scholes as the first name on the list of goal scorers but the flag and the whistle blew that image away.

Bert, who had become an authority in referring decisions, agreed with Graham Poll. "Yes, offside, no argument there."

"He knew it as well," said Walter.

"But you can't fault Sheringham's header; he had two on his back. It was perceptive."

"No, you're right. He came to United to win trophies, he said. Now he's playing for one now, against his old club; it must be a massive incentive for the guy."

"Wasn't he criticised a bit for that, from United supporters I mean?"

"Yeah, but his contribution this season, so far, has been about heart and passion, so..."

The suddenness of Mark leaping to his feet, gesturing like an aircraft Marshall startled Bert and Walter.

"*Handball*! That was handball from Iversen."

It took a second for anyone to respond; they were unaccustomed to seeing such a vocal Mark. "Sorry, lad I didn't notice; I'll replay it," said Tom Curry.

Mark stabbed his finger towards the pitch. "See? He handled the ball *twice.*"

"You're right. He thinks he's playing basketball." Tom thought his comment was funny and intended to drop it into the half-time conversations with the journalists.

Jackie inhaled sharply. "Hey up, the Great Dane's getting a telling off from the referee. He'd better watch himself."

"The big man would be best letting his body do the talking," Dennis added.

"It was definitely hand to the ball, twice. But you have to play to the whistle and trust the referee or linesmen to make the right decision."

"He's never been sent off, has he? Schmeichel? For United?"

"Yeah, against Charlton in the FA Cup quarter-final back in 94."

"Oh, I remember now," said Dennis as he replayed the incident in his mind.

Duncan looked over at the journalists' booth. "What's happening with Arsenal, Henry?" It was Henry's job to keep everyone abreast of all the Premiership games being played. With a separate laptop, he scanned coverage of the grounds and honed in on any relevant action.

"It's still nil-nil Dunc. Villa are taking a bit of a pounding apparently. One's going to penetrate soon." Henry made eye contact and winked at Duncan. "That's only my opinion, of course."

"You can say the same for this game. We've had three shots on goal so far. If they keep taking shots like that, then one is going to hit the target eventually." Sir Matt ran his hand down the buttons of his jacket; he was relaxed; he *knew* Manchester United would score, this season they *always* scored.

Donny sounded peeved. "They're all about defensive play, no desire whatsoever to attack." He had half written his article and it spoke of end to end runs for both teams, but he would possibly have to rewrite it. However, he knew there was a long way to go and anything could happen before the final whistle.

It appeared everyone was caught in private thoughts in Red Cloud Bar and Down Below because, without warning, against the run of possession and opportunities, Spurs scored.

Eddie jumped up. "Where on earth did that come from?"

They watched their own slow-motion replay as Walker kicked downfield and Iversen headed the ball onto Ferdinand out on the left. Ferdinand slipped away from Johnsen and lobbed the ball towards United's goal. Schmeichel realised, a second too late, the ball overhead was on target. He could only backpedal as he hit the inside of the goal at the same time as the ball. Ferdinand, with his fifth goal of the season, had signalled intent; game on.

Sir Matt broke the silence. "I hope that's not the final memory of Peter Schmeichel at Old Trafford. He deserves more than that."

Willie cleared his throat and said. "They all deserve more than that."

Jimmy sighed, "To be fair, it's a good goal."

"I can't believe it." Tommy's eyes and mouth were wide open.

Billy looked to the United dugout and whispered. "Look at them. They look shell-shocked."

"It came out of the blue, from a player that's hardly done anything this season, and he comes on and scores a goal like that!" David was stunned.

With both hands cupped over his mouth, Dennis massaged his nose with his fingers, his voice barely audible. "I'd almost forgotten he was on the pitch, to be honest."

"Come on you lot, never say die." Roger's steady gaze around the Bar took in the journalists and all in the Busby booth; he made eye contact with each and every one of them. "Look at the faces on these guys. They can do this."

Sing your hearts out, sing your hearts out, sing your hearts out for the lads, sing your hearts out for the lads.

George threw his hands behind his head. "Highbury's going crazy, they've just heard."

"What is going on anywhere else, though good to know, is irrelevant to what's happening at Old Trafford now. They have to win. They have to win the game because that's what they need to do. They have to win to be able to chalk this down to one down, two to go. We're not even halfway through the first half. Roger's right, they can do this."

Sir Matt nodded in silent agreement as Jackie's words had the required impact on the listeners. The negative air that had threatened to descend was blown away and overhead the shirts again swayed in the positive wave of energy that swept through the Bar.

A long ball by Neville, intended for Beckham, was intercepted by Edinburgh with a diving header. Campbell readied himself to send the ball up the pitch but Sheringham slid in with a tackle that annoyed his former teammates, the referee and the linesman. Spurs supporters at Old Trafford added their displeasure of both the action and the player.

Tom Curry, in an unconscious action, rubbed his solar plexus. "He can't argue with the yellow but they need to settle themselves a bit."

"The fans are getting behind them; they're singing one of your chants lads," said Alf in an attempt to lift the mood of those in the opposite booth.

The chant from Old Trafford, loud and clear, appeared to jerk the Busby Babes upwards, like marionettes. The front row of the Busby booth, bar Sir Matt and Willie, weaved and danced around the Bar in a haphazard conga line to the Calypso.

Manchester, Manchester United. A bunch of bouncing Busby Babes; they deserve to be knighted! If ever they're playing in your town, Get yourself to that football ground. Take a lesson, come to see, football taught by Matt Busby; And Manchester, Manchester United; a bunch of bouncing Busby Babes, they deserve to be knighted.

Dennis' mouth was open wide. He watched his former teammates dance and sing along to a chant that, just over two months ago, had created a lump in his throat. Right now, in front of him, the Babes were laughing, dancing and singing along.

He shook himself out of his reverie, got to his feet and grabbed onto Duncan's waist. Archangels hurried from behind the bar and joined in too; a moment like this was one of the many reasons *working* at Red Cloud Bar was a prestigious slot.

Their connected camaraderie and energy lit up the Bar; an ethereal glow embodied by a wispy mist had been activated by the joyful scene. The men returned to the booth, their physical form now relaxed; they turned their full attention back to the events at Old Trafford. Behind the bar, the archangels giggled and continued the dance.

Geoff, his jaw set, said. "It's game on guys, game on."

"There's no way United are going to lose this to Spurs and let Arsenal lift the trophy," Duncan said as a statement of fact.

Sir Matt put his arm on Duncan's broad shoulder. "They're dominating midfield so, in my opinion, it's just a matter of time before United score. Keep the faith Duncan."

Roy Keane had possession and found Irwin who was able to pass and, without drama, pick himself up after being tackled. Beckham latched onto Irwin's ball and slid it forward after he saw Keane make a run towards the Spurs goal.

Keane spotted Yorke and a pass was quickly laid off to Scholes who took a shot at goal. The shot was blocked by Freud and diverted out for a corner, shepherded by Giggs.

"How many corners is that for United?"

"Four."

Ryan Giggs passed the short corner kick back to Beckham, his cross landed on the chest of Keane as he waited in the penalty area. Keane tried but was unable to keep the ball in play.

"Unlucky," Eddie said. "Can you believe it? He was on crutches last week. I'm surprised he's even in the mix today."

Billy bent forward to brush a tiny white feather from his trainer. "I can't believe we're only halfway through the first half."

"I know; there was that potential Walker catastrophe, Ginola, running, sorry limping off and a Spurs goal. Who'd have thought it?" As Eddie counted the incidents on the fingers of his left hand he squinted as he tried to remember more. "The rumble with Teddy and Sol…"

"Spurs are playing with a bit more confidence now."

"They've had a bit more possession over the past few minutes; that's for sure."

Attention focussed on Freud as he ran down the left wing towards United's eighteen-yard box. Breaths were held as he back-heeled the ball to Carr; breaths were released when Carr crossed the ball, into the grateful hands of Schmeichel.

Johnny asked. "Was he going for goal or Sherwood?"

"Well, considering it didn't go in, he'll probably say he was aiming for Sherwood. I'm not so sure myself." Jackie knew he should have total focus on the pitch but, as he watched this important football match *with* the people he was watching with, he pinched himself. He didn't think he would ever get used to it.

"Yeah, there was no weight on that ball. I reckon it was an attempt."

Jackie shrugged; he recognised Johnny was talking away the tendrils of apprehension and did not need an articulate response.

Peter Schmeichel's goal kick found Beckham and he peeled off on a determined run towards the halfway line. Beckham crossed the ball to Yorke and asked for it to be returned as he made a run to the centre spot, the Spurs eighteen-yard box his target.

Scholes ran along the wing and made Beckham aware of his presence; Beckham noticed and delivered the ball. Scholes intended pass to Yorke was stymied by Spurs and United were denied further progress.

It didn't take long before United regained possession. They began the march forward over the halfway line. On the touchline, Yorke successfully held off a challenge by Scales, turned to face the Spurs goal and ran like the hounds of hell was on his heels.

Yorke found Keane and as he looked up Keane spotted Giggs out wide. With the luxury of no Spurs player near him, Giggs delivered a cross from the left into the Spurs box. Sir Matt applauded the effort. "What an intelligent cross by Giggs."

"Yorke got a touch but couldn't control it. And, it was good defending by Edinburgh." Eric talked as he typed. He wanted to be optimistic for United but he felt they needed to find another level to their game if they were to win this.

Mark suddenly moved to the edge of the booth, his hands gripped the seat on either side of his legs, his eyes swept around the pitch. "I can feel a goal guys."

David glanced to his right and felt the belief emanating from Mark like a ripple of electricity. His head whipped back to the screen. "*Another* corner," he exclaimed.

Eddie jumped up in a mirror manoeuvre of Keane's header towards goal and watched it sail over the crossbar. "Come on Keane," he shouted. He perched himself on the edge of the booth.

Dennis hid his smile behind his hand and turned to the bar when he heard the archangels whistling along to the impassioned chant.

We love United, we do. We love United, we do. We love, United we do. Oh, United we love you.

Optimism grew as Giggs crossed the ball from the left wing to the centre just outside the Spurs penalty box. A mistimed touch by Yorke and the ball fell to Scholes; he blasted a kick towards goal, and Walker produced a fantastic save.

"Great attempt by Scholes."

"An amazing save by Walker he…" Before Bert could finish Sheringham passed back to Scholes who, directly in front of goal, was denied, yet again, by Walker. The look on Scholes' face was replicated by those watching the game Down Below and Up Above.

Billy and Eddie were on their feet; they clapped and shouted at the pitch. "Come on Scholesy. You can do this."

"Walker has pulled off *two* world-class saves against *two* Scholes efforts in the space of a minute. The sooner the half-time whistle blows and Alex Ferguson regroups them the better." Walter knew he had verbalised what some United supporters were thinking.

However, the onslaught of the Spurs goal continued; the United players were not ready to call time on this first half. An opportunity fell to Beckham from a Giggs cross but it rose over the bar by inches. The frustration and disappointment he felt were clear on his face.

"He'll be the first to say he should have done better with that one."

Willie massaged his temples. "You're right Matt. But, we're still in the first half; their determination hasn't failed them so far this season." He stretched his arms up above his head. "I have to say, I'm starting to feel a bit sorry for Spurs. By the final whistle, those players will have been through the ringer."

"That's as it should be. For Spurs, it's the last game of the season so they should throw everything but the kitchen sink at it."

"They were doing nothing of the sort when they scored the goal so Manchester United need to up their game and pick their way through Spurs' defence."

Sir Matt turned and winked at Bert. "Ah, I reckon that's what Alex Ferguson will say at half-time."

David stood and, as he kept time with clapping and tapping his foot, he started to chant. It was quickly picked up by Tommy and Mark and then by the rest. The archangels behind the bar turned to each other; they stopped the preparation of the halftime drinks, emitted an orchestra of giggles and joined in.

We love United we do. We love United we do. We love United we do. Oh, United we love you. We love United we do. We love United we do. We love United we do. Oh, United we love you.

The men felt looser as they returned to their seats and focussed their attention on the action at Old Trafford. At that very second, Neville was chasing a ball towards the right wing when Dominguez decided, for no obvious reason, to barge into Gary and gave away a free kick. It reached Beckham on the right but his pass was inaccurate and it dropped to Campbell in the centre of the pitch.

"I hope they don't concede another. If they hold on until half-time, hear pearls of wisdom in the dressing room, come back then it'll be okay." Tom Jackson heard how trite his words sounded.

Hello, hello, we are the Busby Boys. Hello, hello, we are the Busby Boys. And if you are a city fan, surrender or you'll die. We all follow United.

Dominguez had just taken a shot at Manchester United's goal but it was way off the mark.

Henry pursed his lips, his eyes danced when he caught the attention of David. "Is that guy's first name David?"

"No, it's Jose. Why?"

"Have you seen his hair?"

"Oh, that was very funny Henry. My sides are splitting." David was aware Henry would not let the *David, hair, football thing* go. He changed the subject. "Yorkie looks tired."

"True. That was a mistake only a tired player could make but we're only half an hour in."

"He should have done better with it."

Willie hoped *they should have done better* would not be the sentence to epitomise the day for Manchester United. The ball was with Spurs but Beckham harried at the heels of Dominguez and forced him to play it quickly, he gave him no time to think.

Keane tackled the ball from Iversen and raced forward towards the Spurs goal; between two defenders, Keane swerved to his left and was inside the penalty box; he laid it back to Yorke.

Tommy sounded perplexed. "Who was that on the floor, defending?"

"Carr; then Campbell cleared it," Mark replied.

"They were all back there, blocking the way." Duncan felt the Spurs defence would be in for a torrid time in the next few minutes.

The ball made its way back to Schmeichel. He delivered a long ball to just outside the Spurs box; Beckham headed the ball down towards Yorke who held off the Spurs defender and laid it back to Beckham.

The cross into the box took a fraction of a second too long to drop and a swarm of Spurs defenders was there to deny United a shot at goal.

The game was exhilarating for a neutral as Spurs, on the counter-attack, surged forward; their confidence grew with every minute that passed. A cross by Anderton from the right was inadvertently passed to Iversen by Johnsen as he sat in his own penalty box.

Geoff put his elbows on his thighs. "Fantastic challenge by Neville on Iversen. He's really on form today."

Roger agreed. "Ronny Johnsen should be grateful Neville was there."

"Did he slip?"

"Not sure, it looked like his left leg was stuck in glue."

"The ball seemed to take a nanosecond too long to drop."

"Well, it's turning out to be end to end stuff. I didn't think *that* would happen."

The Spurs corner was taken by Anderton and Johnsen just got enough on it to head the ball out of the penalty box but only as far as Sherwood on the left. The play was switched to the right when Sherwood crossed the ball to Anderton running towards the goal line. Anderton kept it in play but passed the ball to Yorke who calmly kicked the ball into the safe hands of Schmeichel.

Eddie glanced at the clock and was taken aback at the time. "Wow, ten minutes left of the first half."

"And there were those who thought Spurs would just lie down and take a beating to prevent Arsenal from lifting the trophy. This past half hour should disabuse them of that nonsense." The pressure Alf put on his pen to his notepad was an indication of how he felt about those who believed Spurs would not turn up for the game.

George slid to the edge of the booth and stretched his back; he felt the need to move. "United *are* dominating possession *but* Walker has been a giant in goal today."

Brief flashes of games they'd played in *and* watched where United, dominant in possession, had failed to win blew away.

On the pitch, once again, United won the battle of the midfield and turned towards the Spurs goal. Sheringham hit a long ball from the halfway line towards Giggs running down the wing. An interception by Carr and the ball travelled towards Walker who failed to collect.

"Another corner." Duncan clenched his fists on top of the ball in his lap. "Come on lads, let's have it."

David Beckham swung in the corner, it found the head of May. The deep sighs, the heads clasped in hands were widespread as May sent the ball over the bar. Jimmy smirked inwardly but vowed to not mention the David to David axis.

Duncan dropped the ball and trapped it under his feet. He sat with his forearms on his thighs, head forward, hands clasped between his knees. "Maybe should have tried a header down, towards Yorke or Sheringham." He shrugged.

"Probably," Sir Matt said. "By the looks of things, I don't think Keane was too happy with May's decision to have a go."

Ferguson's Red Army. Ferguson's Red Army. Ferguson's Red Army.

"Keane is putting in an excellent performance today; a real captain's show out there," Billy said.

Eddie nodded. "He's getting in for the tackles; chasing balls down. He's everywhere; Keane and Scholes are well-oiled engines in that midfield."

"I take it the Arsenal Villa game is still nil-nil."

"It sure is," Henry replied.

All movement ceased as Iversen took a long-range shot at goal and Schmeichel was forced into making a save. Neville was there to clear away Schmeichel's parried clearance. Spurs were now playing with the belief they could take something out of the fixture, even though by winning they could hand the trophy to Arsenal.

There was still five minutes of the first half left to go and those in Red Cloud Bar sat back in their seats locked in their private thoughts.

Dennis closed his eyes and inhaled the smell of pipe and cigarette smoke mixed with the aroma of hops and freshly brewed tea with milk just added. It was the signal half-time was mere minutes away. In a split second, before he tasted the smells he felt a *sense* turn on. His eyes flew open; he noticed everyone had inched their way to the edge of their seats. The archangels were silent

Jimmy started it, his gaze intent on the pitch, his voice soft to begin with but as everyone else joined in he grew stronger and louder.

"United, United, United, United. United, United, United, United."

A well-timed tackle by Scholes on Anderton brought the ball back towards the Spurs goal. Giggs raced down the wing and squared the ball back to Scholes. Scholes saw Beckham out on the right make a run into Spurs' penalty box; he waited and then passed.

Beckham, with no one else around him, had time to consider the shot, he moved forward and on his right took a curling shot. It hit the top of the post and ricocheted into the back of the net.

The Bar felt airless for a second and then a rush of energy throughout made the memorabilia flutter in celebration. The outburst which followed was heard throughout other clouds. A Mexican wave of noise rippled Up Above and cascaded Down Below and back up again. A flurry of hugs, pats on the back, hands on hearts and smiles stretched from ear to ear.

Sir Matt put his arm around Willie's shoulders and squeezed. David and Eddie, well, they copied Beckham's celebration of the goal, much to everyone's amusement. The archangels, never shy to demonstrate their biased love of working at Red Cloud Bar *jumped* up and down in circles.

The journalists stood and applauded the goal, smiling at the celebrations at the Theatre of Dreams *and* in and around the booth facing them. Donny noted a slight tremor in his hands as he placed his fingers on his laptop.

Willie, aware he resembled a Cheshire cat said, "What a lovely goal."

Sir Matt nodded, his grin hurt his cheeks, "Difficult angle, but he did it. Fantastic."

"Game on Matt; what do you say?"

Dennis lowered himself into the booth, right hand over his heart. "Remember that feeling when you've been running and you can hear your heart in your ears?." He didn't expect a response; he knew they understood.

David laughed, "Have you heard Old Trafford, I bet it's both sets of supporters singing." He joined in. *"Are you watching? Are you watching? Are you watching Arsenal? Are you watching Arsenal?"*

The air in the Bar felt effervescent, the shirts brighter, the stained glass windows shimmered; a glow circulated. Now, shoulders were relaxed, legs outstretched, less perching on the edge of the seats; their cheeks hurt from wide smiles.

"That's gonna make such a big difference now," Walter said.

Sir Matt remarked. "They needed that lift before the half-time whistle."

"I know. With this goal, United have their just reward for the hard work they've put in." Willie knew a handful of minutes remained before Graham Poll blew the whistle so stood to make his way to the bar area and continued. "It would have been a travesty if they'd gone in at half-time to Ferdinand's opportunistic goal."

At Old Trafford the ball was with Giggs as he ran down the wing, he was not content to sit back and settle for a draw. He slid the ball forward to Yorke who, before slipping on his backside, got an important touch to play it forward to Irwin, in a position one would normally see Giggs. A speedy Carr saw the potential for further damage and tackled Irwin; the ball out for a throw-in.

Tom Curry sounded perplexed. "Anyone notice there've been a few United players slipping on the pitch. Have you noticed? What's going on?"

"I don't think there's anything out of the ordinary," shrugged Bert, "it's just because we're watching intently."

"Yeah, you're probably right. But look; Johnsen slipped earlier and gave the ball to Iversen, not characteristic of him at all. Yorke's just slipped, again and there've been quite a few, to be honest. It's not good."

"It'll be fine. There are two teams playing on that pitch so if United are at a disadvantage, no matter how small, so are Spurs."

Walter broke into the conversation. "The pitch is the best in the Premier League."

"It is, but I'm just saying I can see a bit of a problem." Tom shrugged. "But I will say it's a vast improvement on that mudslide they were playing in back in December."

Sir Matt inhaled the circulating aromas; his tongue instinctively wet his lips as he recalled the taste of a cup of tea. He brought his hands together on his lap; his full attention back on the action at Old Trafford. "Iversen's having a blinder of a game."

"I've not really paid him too much attention before today. He seems to be popping up a lot, getting himself into position, holding up play."

Darren Anderton whipped the ball in and somehow it made its way out of the United box helped by Neville.

Johnny, almost to himself, remarked. "He's having a tremendous half is Gary."

"He is, thankfully, because the rest were about half a second behind him in reading what was going on then."

Willie, unsure when he had hunched over, straightened his back against the booth and said. "I'm not happy at the defending of that corner, it was lacklustre. How much longer before the ref blows the whistle?"

Sir Matt understood Willie's nervous chatter and patted him on his knee. "It'll be okay, don't worry. Just a couple of minutes left in this half to go. I reckon Alex Ferguson will settle them when they're in the dressing room; tell them what's exactly at stake. It'll be fine."

Willie opened his mouth to respond at the same time the whistle for half-time was blown. Everyone began to move and speak at once. Tommy made his way over to sit with Dennis to get his take on the game. The journalists moved over to the Busby booth, on their way to the bar. Archangels hovered for no other reason than to hover around the Bar.

Roger clapped his hands together. "I know we've had a lot of talking points but don't forget to fill in your ballot slips before the second half starts. Thanks."

CHAPTER THREE

The Bar was noisy.

"I don't think Fergie needs to give the hairdryer treatment to anyone today."

"A beauty."

"I'm sure I felt palpitations!"

"It's in the bag, mates. It's in the bag."

"I hope so."

"A great goal, wasn't it?"

"The score still nil-nil at Highbury?"

The journalists positioned themselves at the bar. They revelled sitting on their stools observing the bubbles in the pints, the feel of the wood under their fingers, the *damp* beer mats. Their ballot slips lay on the bar as they analysed the first half. The archangels pretended to polish the various brass pumps.

"Alex Ferguson's not going to sit back on a draw; he's going to go all out for another. He's got a few attacking options sat on the bench, I bet one of them will get a call early in the second half," Tom Jackson said as he wiped the condensation from the pint of Boddingtons in front of him.

"He'll probably remind them that there's another Premier League trophy at Highbury." Archie shook his head as he said it. "I don't get that. Apparently, there are two originals. How can there be two originals?"

"There can't be. Just by nature of the word *original,* it denotes anything else has to be a copy of the said original." A second of silence followed before Henry realised he'd spoken out loud; he continued. "Sorry, you know how pedantic I can be."

George changed the subject to the half-time results in the other games.

***

Duncan stretched his arms out wide, a twinkle in his eyes and said: "That'll *spur* them on." He ducked as David and Eddie threw small foam footballs at him.

"Very funny," said Sir Matt.

Roger stood between the Busby booth and the bar. "Okay, lads come on, you know the score. Write on the ballot slips," he waved his slip, "Your votes for Manchester United's first, second and third goal of the Premier League season so far. I know we've got forty-five minutes left to play; so, if a wonder goal is scored we can change the results." Roger raised his voice over the muted conversations that had started. "But it has to be by consensus. Clear?"

"As mud Roger, as mud." A foam football hit Eddie on the back of his head; he nearly gave himself whiplash as he spun round to look for the culprit. He was sure it had been one of the archangels.

"When you've finished writing down your first, second and third, I'll collect your slips and hand them in at the bar. The results will be read out after the game."

The giggles of the archangels seemed to reverberate off the walls and windows. They loved being part of the ballots. They had their own favourite goals but their *thoughts* never influenced the outcome.

The sounds of pens and pencils being tapped against tables, fingers and teeth filled the Bar. Chins were rubbed and scratched; smiles brightened when thoughts settled on a specific memory. Memories of Manchester United goals scored over the past ten months appeared as visions, as clear as the second they were scored.

Mark got up to stretch his legs and walked over to the bar. "Is anyone going for Blomqvist's goal against Everton?" He stood *admiring* the relief carvings of memorable Manchester United moments etched into the lower half of the bar; he thought he looked nonchalant, the journalists did not.

Eric looked up from his slip. "No I haven't, but if we had to vote for the weirdest celebration after a goal then *that* would be at number one."

"Phil Neville did the same…*"* George had become fond of using air quotes, "*celebration* after he scored against Brondy back in November. Anyone have *any* idea what that whole sleeve flailing thing was all about?" George was genuinely interested and thought he might have missed it's significance.

Eddie shook his head and smiled, "I've no idea mate. It was a good goal but it doesn't make my top three."

Mark laughed. "I agree, it was a good goal but there have been better."

"It was a great team effort goal, Keane, Beckham to Blomqvist, back of the net. I'm putting that as my third." Bert knew the likelihood of Jesper Blomqvist scoring another memorable goal for United was low and decided to vote for him as a dark horse.

"There are so many examples this season of great team effort goals. Look at the Yorke and Scholes second goal against Blackburn back in November at Old Trafford. The passing between them before the eventual goal was sublime, they made it look effortless." Willie always became enthused at team goals.

"Roger, I've been thinking…"

"Oh, steady on Henry. Do you need to sit down?"

Henry fake laughed at Eddie's joke and continued. "What do you think about adding a category for team effort goals next season?"

Roger cast his eyes around to gauge everyone's reaction to Henry's suggestion. "I think it's a good idea. Let's get together and chat later."

"Great."

"For me, one of the best, but not the best was David Beckham's against Leicester City back in August." Tommy knew it had to go somewhere in his top three.

Billy agreed. "True; that free kick was sublime. Right now, it's in my top five."

"It wasn't just that he'd scored, but he scored after all the scapegoattery after the World Cup *and* it was in the ninety-fourth minute." Eric was determined his new word was going to gain traction.

Sir Matt waited for the laughter to die down; he thought the goal was worthy of a vote and didn't want it to get lost in the pulling of Eric's leg, "It was his way of saying, I'm back and I'm doing it for my club."

David nodded. "I suppose for that reason that goal is going somewhere in my top three. He kept quiet and let his football do the talking for him."

For Dennis, one name would definitely appear on his list. He scratched his head. "I'm trying to pick *only* one of Ole Gunnar Solskjaer's goals; nearly every one of them world class." He held up a finger. "You've got his goal against Charlton Athletic at home in September. Boy, that kid was tenacious getting that one." Dennis closed his eyes and replayed Ole's Premiership goals this season.

Walter ambled to the bar to speak to Henry. "It was a good example of a cohesive team goal, Phil Neville to Scholes to Solskjaer to Yorke back to Solskjaer and, from outside the box, scores. Beautiful." Henry inched along the bar and made room for Walter.

"Remember Scholesy goal against Liverpool back in September? Another great team goal but the finishing by Scholesy was pure United. Especially given the fact seven or eight Liverpool players were hung out, *chilling*, inside their own box." Johnny danced his pen through his fingers, a half-smile on his face.

Geoff chuckled. "No, yeah, I remember. I couldn't understand what they were all doing there *and* doing nothing while being there."

Tapping his black pen against his knee Jackie noted. "I could pick any of the goals scored against Wimbledon in October. Beckham, Yorke and Cole; all scored delicious goals that day."

"Jordi Cruyff scored a couple of tasty goals too; is he on your list?" Bert could not disguise the affection he felt for the son of Johann Cruyff. "To be honest, I feel his career as a United player is over, so I'm going to put him down as a farewell gesture."

Jordi's two goals flashed through Roger's mind; he put his chin in his palm. "No, sorry he doesn't make the grade on my list."

Roger tapped his finger on the imaginary watch on his wrist. "Come on guys, less chatting, more individual thinking and writing. We can dissect the results and the also-rans after the final whistle. The second half is seven minutes away."

Dennis had completed his slip. He sat back, elbows on the back of the booth, and enjoyed the conversation, debate and sense of calm in the Bar. As time Down Below moved forward without him, days like this were treasures.

Finally, the men became silent and slipped into their private thoughts of the seventy-nine goals scored by Manchester United during the Premiership season. The archangels peeked over shoulders; surprise shown at some notations and nods and winks at others. They would be *busy* counting up the votes during the second half.

***

The completed slips were delivered to the bar and everyone made their way back to their booths, eagerly awaiting Graham Poll to blow the whistle for the second half to get underway.

Jimmy was unable to sit still as he spoke to Bert. "Any rumblings about who's going to replace Schmeichel next season?"

"I have no idea. But, whoever it is, he has huge boots to fill." Bert rolled up the sleeves of his tracksuit jacket. "Van der Gouw has done great in the four games he's played in but, the idea of him playing week in, week out doesn't fill me with joy." He shrugged.

"Any outside contenders?"

"Well, as it happens I've had my eye on a young Dutch keeper; Edwin Van der Sar."

"Sar? Sar?" Jimmy clicked his finger as the memory came back. "Ah, yes. He won the Dutch Football Goalkeeper of the Year. How old is he?"

"He's the same age as Peter was when he first joined United, twenty-nine."

"Really?"

"Yeah; he's still playing for Ajax but, in my opinion, it's just a matter of time before some bigger club comes along and snaps him up." Bert became unfocused as he recalled the abilities of Van der Sar; he couldn't imagine anyone else to fill Peter's gloves. "Yeah, he's done a great job for them these past nine years. He's definitely my first choice."

"Well, I hope Alex Ferguson has the same discerning taste as you."

Everyone settled into their seats. It was habit that kept those in the front row of Busby booth in the same seats they sat in as they watched the F.A. Cup game against Sheffield Wednesday two weeks after their arrival.

The exception being when Sir Matt arrived; he chose to sit between Willie and Duncan and, to accommodate him, Eddie moved to sit between Billy and Geoff.

Tom Jackson picked up his notepad and nodded towards the screen. "And we're off." The players were on their way down the tunnel, their faces determined.

"*Andy Cole's on for Sheringham. I bet he scores.*" George clapped his hands together; he was giddy. It was possible his article about the *beautiful psychic partnership* of Cole and Yorke could be topped off by a goal.

Jimmy nudged Dennis. "Is it true there's animosity between Cole and Sheringham?"

"Not sure; to be honest, I don't care. As long as they're professional on the pitch then I don't care if they hate each other."

Billy mused on the Yorke/Cole partnership that was not even a year old. "It's like they can read each other's minds. It must be amazing to have that kind of rapport with a teammate."

"There you go again, hogging the conversation." Eddie grabbed Billy in a playful headlock.

Willie loosened his tie and unbuttoned the collar of his shirt. "A couple more from those two should put this game to bed."

"I think you're right, but I don't care much who scores it as long as we get to lift that trophy." Sir Matt would even welcome a Spurs own goal; the idea of beautiful football being played when a trophy was at stake was not high on the list of priorities. "What do you think Swifty?"

Swifty paused on his way back to his booth and placed his right hand over his heart. "*If you can keep your head when all about you are losing theirs and blaming it on you: If you can trust yourself when all men doubt you...*" The flurry of foam balls, from every direction, flew towards Frank's head. He jogged towards his seat in a zigzag manoeuvre in an attempt to dodge the balls.

Donny sighed. "I *think* what Frank is trying to say is, if they can settle themselves down and not make any mistakes they should do it. Keep their heads for the next forty-five minutes and they will be Champions. But I don't have to tell you, a lot can happen in forty-five minutes."

"Ferguson's not just sitting back though; he wants to add to the scoreline. Putting Cole on is a sign of his intent. He wants more, and I think he'll get more." Archie was surprised how confident he sounded.

***

Since April, the word *Treble* had been heralded from the rooftops by journalists Down Below but only spoken in a revered whisper among the supporters. However, now, forty-five minutes stood in the way of one down, two to go.

"Cole must be nervous but, I have to say, he's a different kind of player now he's partnering Yorke. I hope he gets to wipe away some of the not so brilliant memories. It takes a lot to come back and score goals when you've been offered out for sale. He did it though, you know? I wonder if he ever thinks about *that* last game of the season, against West Ham."

Willie's babble was an indication of his nerves; Sir Matt placed his hand on Willie's shoulder and said. "He'll be fine, Willie, he'll be fine. What a fearful sight it must be for any opposition to see those two facing each other over the centre spot."

Graham Poll blew the whistle for the second half.

Oh Andy Cole, Andy, Andy, Andy Cole, Andy, Andy, Andy Cole, Andy, Andy, Andy Cole.

"Move up Duncan, you're taking up the space of two there, or would you like me to sit on your knee?" David swung his legs over Duncan's thighs and attempted to nuzzle into his neck.

Duncan placed both arms on David's knees; he knew David would not be able to sustain the position for long. "Yeah, no problem, get yourself comfy."

The weight of Duncan's arms meant David could not move. "Alright Dunc, I surrender; I was only joking." Duncan lifted David's legs, delicately placed them on the floor and stretched his own in front of him.

Tom Curry nodded as he massaged his neck. "Spurs are out of the gate quick, that's for sure."

"They are and look at Sherwood. He's had a decent game so far."

"Even though Ferdinand got the goal I have to say the best Spurs player, for me, is Iversen and then Sherwood. He's playing a more attacking midfield role today."

"I know; he's in a much more advanced position than usual. He's…"

Billy's laughter interrupted Bert's praise of Tim Sherwood. "Look there's a sniper at Old Trafford."

Eddie, with a brief round of applause and a smile on his face, pointed to the replay of Dominguez having been *shot* in Manchester United's penalty area. "To be fair, it was a fantastic triple roll by Dominguez. On a gymnastic mat, you would probably give him eight out of ten."

Geoff proffered his opinion as to the content of the conversation now taking place between Graham Poll and Gary Neville. "He's probably telling Gary not to blow on the lad or he'll fall over again."

Johnny remarked. "Disappointing tactics but it's the way football is going these days."

"I hate to see it. It's a European thing."

"You know, Gordon Taylor said four years ago the *flood* of foreign players, his words, not mine, would be a detriment to the game of football." Henry's eyes flicked through the other games as he spoke.

Sir Matt, ever the pragmatist knew the genie could never be put back in the bottle. "I can see why he would think that but look at the European players we have playing for United now. It's brought good and bad. It is what it is."

"You're right; it's unlikely United would be going for this Treble if the European Court hadn't abolished the three foreigner rule."

Silence settled on both booths as they mentally chose the three foreigners they would pick for *their* Manchester United side. Within seconds they realised what a difficult task it was and their attention was brought back to the activity at Old Trafford.

Les Ferdinand held off attention from Keane, Beckham and Gary Neville. The ball came to Sherwood only for him to put too much on it for Dominguez to keep it in play.

"Don't get me wrong, I think the influence of some players from Europe has been unbelievable; just look at the impact Eric Cantona had on United but with it, some, not all, bring bad habits."

Willie smiled and turned to respond to Jackie. "Don't forget Peter Schmeichel; he's been phenomenal for United over the past eight years. He's saved United's skin on many occasions. Remember the 1992/93 season? Those twenty-two clean sheets he kept helped United lift the Premiership title, no doubt about it."

Eddie began to sway. *"No there ain't no doubt about it. Something was missing it was making me blue. But all I ever needed was you."*

Geoff stared at Eddie and shook his head. "I take it that's a song."

"Yep, a country and western; I'm not so keen myself but I couldn't resist it."

"No doubt about it."

On the Old Trafford pitch, Ryan Giggs crossed the ball into the Spurs penalty box; it was intended for Yorke. Scales tried to intercept but missed; Edinburgh saved Scales' blushes as he cleared the ball for a United throw-in.

"They're a great combination those two – Gary Neville and David Beckham," Roger said.

"It happens when you have teammates that are best mates off the pitch as…"

Willie's sentence trailed off as a feeling and movement caused everyone's jaws to loosen. Eyes grew wide as Neville's ball reached Andy Cole on his way into the Spurs eighteen-yard box. The ball dropped over Cole's shoulder, he brought it down with his right boot; the ball appeared to be magnetised to it. In a one, two three Cole lobbed Walker and the ball hit the back of the net.

Red Cloud Bar erupted. Tommy emulated Cole's celebration and the rest of the Babes chased him down. Willie was on his feet pumping his fists in the air. Sir Matt clapped so hard he swore he could feel it. Energy danced, colours sharpened and the crystal bell giggles of the archangels touched all of the senses. The vocal supporters in Old Trafford contributed to the amalgam of happy sights and sounds.

Alf uttered the first coherent sentence. "Oh, my word."

Walter replayed the moment and watched it again and again and again; it astounded him. "You can't teach that kind of thing."

Henry sat down and stretched his fingers, ready to pepper his prose with words that could do justice to what he had just seen. "That first touch was sublime, the second, not so great but, well, the third; what can you say."

Everyone else appeared to find their voice at the same time.

"That was one of the best goals he's ever scored."

"It is the best and most important goal Cole will *ever* score."

"What a beauty."

"Amazing!"

"Did you see the way it almost stuck to his foot?"

"You can't teach that kind of control."

"Beautiful."

"He exhibited excellent composure."

Willie slipped his jacket off and loosened his Club tie, his smile stretched from ear to ear. "I mean each of the touches on their own was goal worthy but all three. The guy's a maestro with the ball at his feet."

"His partnership with Yorke has definitely helped him to develop his game." Jackie's glare led Dennis to hold his hands up in a defensive posture. He continued. "I'm not saying he didn't have it in him already but I think Yorke has given him that extra ten percent."

"Look, he's telling everyone to calm down," Jackie said.

"He's blown away those images of four years ago and some."

"That kind of image can break you as a player, fortunately not our Andy Cole."

The archangels started to whistle and in a heartbeat, everyone in Red Cloud Bar sang at the top of their voices. The United shirts above fluttered. Old Trafford too was intent on giving respect to the goal-scorer.

Oh Andy Cole, Andy, Andy, Andy Cole, Andy, Andy, Andy Cole, Andy, Andy, Andy Cole.

On the pitch, Ferdinand raced forward with the ball, intent on getting to United's penalty box. A pass to his right, to Anderton, was claimed by Irwin; the ball out for a Spurs throw-in.

"See Denny Irwin slipped just then." Tom Curry was like a dog with a bone regarding the pitch at Old Trafford.

Duncan's back was flush against the booth, head back, his eyes fixed on the pitch he said. "Remember the state of the pitch back in November when Blackburn Rovers came to town? It looked like a patchwork quilt!"

Roger made eye contact and beamed at Duncan. "Remember some of the pitches we played on! In comparison, *this* Old Trafford pitch is a bowling green."

A long Anderton throw-in reached the head of Campbell and the ball fell to Iversen. The touch was light and Schmeichel was able to collect it with confidence.

"He needed more contact on that," Mark said.

"The Old Trafford crowd are doing Andy Cole *and* the boys proud."

Tommy was right; Old Trafford was indeed raising the roof off The Theatre of Dreams; the supporters *felt* their team would not let this lead slip. They believed the Premiership was theirs and chose to celebrate in the best way they knew how, by singing.

Although confident Tommy knew he would not be happy until the final whistle of all Premiership games. "What's happening at Highbury?" He moved to pick an invisible piece of lint from his jean-clad right leg, an unconscious action remembered from Down Below.

David, in complete contrast, oozed confidence and sat with his hands behind his head, legs outstretched and crossed at the ankles. "Still nil-nil, but it makes no difference what happens there so long as United retain this lead.

Bert moved forward and put his hand on Sir Matt's shoulder. "If the result stays like this and Manchester United are indeed crowned Champions of England, Alex Ferguson will equal your record Matt."

"Aye, there's no other man walking the earth that deserves to be on par with Matt."

"Thanks Willie. But Alex Ferguson, if they lift the trophy today will have won five times in seven years; it took me fifteen years. He is an incredible manager, what he's done with the Club is what I wanted to do with these lads."

"We are the Busby Babes and they are Fergie's Fledglings, the same but different." Duncan did not feel the need to say the reason it took Sir Matt fifteen years, everyone knew.

Sir Matt put his pipe to the corner of his mouth.

***

Spurs were not going to just lie down and roll over, they continued to press forward. Carr on the right wing played the ball to the middle of the pitch, to Ferdinand who played a quick one-two with Anderton and then laid it off for Dominguez. He tried to get around Neville to no avail and decided Edinburgh may have better luck.

The cross was whipped into United's box and Johnsen calmly headed the ball away but only as far as Carr.

"What's Ryan Giggs doing there, tackling?" Jackie did not want to see a free-kick or worse a penalty being given away by an out-of-position Giggs.

Eddie shrugged. "He's helping out his teammates but I get what you're saying."

Willie turned to Roger. "Excuse my back," and swivelled to the other side, his elbow on the back of the booth. "Okay, I've been thinking lads."

"I wondered what that noise was."

"Eddie, you are *hilarious*. No seriously, if it stays like this, at two one, then I will be changing my vote for number one goal of the Premiership."

Roger nodded and swept the Bar with a questioning look that was answered. "I think we all will. Not only was it a beautifully controlled goal, it will be the goal that wins Manchester United the Championship *at* Old Trafford for the first time since 1965."

"*And* set them on course for the Treble," Geoff said.

Willie was happy there was no audible voice of dissent but wanted to be sure. "Can we have a vote on this?"

Everyone put their hands up, some put both hands up; it was unanimous.

Roger stood and turned to the bar, ready to open his mouth to speak to the archangels. He saw two archangels holding up a sheet of paper with the words *'Number One - Andy Cole vs Spurs 16ᵗʰ May 1999'*.

Of course, Roger said to himself as he turned back to the screen.

The visual focus was back on the pitch, of the match being played, auditory attention basked in the sounds of the crowd at Old Trafford. Thoughts and images were of the dream unfolding before their very eyes. It was as though each was in their own private bubble but connected somehow with all the rest in Red Cloud Bar, and feeling the positive emotions of the supporters Down Below.

Spurs were awarded a free kick after Beckham fouled Dominguez on the left wing, midway into the Spurs half.

Billy twirled a cigarette through his fingers and shook his head. "At least when he's fouled Dominguez is consistent with his gymnastic rolls, you can't say fairer than that." Eddie nudged Billy with his left elbow. "You're making way too many funnies today Billy, cut it out."

Sol Campbell was in Manchester United's box, tussling with Johnsen. As Anderton whipped the ball in it was the man who had initially given away the free kick that headed the ball out, Beckham.

"The man's like a terrier today." Eric liked the sound of that and tore his eyes away from the screen to type the sentence into his article.

The Old Trafford crowd continued to go through the rest of their homage repertoire and laud the names of some of the great and the good.

Dennis could not contain the envy in his voice when he said. "They're having a right ball down there, aren't they?"

"Can you blame them? They're thirty minutes from the first step into the history books." Jimmy felt part of him was down there, experiencing the emotions of every United supporter on the planet.

"No, definitely not. To be honest, I was just wondering if The Omnipotent One will let us nip down and take in the celebration." Dennis had a lot to learn about rules Up Above; they knew he would figure it out eventually.

"Can you hear it? Dwight's chant! Can you hear it?" Eddie bit the corner of his lip. He surmised that a lot of alcohol had to be involved in coming up with that chant.

Dwight Yorke wherever you may be, you are the king of pornography. You stuck two fingers up at Gregory, now you play for MUFC.

United had possession and in the midfield passed the ball amongst themselves. Spurs were ready to pounce, looking for a chink, a glimmer of hope.

Schmeichel, Schmeichel, Schmeichel, Schmeichel, Schmeichel

Jackie pursed his lips. "It's a shame we couldn't think of a better chant for Peter, you know?"

"I imagine that being a legend at Manchester United is sufficient praise. Anyway, you try and come up with something that rhymes with Schmeichel." Willie knew it couldn't be done because he'd tried with the first name and surname and had to give up before it drove him insane.

A Neville throw-in on the halfway line fell to Cole and a quick one-two with Yorke and the ball was with Beckham. He sent in a cross into the Spurs' box and Scholes, as if from nowhere, *and* between four Spurs players, dived at the ball and directed a header towards the goal; it was smothered by Walker.

"That boy there, I'd love to have played with him *and* he's from my neck of the woods." Eddie's admiration of Paul Scholes was not new. He could watch Scholes' prowess in midfield all day, every day.

"Your man nearly got himself a goal then," Jackie said.

"He's a midfield maestro. One of the best players I've ever seen."

"It's going to be an all-out assault on Spurs' goal now." Dennis had changed from his tracksuit into a suit at half-time and now wondered why. He took off the suit jacket and placed it over the back of the booth, smoothing down the lapels. "In my opinion, I think they should just sit back and defend because the way United are shaping up now there could be a couple more goals in it for them."

Bert waved his arm in the air to get everyone's attention. "I know we've got twenty minutes left to play, but who's your man of the match?"

Without a second's hesitation, Walter said, "Walker."

Tom Curry had a bemused look on his face as he turned to Walter. "Walker? Seriously?"

"If it wasn't for Walker being on form, United would probably be four goals in the lead and be on target for most goals scored in a Championship."

Henry interjected. "Five goals, the other one was saved by the goal post!"

"They've got that record, in my opinion." Bert's voice rose as he became more passionate. "The only reason it's not *official* is Newcastle did it *but* that was when it was a forty-two game season."

No one told Bert that his opinion did not count when it came to the record books, they knew he knew.

The Walker goal kick from the attempt by Scholes went long towards the right and was kept in play by Iversen but Johnsen deftly took possession and ran back into the Spurs half. Keane laid it off for Yorke and, of course, the next touch was to Cole. The attempt to pass it back to Yorke who was by now at the edge of the Spurs box was unsuccessful.

Duncan turned to Sir Matt. "I think Schmeichel is in danger of falling asleep! I don't think Spurs have had an attempt this half."

"It's definitely a risk; trying to keep yourself sharp but, that's what he does."

"How long have we got?"

"Twenty-five minutes of normal time."

Jackie slid forward in the booth, his head sandwiched between Roger and Geoff. "I don't think there's a lot of injury time to put on but you never know with the referees these days."

"If this was boxing the referee would be performing a standing count."

Geoff smiled at Roger's comment. "Spurs are looking exhausted."

"In the first half, Iversen would have been all over that ball, trying to prevent it going out." Willie too could sense the air seeping out of the Spurs balloon.

"Look at Keane there. He's not happy with two goals, he wants more."

Roy Keane made a run forward between two Spurs defenders and slotted the ball to Cole on the edge of the Spurs box. He was unable to make anything of it as Campbell made another crucial interception.

Yip Jaap Stam is a big Dutchman, get past him if you can, try a little trick and he'll make you look a prick, Yip Jaap, Jaap Stam.

"They're dominating possession and not letting any Spurs player get close to their final third." Eddie put his ankle on his thigh and studied the tread on his new trainers. He wasn't a great fan, he preferred his leather brogues, but everyone wore them Down Below.

Sir Matt contemplated the bench, the two games coming up and said. "I wonder if Alex Ferguson is going to make any more changes."

"It's something he needs to consider. He's got two more matches to play in the next nine days; he'll want to keep some fresh and protect some."

Sir Matt heard Willie and, not for the first time, thought he would have been a huge asset to the Board of Manchester United. "I certainly think that's why Jaap Stam didn't start."

"He had a bit of a knock too but you're right Alex Ferguson wants to protect him. He's going to be vital against Bayern Munich in particular."

"Irwin will stay on because he misses the FA Cup game, Johnsen's had a great game so he's likely to stay on too."

"I wouldn't like to be the one to tell Keane to come off so I don't think he'll be going anywhere. It's possible he'll take off Scholes and put on Butt; an attacking midfielder for a defensive midfielder."

"Aye, it makes sense."

Jimmy slid back into his seat and sighed, to hear Sir Matt talk tactics, however, remote his words were to being implemented, was music to his ears.

Ryan Giggs, Ryan Giggs running down the wing. Ryan Giggs, Ryan Giggs running down the wing. Feared by the blues, loved by the Reds, Ryan Giggs, Ryan Giggs, Ryan Giggs.

"I much prefer the other Giggsy chant." David stood with both arms in the air. *"Giggs, Giggs will tear you apart, again. Giggs, Giggs will tear you apart, again."* He sat back down with a huge smile on his face. "I love, love it."

"Nothing to do with the fact that you're a Joy Division fan?" Tommy asked.

"Maybe." David burst out laughing. It was well known that he had been giddy with excitement when he first heard that particular chant. Giggs was his favourite player and now he had a chant sung to the tune of his favourite record by his favourite band.

A quick one-two between Yorke and Cole in midfield brought both Neville and Scholes into play. Manchester United, although in the lead, were not about to rest on their laurels, they wanted more goals.

He scores goals galore, he scores goals. He scores goals galore, he scores goals. He scores goals galore, he scores goals. Paul Scholes, he scores goals.

Donny, happy to call the game early, said, "It has to be Cole for Man of the Match." He looked around the Bar for any differences of opinion.

Swifty turned to Donny. "Why, not just because of the goal is it?"

"Well, yes, partly. I'm not detracting from Beckham's goal or attempts by Beckham and Scholes but I think Andy just had that little bit extra to provide the goal United were looking for. What do you think Henry?"

"It's really difficult to pick one player out of the twelve that have been on the pitch." Henry included Schmeichel even though his role, particularly to this point, had been non-existent.

Who put the ball in the Scousers' net? Who put the ball in the Scousers' net? Who put the ball in the Scousers' net? Ole Gunnar Solskjaer.

David May hit a long ball into the Spurs half and it fell to Cole who played a one-two with Yorke outside the Spurs box. Cole continued his run and made contact with a perfectly timed through ball from Yorke.

Before he could position himself to what could possibly be his second he was challenged six yards from goal. Scholes pounced on the stray ball and struck it with pace and precision, however, Walker, already going to ground, saved the shot.

Alf shook his head and glanced down at his notepad with a content smile on his face. "That's what one of the things I love about United. Most teams would just sit back and defend the lead they have but they're not; they're still attacking the Spurs goal as though they were behind."

Eric couldn't agree more. "They've all put an incredible amount of work into this game."

Tom Jackson sat forward and placed his hands on the shoulders of Eric and Alf; his head between theirs. "The fat lady's not singing yet lads."

"Maybe not but she's certainly gargling," Alf said as he tapped the top of Tom's head with his notepad.

Roy Keane was on a run forward when he slid the ball to Cole twenty yards from Spurs' penalty box. The ball had too much weight on it and as Cole chased it to the goal line Campbell prevented him from getting a cross in.

Archie stood and stretched his arms to the ceiling. "Pity Andy couldn't get on the end of that. That would have finished the game." He walked to the bar in the hope that the archangels would let him have a peek at the goals that came second and third.

George with one eye on the game and one eye on Archie murmured. "I hope those Walker saves don't come back to bite United in the backside in the next few minutes."

Spurs were on a rare foray into the United third; Dominguez tried his best to make something happen for his team. Neville calmly and precisely took the ball from him and played it away.

Swifty commented. "Like candy from a baby."

The journalists were confident the Premiership was United's so decided to look at some of the other games being played.

Johnny said, to the room. "You have to wonder what Brian Kidd must be feeling right now."

Sir Matt paused, scrutinised his pipe and turned, his arm draped over the back of the booth. "No, you don't Johnny. It was his choice to leave. He said he didn't want to die and be left wondering. I understand that but I also believe in loyalty." As he re-positioned himself he continued. "The irony would not be lost on him that *his* Blackburn Rovers were relegated after their penultimate game *and* it was United that did it."

Willie shook his head. "I'm not sure *exactly* how Alex Ferguson felt about him leaving but I'm sure he raised a glass or two of red wine after that particular game."

Before anyone else could contribute to thoughts of Kidd's abandonment of Alex Ferguson Tommy asked. "What happened there? Why was Anderton booked?"

David shrugged and looked behind him, his attention drawn to the bar. "Sulking *and* because he's not been injured for X days."

"I think he's letting frustration get the better of him," Mark said. "He had a little tug at Denis Irwin before the actual tackle."

The ball was with Spurs deep in their own half; the players measured in their own minds, which play would reap the reward they desperately wanted – a goal. Carr spread play to the left, in search of Ferdinand but Beckham intervened.

Dominguez was first to pounce and intent on driving forward into United's box he squared the ball to Ferdinand who tapped the ball wide to Edinburgh.

Jimmy, almost to himself, said. "He put way too much on that ball, considering no-one was there." He wanted the game to continue at the same speed and accuracy of the first half but knew it was impossible. "I'm surprised George Graham hasn't made any changes, those players are knackered out there."

Jackie responded. "You don't feel the tiredness when you're winning but when you're losing, every muscle and sinew in your body feels it a little bit more."

Tom Curry threw his hands in the air, in a gesture resembling umbrage. "Giggs has slipped now!" He shook his head. "It must be something to do with their boots because Manchester United have slipped so many times today."

Dennis was half-hearted in his response. "It can't be their boots, they *all* wear different boots."

"Aye, and don't get me started on *that,"* Bert said.

"Well something's going on with them and their boots; they can't seem to stand up straight."

Walter diverted the conversation. "Spurs are up for it again, that was a decent chance by Iversen."

"Good save, considering he's been napping for most of this half."

"Look at the smile on Schmeichel's face, says it all really."

"It's good he's feeling relaxed. His last game at Old Trafford, people will not dwell too much on the way Ferdinand scored against the run of play."

"He's definitely a relieved man."

"They're *all* feeling relaxed now; they sense and believe it's their time." Sir Matt put his pipe to his mouth. "It is their time."

Forever and ever, we'll follow the boys; Of Manchester United, the Busby Babes; for we made a promise, to defend our faith, in Manchester United, the Busby Babes. We've all sworn allegiance, to fight till we die, to stand by United, and the Red flag we fly. There'll be no surrender, we'll fight to the last, to defeat all before us, as we did in the past.

For we're Stretford Enders, with United we grew, to the famous Red Devils, we're loyal and true. To part-time supporters, we'll never descend, we'll never forsake you, we'll be here to the end. For we all remember, that '58 day, and the plane that once stood, on that

Munich runway, as it tried to take off, for the third fatal time; the immortal young Babes were, cut down in their prime.

In the cold snow of Munich, they laid down their lives, but they live on forever, in our hearts and our minds. Their names are now legend, for the whole world to see, why this Club's a religion, spelt M.U.F.C.

So bow down before them, and lift up your eyes, for Old Trafford's glory, will always survive.

***

David May out on the wing delivered a ball to Neville; his cross into the Spurs box blocked by Edinburgh, the ball whizzed out for a United corner.

"Hey look, Willie, you were right; Alex Ferguson's taking off Scholesy and putting on Nicky Butt. He's shoring up the defences." Roger enjoyed watching Nicky Butt play and was happy to see him getting a few minutes under his belt before perhaps the most important game of his career, part of the midfield standing in for Scholes and Keane in the Champions League final.

"It makes perfect sense when you look ahead to the next two games," Billy said in a matter-of-fact tone.

Eddie moved closer to the edge of the booth and raised his voice so everyone could hear him. "Luke Young's coming on for John Scales." He paused and straightened his Stone Roses t-shirt, he continued. "I don't know much about the Young youngster."

Geoff's head slumped, he let out a fake laugh before saying, "I bet you've been waiting for ages to come out with that."

Eddie raised his shoulders towards his ears. "They flow so easily these days. And, who knows when I could use that line again."

David Beckham's corner was dealt with by Sherwood, it fell to Neville who kicked the ball back out to Beckham at the edge of the penalty box. He brought the ball down and was poised to hit a cross into the Spurs box but the foot of Anderton blocked the shot. He was unable to control the ball and Beckham attempted to win it back.

"Every time a United player has lost the ball, they've fought hard to get it back, every time," Mark noted.

"That's the way it should be," Tommy exclaimed. "You couldn't live with yourself if the ball you lost led to a goal. At least if you try and get the ball back there's little chance of a catastrophe happening."

"Oops, Dominguez caught napping then by Gary Neville."

"There's a teeny tiny fraction of a second that United seem to have on the Spurs players that hopefully will see them through to the final whistle."

We're gonna win the League again, this time in Manchester, this time in Manchester, this time in Manchester. We're gonna win the League again, this time in Manchester, this time in Manchester.

Ryan Giggs on another wizard-like run down the wing and, it was again the turn of the Spurs players to watch, as he slid the ball forward to Cole. Cole squared the ball in a one-two with Butt and found Keane; the captain looked up, assessed the situation and decided to play it back to May and he decided Schmeichel was his best option.

Archie, now back in his seat after being politely rebuffed by the archangels remarked. "Spurs are all out defending now, it's only fifteen minutes or so remaining but I think they're concerned United are going to start popping them in for fun."

"Well, their concern is not unfounded; Alex Ferguson may have taken off an attacking midfielder for a defensive midfielder but I don't think the team got the memo; they want more goals." Eric knew the game belonged to Manchester United, he took off his suit jacket and loosened his tie, he could now relax and watch the Babes enjoy the rest of the match.

Peter Schmeichel's goal kick found Yorke who unfortunately fouled his marker and Spurs were awarded a free kick. Campbell picked out Iversen who, positioned in United's half of the centre circle, strangely, headed the ball back into his own half.

"I know there are minutes left on the clock but I think Iversen needs a break, he's worked his socks off today; that was an uncharacteristic mistake he's just made, borne out of tiredness I say." George had a great deal of respect for Iversen and did not want his hard work to be topped off by a mistake that cost his team another goal. He wanted United to win but he wanted them to win by effort and hard work and not by a sloppy mistake by a Spurs player.

Eric had the Arsenal game on the laptop in front of him, he looked up. "You're right you know but I don't think Iversen would want to be taken off yet, he's not ready to throw the towel in."

Henry leant back; his eyes flicked between his laptop and the big screen. "He's another example of the positive impact foreign players have made in English football." It was a quote Henry had just written in his article and he verbalised it to see how it sounded; he was happy with it.

The archangels approached the booths to clear tables; *unofficially* they wanted to sit and enjoy the last few minutes, it had become a new routine for them. A tier of seats appeared behind the Busby booth.

Dennis peered behind and believed he could feel a glow emanating from them. Three seconds after they sat down they left their seats and began to dance the calypso. His eyes wide he turned to Jimmy, who winked and said. "Once the love of United gets you, it gets you."

"They're sitting back a bit now, United." Jackie's voice brought Dennis out of his semi-trance.

"Well, they don't need to overexert themselves, they just need to defend, no heroics in trying to get a third goal, just defend."

"I hear you, but a one-goal lead is slim; if the opportunity presents itself then they have to go for it."

"True." Johnny glanced at the United bench. "He's kept both Yorke and Cole on so Alex Ferguson is up for more goals but his focus is to defend the lead they have already, that's what I think anyway."

"That was a terrible ball by Sherwood! They were just picking up momentum."

Johnny could feel Jackie's tension; he turned and patted him on his back. "Actually I don't think they're picking up momentum I think Manchester United are sitting back and that's giving the impression Spurs are pushing forward."

"I guess, you're right, but it was still a poor ball by Sherwood."

Roger turned to his old teammates. "Iversen, Campbell, Sherwood and, of course, Walker, have had an excellent game today, but they're not a match for a United team with a trophy within their grasp." Jackie and Dennis said, in unison, "Well said captain."

We'll never die, we'll never die, we'll never die, we'll never die. We'll keep the red flag flying high, cos Man United will never die.

Duncan pointed at Dominguez jogging from the Old Trafford pitch. "That's a first, a substitute being substituted."

"Well, he was only on because Ginola went off injured." David crossed his arms. "But taking him off to put Sinton on is just swapping like for like and, no disrespect to Andy but he's a wee bit older than Dominguez."

"Dominguez made a couple of mistakes but, obviously George Graham has a plan, we'll just have to wait and see." Duncan put a foot on the ball, his back flush against the back of the booth and stretched his right arm behind David. With his right hand, David pulled Duncan's arm down onto his shoulders, angled his face, closed his eyes and puckered his lips. When they were met by Duncan's big left hand David snickered.

On the pitch, Anderton delivered a ball meant for Sherwood, May intended otherwise and intercepted. In the process, May was fouled by Sherwood.

"I would have given him a yellow for that," said Bert with his refereeing hat on.

"It did look deliberate but there you go; the referee doesn't have the benefit of watching replays." Tom Curry stood up to make his way over to the journalist's booth.

The long kick by Schmeichel was dealt with by the Spurs defenders but it fell to Neville who guided the ball along the wing to Yorke. On the edge of the eighteen-yard box, Yorke passed to his right to Beckham who whipped in a cross for Cole positioned on the edge of the six-yard box; Sherwood had other plans and the ball went out for a corner.

"They've got everyone defending this, everyone."

In an almost synchronised movement, everyone sat forward, upper bodies magnetised towards the screen as Beckham took the corner. Johnsen wanted to add to his tally of three goals for the season but headed the ball just wide of the upright.

Alex Ferguson took the opportunity and made his second substitution of the game; he brought off Giggs and put on Phil Neville.

Many stood to applaud Giggs off the field. "No more tearing them apart for today Ryan." David ran his hands down his black *Unknown Pleasures* t-shirt. He could hear the archangels whistling. With a smile that stretched from ear to ear, he turned, clasped his hands and said, "I thank you." Their excited giggles made everyone smile; the perfect accompaniment as they focused their attention back on Old Trafford.

All eyes were on the screen but minds started to wander to the feelings and emotions of United supporters Down Below. A camera panned and captured the face of Bobby Charlton and, without a word being said, those in the Busby booth linked arms.

Eddie broke the silence. "Well, come on lads, there's less than five minutes and this looks like one down, two to go. What do you think?"

Jimmy had to say it. "Sorry lad but the fat lady has her frock on, she's just finished gargling but she's not singing yet. If Spurs equalise then the trophy goes to Arsenal." Jimmy mumbled, "The *copy* trophy goes to Arsenal."

"I agree, but do you really believe United are going to concede a goal now when they know they are so close?"

"No, I don't think they are but theoretically it's possible they could concede."

"This season more than any others, United have played to the whistle. They will continue to for the next couple of minutes; they're not going to take their eyes off the trophy. You're right though Jimmy we shouldn't be counting our chickens." Nothing was going to take away the belief Willie had, United were minutes away from lifting the Premiership trophy; at Old Trafford.

All eyes were on Alex Ferguson as he looked at his watch and chewed gum like his life depended on it.

"If he was a pipe smoker he'd be chewing on the stem the exact same way," said Sir Matt with a smile.

"His nerves must be shot right now." Dennis twisted his hands together as though he was cold.

"I hope not, he's got another two games to go."

"Well, I hope his nerves can take it because mine are on edge and I'm *here*."

Sir Matt took his pipe out of his mouth and turned to Dennis. "He'll be fine, he's a Scot; we're born with nerves of steel."

Old Trafford beseeched for the whistle to be blown, for the trophy to be presented to them at The Theatre of Dreams, seconds were being counted down.

The younger Babes stood and made their way to the bar.

Roy Keane told his players to retain possession and calm down. Phil Neville looked up, saw Cole and launched the ball; it was an almost perfect pass if not for the linesman blowing for offside.

Swifty, his hands in a prayer position, focussed on his laptop as he watched and heard the screaming of the Arsenal supporters at Highbury. "I'm sure I can hear *c'mon Spurs* being shouted in the Clock End; unbelievable."

Ian Walker launched the ball forward knowing his team only had seconds left. The ball fell to Iversen and he delivered a header into the United eighteen-yard box. Anderton went to ground in the penalty area and, with Spurs on his heels, Keane shepherded the ball out of immediate danger.

The Spurs pressure on United continued until Keane took possession and fired the ball towards the Spurs goal, happy for a second or two of respite. Walker collected and, in a rash move, kicked it straight to Beckham. There was no need for a second invitation; he ran forward and laid off to Yorke on his right.

Willie, head forward, forearms on his thighs, whispered. "Come on referee, get that whistle blown."

Henry, much louder than was necessary, shouted. "It's all over at Highbury, one-nil."

The Babes walked in slow, measured steps back towards the booth; they began to shout words of encouragement.

"Come on United."

"You can do this."

"Come on lads."

"Where on earth have they got two minutes extra time?" Dennis looked bemused.

Johnny had been poised to jump up to celebrate victory but now settled to wait out the two minutes. "I know, I can't remember any injuries so I'm not sure."

The clock showed the two minutes extra to be played, a decision that was met with derision by the United supporters in Old Trafford, in Manchester and around the world. Eddie and David started the chant and Down Below the same chant could be heard around Old Trafford.

United, United, United, United, United, United, United, United, United, United

The journalists joined in, the older Babes too; Jimmy stood and punctuated the word with his right fist in the air. The sound got louder and louder. The shirts on the walls and suspended from the ceiling fluttered as though a strong wind had blown into the room.

A challenge by Irwin on Carr resulted in a Spurs free kick about thirty yards out. Anderton hit the ball deep and, although Campbell got a head to it he couldn't control the flight and it was picked up by Johnsen.

His header was collected by Gary Neville who slid his way to make contact with the ball; it connected with a Spurs player before it crossed the line. The resultant United throw-in was delayed for seconds until Graham Poll could talk to Johnsen and Campbell to ascertain if they needed medical attention.

We're gonna win the league again, this time in Manchester, this time in Manchester. Oh, we're gonna win the league again.

Then the sweet beautiful sound of the referee's whistle could be heard. It was greeted with hugs, handshakes, sounds of popped champagne corks, screams of delight, applause and, of course, giggling archangels. The energy wave of the roar from Old Trafford added to the noise. The journalists made their way over to the opposite booth to join in the celebrations.

    ***

The second Roy Keane held the trophy aloft those in Red Cloud Bar lifted their arms and applauded until they could almost feel their hands hurt.

"I wonder if that's the real trophy or the *copy*." Henry scoffed.

Sir Matt put his arm around Henry. "It doesn't matter; at least I'm sure it doesn't matter to Alex Ferguson." Henry shrugged.

"Boss what do you think of him saying that this was the most difficult game and he's glad it's out of the way? I mean; no disrespect to Spurs but, they are eleventh in the league, Newcastle finished thirteenth and Bayern Munich are competing for their own treble. Do you think he's playing mind games?"

"I wouldn't be surprised Tommy. This game is out of the way and the other two teams are probably thinking to themselves, well he's not taking us seriously, they get angry and well, you remember what happened to Kevin Keegan in 1996?"

"How could we forget? That was a spectacular meltdown, I have to admit, but Ruud Gullit is in charge of Newcastle now and I'm sure those types of mind games don't work with Ottmar Hitzfeld."

"Whatever Alex Ferguson is thinking and doing you can be sure he's doing *and* thinking them for the best interests of Manchester United. He's not come this far without a few aces up his sleeve, he'll be alright on the night, as they say. Where's Roger?

"I'm here Boss." Roger stood at the bar waving the results of the goals of the season from the archangels.

"Excellent."

Everyone took a seat, speculating as to which goals had come second or third.

"So many to choose from for Ryan Giggs but I think his strike against Nottingham Forest on Boxing Day was just superb."

"I bet the goal David Beckham scored against Leicester back in August is second."

"I doubt Nicky Butt's goal against Leeds is up there but, for me, it was an excellent strike by a defensive midfielder."

Roger stood at the bar and cleared his throat. "Okay, gentlemen the number one goal of this Premier League season you have already unanimously voted for, Andy Cole's strike against Spurs an hour ago."

He grinned as he waited for the chanting of the recipient's name to die down, then with an arm sweep towards the archangels he said. "Drum roll please." An archangel obliged with a small drum they had acquired for these occasions.

"You have voted Manchester United's third-best goal of the season a tie; with seven votes each, they are Dwight Yorke's goal against Wimbledon in October and Ryan Giggs against Nottingham Forest in December. Let's have a look at the replays of these goals shall we?"

"See, I told you that goal would make the list," Billy whispered to Duncan.

The screen showed the replay of both goals, each person could change angles and speed to suit their own preference.

Roger gestured for silence. "Before I continue there were some honourable mentions, in particular, the combination goals of Dwight Yorke and Andy Cole, so many to choose from I think *that* was the problem. Against Leicester City in January they were on a psychic level most forwards, sorry strikers, can only think about. Yorke's goal against Charlton at the end of January wasn't the best visual goal but in terms of importance for the points tally, it was immense. The goals they scored against Nottingham Forest. And, of course, Solskjaer's goals against Nottingham Forest deserve a mention too."

Sir Matt applauded Roger, who bowed his head to hide his reddened cheeks. "Well said Roger, some goals are excellent not for their aesthetics but for the importance in the grand scheme of things."

Walter stood; hands on hips, eager to go and play golf, a new pursuit he enjoyed. "Come on Roger, who was the original number one?"

"Okay, calm down, calm down, I'm nearly there. Andy Cole scored an important goal in February against the team we have just pipped to the post, Arsenal." He paused until the singing of *Champions* had died down. "It was a, I think, a signal of our intent of what we, United, were aspiring to achieve, to do that we had to beat Arsenal."

The praise by Sir Matt had given Roger confidence to laud the goals that had not made the list. He cleared his throat. "Okay, another honourable mention is Gary Neville's goal against Everton in March, it was a difficult angle but he put it away with aplomb."

"A plum? I thought he put it away with his right foot, not a plum." Eddie glanced around expecting laughter, but instead, received an avalanche of foam balls.

The balls *appeared* when more than two people thought of them, it was entirely the choice of the individual and archangels if you wanted to throw them at a teller of bad jokes. Since their introduction, Eddie had received more barrages of foam balls than anyone else.

"Very funny guys, very funny."

"Okay, before I was so rudely interrupted, I was just getting to the goal scored by Manchester United that ranked number two this season." Roger nodded in the direction of the bar and the archangels played another elaborate drum roll. "You have voted the second best goal in the Premier League for the 1998/99 season." He paused for dramatic effect and the drum roll quietened down, Roger ducked as the soft foam balls thrown by David and Eddie hit the projector screen.

"It's David Beckham's against Leicester in August, and here it is." He took a seat as a montage of clips from Beckham's involvement in the World Cup in 1998 appeared on the screen; it segued into stills of newspaper articles vilifying *their* boy wonder and then the free-kick that silenced his critics.

"You can't say fairer than that, he came back and came back in style, his style, great goal," Walter said as he, Bert and Tom Curry stood ready to take their leave; they shook hands with Sir Matt and Willie. "We're off to play golf, anyone else interested?"

"I'm off away back to mine lads but thanks for the offer." Sir Matt turned to Willie. "You're more than welcome, I'm sure we can find a horse race or two going on Down Below."

"Actually, there's a race I want to have a look at, but I wouldn't mind having a peek at the Formula One race too."

"Okay Walter, I'm up for a round with you lads. I need to work on my chip a bit more." Jimmy zipped up his tracksuit jacket and waved to those left. "See you lot next weekend," and left the Bar.

Tommy shook his head. "We're off to the beach for a couple of hours, play a bit of beach football, and then," He turned to the rest of the Babes and smiled. "We're having a *huge* debate as to what to do later."

"I *think* we should have a disco at my house but *we're* arguing," David pointed to Eddie, "about what decade the music should come from."

"We have to do the nineties; it's the last year of the decade, it's the last year of the century actually, so it has to be the nineties."

Geoff looked at Sir Matt and shrugged. "What can you do?" He clapped his hands loudly to get the attention of the now mock wrestling David and Eddie. "We can sort out the music situation when we're at the beach, let's get a move on lads."

They retrieved their kit and bags from the bar area and wondered, not for the first time, why they carried the things they did.

Billy slung his backpack over his shoulder and offered another option. "Or, maybe we could watch the Formula One too. Eddie Irvine is tipped to be on the podium for Ferrari."

The layered conversations, light-hearted banter, the howls of laughter accompanied the Babes as they made their way over to the door; they turned as one and said "See you next Saturday Boss. See you Willie." They waved and exited and the doors closed behind them.

The journalists had been quietly discussing the articles they had written, the pre-match game and the Manchester United game.

"I've finished mine so I'm going to head down to the golf course and maybe have a swing myself, anyone else?" Henry struck his best golfing pose and grinned when several hands went up. "Great, let's get a move on then." They rose, collected their notepads, laptops and other *stuff* they carried; after waving goodbye to Sir Matt and Willie the doors opened and the journalists left.

With the archangels *working* in the background, Sir Matt and Willie sat back and took in the silence for several minutes. A gentle breeze brushed their faces and brought them out of their reverie; Sir Matt got to his feet first, looked down at Willie and said, "Come on Willie, let's find you some horse racing."

Willie smiled and put his hands on his knees to get up, as though it was a huge effort. "Okay, it's been a hard day; it would be nice to watch something relaxing and noncompetitive." He made it to the end of the sentence then bent over laughing, Sir Matt joined in, they waved goodbye to the archangels and left Red Cloud Bar, exhilarated.

CHAPTER FOUR

In the beginning, David and Tommy occupied the same space, but, over the past decade, they had created separate abodes joined together by a cinema and a dance hall.

On 22 May 1999, David invited the rest of the Babes round to watch a movie before the game. The movies played in a replica of the Gaumont Cinema but with all of the latest technology available, which Up Above was a lot. It became a popular venue, not just for the Babes and their families but the journalists and backroom staff too.

Mark strolled into the cinema closed his eyes and lost himself as he inhaled the smell of popcorn; he settled, content, into one of the lazy boy recliners and faced the big screen. "I'm looking forward to being dazzled at what you've picked for us today David." He flexed his fingers and mimicked a sneer.

Tommy smiled. "There's some pressure on you here lad. This film, as I'm sure you are aware, will always be linked with the 1999 FA Cup Final, so – there's that."

"Leave him alone, he's picked some good pre-match movies over the years." Roger knew if the movie did not make the grade David would be ribbed mercilessly.

"I'm sure whatever David has picked for our entertainment today he will do us proud." Everyone turned to Eddie, paused and waited for the punchline or joke. After several seconds he looked at the bemused faces and said, "What?"

"Nothing Eddie, we just thought… It's nothing." Billy turned to his former teammates with his hands spread and a confused expression; from the looks on their faces, he knew they were just as stumped.

Duncan glanced up at the ceiling. "We watched Planet of the Apes before the 1968 European Cup Final. I liked that movie."

"Was that the one with Charlton Heston in?" Johnny asked.

Geoff, head in the matchday programme, looked up. "Yeah, great movie, I really enjoyed it." His voice trailed off as his attention was drawn back to his programme. "I've watched it a couple of times since."

An awestruck Dennis stood in the orchestra pit of David's cinema. His eyes ate up the crimson red velvet-draped stage, the gold coloured balconies furnished with sage green upholstered chairs.

He shook himself out of his trance. "They made a few follow-on films but they never really had the same impact as the 1968 one." He inched closer to the archangels *working* the ice cream and popcorn stands, the smells caused him to salivate, a conditioned emotional response to the memories. He closed his eyes and held out his tongue.

Jackie watched Dennis with a knowing smile and turned to Roger. "So what did you watch before the 1977 FA Cup Final, against Liverpool?"

Roger and Duncan said, simultaneously. "Star Wars – A New Hope."

Tommy laughed. "We got an advance copy. It was fantastic, even appropriate."

David strode to the orchestra pit as the velvet drapes swished back to reveal an enormous screen. He stood between the popcorn stand and the ice cream chest and clapped his hands together to draw attention to the front.

"Well, gentlemen this movie is called, Lock, Stock and Two Smoking Barrels. It's a British movie by a director called Guy Ritchie, who also wrote it. It's set in the East End of London, and," He paused for effect, turned to sit and said. "It's got Vinnie Jones in it."

"Vinnie Jones; plays for QPR? The Welsh international?" Billy was confused. "That Vinnie Jones?"

Mark reclined his chair and said with a confident air. "The very same, trust me guys you are going to love this movie." He, Tommy and David had watched the movie the previous year when it was first released and had decided to save it for a special occasion.

"No way, you're joking, aren't you?" Eddie could not contain his laughter. "This is *not* going to be your finest hour David."

Geoff nudged Eddie. "Give the lad a chance; he's not let us down yet, has he?"

"Well, you know, there's a first time for everything." Eddie reduced his grin to a wry smile. "But, I'm just going to sit here and watch a footballer *act*."

"Pele and Paul Breitner have done it; they've both been in the movies," Jackie said.

Eddie frowned. "Who would have thought Pele and Vinnie Jones would be in the same small elite group."

Duncan took advantage of Eddie's silence. "He's probably picked up tips from the European players rolling around the pitch."

Roger reclined his seat and said. "Let's get this show on the road."

The lights dimmed and the 1999 FA Cup Final pre-match movie started.

***

Duncan's chair clicked upright when he jumped up. "That was really good guys. I was surprised how funny it was."

David, arms out wide, made a sweeping bow. "I thank you. And, *it's been emotional*."

"*The entire British Empire was built on cups of tea, and if you think I'm going to war without one mate, you're mistaken*." Eddie's mind raced through the quotes he could and would use.

"I really rate the music. I'm going to watch it again later." Geoff stood and stretched his arms towards the ceiling.

Roger clapped David on the back. "You've not failed us, really good movie; I loved the music."

Eddie stuck his chest out. *"They're armed."*

"What was that?" Billy knew exactly what. *"Armed? What do you mean armed? Armed with what?"*

"Err, bad breath, colourful language, feather duster… What do you think they're gonna be armed with? Guns, you tit!" Eddie laughed at Dennis' perplexed face. "The character's even got the same name as me!"

Eddie was excited, "Great choice David. Vinnie Jones was alright in it, I suppose. You know what? I think you and Tommy would have made great actors; better looking than Jones that's for sure."

"Let's be weaving lads, I want to see some of the build-up." Duncan was playing keepy-uppy; he loved movies but loved to play or watch football much more. "I know it's not what we usually do but anyone fancy a kick-about, you know, after the game?"

Roger nodded. "I'm up for it, anyone else?" The show of hands was unanimous.

"I'll be ref and Jackie and Dennis can be cheerleaders or whatever," said Johnny.

***

They approached the large door to the abode and as each stepped over the threshold casual clothes were replaced with charcoal grey two-piece suits, white shirts and the Manchester United Football Club tie. Sir Matt had requested, for every final, the Babes wore formal attire. Two or three were secretly grateful they were no longer at the mercy of Eddie's idea of fashion.

The doors closed and they stepped into a meadow which stretched from the front door to as far as the eyes could see. It meandered over hills far in the distance, towards Red Cloud Bar. The fragrance of honeysuckle and jasmine wafted through the air, sounds of cicadas and crickets musically interweaved with the rhythm of drumming snipes.

Duncan, David, Mark and Billy played one-touch football; the others strolled and discussed the movie and the upcoming game. Eddie, still in pre-match movie mode, started and it was quickly picked up by the rest. Several archangels watched as the eleven suited men danced their way through the meadow accompanied by singing and clicking of fingers.

In the cool of the evening. When everything is getting kind of groovy. You call me up and ask me; Would I like to go with you and see a movie; First I say no, I've got some plans for the night: And then I stop, and say, alright; Love is kinda crazy with a spooky little boy like you.

Progress was slow; scenes from the movie acted out along the way. They were in a happy mood.

Roger stopped in his tracks. "I wonder how Scholes and Keane are feeling right now." He answered Johnny's questioning look. "This being their last game of the season."

"They're going to go for it, body, mind and soul, no doubt about it." Tommy's firm assured gait an indication he believed what he said.

Mark fell back to walk alongside Geoff, Dennis and Tommy. "It's going to be a tough call for Alex Ferguson, who to rest, who to play."

A British large copper undulated around Geoff; it seemed to ask for permission to land. Geoff held out his forearm and the butterfly settled on the back of his hand; he whispered. "The second he knew when each was suspended was probably when he half drew up his squad for Wednesday's game; exactly as he should."

"True. The way he shapes the midfield today is going to be just as crucial for the Treble." Dennis said.

Dennis paused in mid-stride. "Can you lads believe it? One piece of silverware already this season." He held up two fingers. "Two more to go and Manchester will be partying like never before."

Eddie ran forward a few feet, pivoted and with a grin adopted his best Ian Brown swagger.

I'm standing alone; I'm watching you all; I'm seeing you sinking. I'm standing alone. You're weighing the gold; I'm watching you sinking: Fool's gold.

The happy and relaxed ensemble arrived at the door to Red Cloud Bar seconds before Sir Matt and Willie turned the corner.

Sir Matt took in the suited Babes and swallowed hard. He thought they looked magnificent, their twinkling eyes added to their beauty. "Good afternoon lads. You look like you've had a good afternoon?"

David proceeded to give Sir Matt a synopsis of the movie as the doors to Red Cloud Bar swung open and they made their way to the bar.

***

The journalists were already at the bar; they shook hands and split into smaller conversation groups.

"Do you mind Duncan? I'd like your perspective on this. What was it like, for you, stepping onto the turf at Wembley, the first time?"

Duncan was taken aback by Alf's question but gathered his memories. "It was an amazing experience. I was only fourteen. The idea of playing at Wembley can make you giddy. No, it's more than that. Well, it starts as a sensation in your toes and, in waves, reaches the crown of your head. That's the only way I can describe it, but for me."

His hand on his chest he added. "The first time I stepped onto the pitch at Old Trafford, for a First League game, was much more of a physical sensation than the Wembley one. I don't know; they are both special to me."

The Bar was quiet, conversations had stopped to listen to Duncan remember. Minds recaptured the sensation of the roar of the crowd preceding *their* favourite first moment of boot touching turf. In their short lives, they had experienced time as only people in their twenties experienced time; it would go on forever. Over the past forty-one years, their limited duration of earthly feelings and sensations had not faded.

Roger spoke, his voice soft, the memory of his first-team game at Old Trafford fresh on his mind. "It was the first of December 1951 and we were playing Blackpool. We won three one, Jack Rowley got one and John Downie got a brace. It wasn't the greatest attendance at Old Trafford but the roar of the crowd was something that rang in my ears as I went to sleep that night."

Geoff unbuttoned his jacket and hung it over the back of his stool at the bar. "As you guys know, I grew up in Salford. And my very first job, before I was sixteen, was as a member of the ground staff at Old Trafford. I wasn't even a *player* and every time I dared to put a foot on the turf my stomach tingled." He placed his hand on his stomach as he remembered.

"When I signed a *professional* contract with United, well, it was unreal. I knew I might not have many opportunities to play but I was playing for Manchester United! *Manchester United*. When I made my first team debut five years later…" Sir Matt placed a hand on Geoff's arm and interrupted him.

"You know the quality of Roger's play kept you out of the first team. It's…"

"Boss, I loved every minute of my time on the books. You never have to justify what happened. I know how great Roger was and so nothing further needs to be said." Geoff was in full flow.

"My best game was against Preston North End and I managed to get the ball off Tom Finney. I've got a copy of the article here somewhere." His voice trailed off as he rummaged through his wallet; he pulled it out and looked at it as though it was gold.

The Bar was silent. Geoff had a faraway look in his eyes, he continued. "In my seven years at Manchester United, I played for the first team twelve times. I remember each and every one of them as though they were yesterday. It was an honour to be worthy of a place in the squad, if not the team. I knew I could be called upon at any time. When the team sheet was read out I used to think, okay, not this time, maybe next."

It was quiet as souls soaked in the nostalgia that appeared to have gripped the Babes. David felt compelled to speak.

"When I signed for United it was one of the happiest days of my life; after that, they kept coming, the games, the trophies, even Europe. I accomplished so much in my twenty-two years Down Below. I didn't take it for granted."

"I suppose with hindsight, things could have been so different but you don't regret taking a particular turn." Attention reverted back to Duncan. "I loved Morris dancing but there was something extra special about football for me. I decided to concentrate on football; it was the best decision I ever made." Those around Duncan leant forward as his voice lowered. "Every game I ever played, for every team I ever played for was special to me *but* the FA Youth Cup game, against Nantwich Town, was one of my favourites *and* I scored five goals."

David chuckled. "I scored five too in that one! Twenty-three nil, unbelievable result, it was a memorable game, to be sure, to be sure." He ducked as Billy and Jackie threw foam balls at him.

"I was just thinking back to my hat-trick at Filbert Street in August 1957." Billy shook his head. "I felt ten feet tall that day; first game of the season, beautiful memory. Moments like those are treasures."

Eddie propped himself against the bar. "Wow, my first team debut against Bolton Wanderers was a three one defeat but it didn't take away the shine of playing for the first team in any way, shape or form."

Everyone in the Bar smiled at the memory of Eddie as he bedazzled the crowd with his body swerves, confounded Nat Lofthouse and played into the hearts of many a football supporter.

The Babes were on a trip down memory lane separately but together. Some of the journalists knew the stories off by heart, they had heard them several times and some had experienced them first hand. Jimmy smiled as he thought; this is like having your favourite book read to you.

***

The erstwhile recollections were cut short as time Down Below crept close to kick-off at Wembley.

"How many countries are watching Bert?"

Bert straightened his tie; he took dispensation of information seriously. "It's being televised in over one hundred and forty countries."

"Did you count Wales?" Jimmy queried.

"Count Wales as what?"

"Count Wales as a separate country."

"Yes." Bert hadn't but he could see the long discussion ahead of him if he answered with the truth.

Tom Jackson opened his notepad and took a pen from the inside of his brown leather jacket. He had part written his article but jotted Bert's information down anyway.

A camera panned to images of the players in the Wembley tunnel and he knew the image he saw before him would be the photograph he would use for his article. "Look at Keane's face, total concentration."

The teams in the tunnel focussed on the minutes before them. They were ready to step out on the lush green Wembley pitch and prove themselves worthy of lifting the FA Cup.

"He looks determined." George glanced down at his own scribblings of the pre-match statistics.

Alf agreed. "Scholes too."

"It's going to be a struggle on Wednesday without them but for today we've got them and they're going to play out of their skin, I reckon." Donny was determined to think one game at a time.

"Both of them have had a long hard season; it would be a fitting tribute if they bowed out by lifting the Cup."

"Yeah, it's been a phenomenal season so far."

Archie took his seat in the booth. "What day is the replay, if it's a draw?"

Swifty looked up from his laptop. "Didn't you hear, today's Final is today's Final. For the first time in its history, there will be no FA Cup Final replay, if there's a draw."

"Really? I missed that."

Bert, in the opposite booth, had not missed the conversation. "Talking about firsts, this is the first time two Uniteds have played in an FA Cup final. And Manchester United, if they win, will be the first team to win the Double three times."

George's pencil broke as he wrote down the information. He had designed his pencils to do this, to keep him in touch with sensations he had felt Down Below, and to make him smile. As a rule, things Up Above didn't break unless *programmed* to.

The physical body could never be programmed to fail or break but it could keep certain sensations alive. It was like a comfort blanket and, during the preceding years of existence Up Above, some let go of the need to hang onto those comfort links. Some didn't. The Omnipotent One left it to each soul to decide what works best for them.

Sir Matt raised his pipe in a gesture of appreciation. "You're surpassing yourself today Bert."

Bert gave him the thumbs up. "Thanks, Boss. It's unbelievable the amount of information the world has access to these days. My favourite source of information is pub quizzes. It's amazing the type of facts I've picked up. Ask me anything about the films of a man called Oliver Stone and I can tell you everything." He sat back with a smile on his face and waited for the first question.

"Is he an actor?"

"No, he's a director, like Orson Welles or Alfred Hitchcock."

"Oh, right."

Bert unbuttoned his waistcoat and moved to the edge of his seat. "Bringing it back to firsts and lasts; this is the last game of the century at Wembley. United's game against Arsenal was the last ever FA Cup semi-final replay."

Henry tilted his head towards Bert. "We doff our cap to you Statman; always illuminating information."

"It's my pleasure chaps."

Willie hung his head. "I have a confession. I'm not proud of it but, I'm looking forward to Alan Shearer being on the losing side today." He looked up and hid a smile behind his hand.

"I hear you Willie," Dennis said.

"Aye, the dilemma of making choices; we have to live with the consequences."

The smell of ales and beers, the pungent aroma of pipe and cigarette smoke dissipated as everyone made their way to the booths.

Jackie slumped down. "You know, two years ago Ruud Gullit won this trophy as player-manager for Chelsea." He ran his finger under the collar of his shirt and loosened his tie. "It used to be said it's a sign you're getting old when policemen look like babies; well, it's getting the same with football managers."

In a low, quavering voice Eddie said. "Back in my day, cough, cough, cough, you couldn't be a manager until you had a hip replaced."

"Yeah, well, I've seen the way you swing your hips. I'm sure you would have been a record breaker- as the youngest person to have a hip replaced."

Eddie leapt to his feet and impersonated Robbie Williams. *"I'm a man machine, drinking gasoline, superhuman being, shooting laser beams."*

He tried to use Billy as a human shield against the deluge of foam balls.

"No, no, no Eddie, not today." Billy slid close to Willie and Sir Matt, sure in the knowledge that Eddie would not follow.

Johnny brought the carnival atmosphere back to what was about to occur at Wembley. "What's United's line-up Tom?"

Tom Curry glanced down. "Schmeichel, the Neville brothers, Johnsen, May, Keane, Scholes, Beckham, Giggs, Cole and Solskjaer."

"Oh aye, that's right Irwin's suspended for this one. Shame that."

"It was a ridiculous card, petty even, but it's the rules." Tom continued. "Bench is, Stam, Brown, Sheringham, Butt and Yorke."

Billy was stood at the back of the booth in an attempt to avoid Eddie. "Why do you reckon Stam's on the bench?"

Walter responded. "I think Alex Ferguson's got one eye on Wednesday's match; maybe he wants to keep Stam fresh for that." He made eye contact with Billy and winked. "It's only my opinion of course."

Willie had half his attention on the conversation around him and half on the horse race at Musselburgh later that day. "I think Stam is carrying a bit of an injury but yeah, why risk him today when he can be fully fit by Wednesday."

"Yeah, I agree he's going to be more valuable to Alex Ferguson in Wednesday's game." Jaap Stam had become a firm favourite for Mark since he signed for United the previous year. "His experience in Europe will be a stabilising factor for the team with Keane suspended."

"That's a good point, Mark." Sir Matt did not need to look to know a wave of redness had swept across Mark's face. "His European experience, and the way he's handled himself since joining United, I think he'll be with the Club for many a year to come."

"I hope so," Mark said.

"Henning Berg's still injured but I think he'll be okay for Wednesday's game," Walter continued. "And I'm chuffed David May's got a start."

Willie, the Racing Post read from front to back page, leant back. "It was unlucky he didn't play enough games to get a Championship medal. At least he's in the running to contribute to the silverware tally; if they win this one."

"So there's no Van der Gouw?"

"Actually, he is. I forgot him, sorry."

"No disrespect to Van der Gouw but if, as a replacement goalie, you're forgotten that's a *good* thing." Dennis stretched forward, over Willie's shoulder to pick up the Racing Post.

Henry made his way to his seat. "It means Schmeichel's doing his job properly. Van der Gouw will get his chance to shine next season."

"I don't think so Henry. Alex Ferguson will be on the lookout for someone a little more tried and tested than Van der Gouw. He's been a great standby but, for the main event, I would prefer to have a look at Europe, but that's just my opinion." Sir Matt brought the stem of his pipe up to his mouth.

Jimmy tapped Sir Matt on the shoulder. "From the point of view of goalkeeping; who impressed you the most in the World Cup?"

"Edwin Van der Sar for the Netherlands had a *great* tournament."

"See, I told you, it will be Van der Sar." Bert was cock-a-hoop.

Billy agreed. "He would be an amazing replacement for Schmeichel. If anyone can pull that deal off it would be Alex Ferguson."

"Bernard Lama had a good tournament but he's too old."

Duncan asked. "Anyone closer to home, so to speak?"

"Nigel Martyn. He's destined for bigger and better things that lad. Yeah, I'd try to explain life could be better on the other side of the A62."

The journalists reflected on what it must be like to interview Alex Ferguson. They had heard his straightforward approach was similar to that of Sir Matt and they put that down to the fact they were born fifteen miles apart from each other.

Eric coughed to attract attention and broke into the self-reflection. "Just in case you guys are wondering, the line-up for Newcastle United, you know, the team United are playing today, is Harper in goal, Griffin, Dabizas, Charvet and Domi in defence. Lee, Hamann, Speed and Solano in midfield with Shearer and Ketsbaia up front."

"And talking about firsts," It had escaped Bert's attention that the last five minutes of conversation had *not* been about firsts. "Solano is the first Peruvian to ever play in an FA Cup Final. Ketsbaia is the first Georgian, although that was last year and not today."

Sir Matt placed the stem of his pipe to his mouth to hide his smile. "Thanks, Bert."

"You're welcome Boss."

Duncan asked. "Is Duncan Ferguson on the bench?"

"Oops, yeah, sorry; the rest of the bench is Given, Barton, Glass and Marić."

Archie looked up from typing the preamble to his article. "It's a good thing Ferguson's on the bench, to be honest; he can be a bit of handful that one."

"I know, but apparently he's having a hernia operation on Monday," Donny proffered.

"Is that right? I thought hernias were serious."

"Yeah, they are, I mean, they were. Some things that were serious in the fifties are no longer so in the nineties or, should I say the twenty-first century."

Tommy put his elbows on his thighs and soaked up the images from Wembley. "Look at that crowd." He turned to Mark and David. "There must be something special about watching a game at Wembley. The equal division of match tickets, fans with their replica shirts and having a right ball before kick-off. I'm not too sure about all that face painting though."

David squinted as he looked at the ceiling and began to click his fingers. "Let me think, let me think. I've got it!" With a grin, he pointed at Tommy. "The England game against Brazil back in 1956?" David raised his eyebrows. "Am I right? Am I right? Oh yes, look at his face, I'm right."

Tommy blushed.

Mark came to Tommy's rescue and pointed to the screen. "Look around though, it seems to be just a Newcastle thing. There aren't many United supporters with painted faces."

"That pitch looks immaculate." Roger took his seat. "I'd love to pop down and just feel the pitch, you know feel it pulsating."

A camera panned the faces of both teams as they lined up in the tunnel, concentration on the ninety minutes ahead. Handshakes were made, mascots reassured, the muffled sounds of seventy thousand people chanting, roaring and then the walk.

Their emergence out of the tunnel into a gladiator's arena, the smell of sulphur emitted from the exploded fireworks tickled the nostrils and blurred the eyes. The roar of the crowd was almost frenzied. Peter Schmeichel wiped his eyes with his towel. In the Bar, they *felt* their eyes smart and wrinkled their noses at the smell.

Manchester United supporters around Wembley began the chant for their captain.

La la la, la la la Keano. La la la, la la la Keano. La la la, la la la Keano.

The first few lines of the national anthem were sung before Alf frowned and looked around to see if anyone else had noticed. Out of respect, he said nothing but, at the end, he blurted out. "What was that?"

He looked around as the journalists settled themselves behind their laptops and notepads. "I'm not happy with their choice of singer. The national anthem is the national anthem; you can't just change the words to suit whoever's singing it! It's *our* gracious Queen, not *your* gracious Queen. Terrible." He plopped down in his seat and began to write furiously.

"She's probably not from the United Kingdom and that's why she sang *your* and not *our* gracious Queen." George thought this would placate Alf; it did not.

Alf spluttered. "What? Surely they could have found an English lass to sing the anthem."

David, Tommy and Mark exchanged amused glances but knew better than to toy with Alf on this subject.

Willie inclined his head towards Sir Matt. "I don't think we'll have a classic on our hands, I get the feeling it's going to be a comfortable game. What do you think?"

"It's a step they need to take to get to the Holy Grail. You're right though I can't see us having a classic today but, they'll get the job done."

Eddie threw his head back and laughed; he grabbed the knees of Billy and Geoff on either side of him. "Oh, yes, maybe we could give that a watch again tonight." His head swivelled from one to another, ready to hear the word, yes.

"Monty Python, you mean? No count me out; I'm not a fan." Geoff said.

Billy tried to think of a reason not to and failed under the eager gaze of Eddie; he murmured. "Maybe; let's ask the others later." He straightened his tie and had a word with himself about saying no sometimes.

Eddie, confident he could convince the others sat back, put his arms around the shoulders of Billy and Geoff and sang. *"We're knights of the Round Table. We dance whene'er we're able. We do routines and chorus scenes with footwork impec…"* His carolling was cut short when Sir Matt leant forward and made eye contact with him.

"Anyone willing to make a prediction of what the score is going to be?" Duncan asked.

"I can only see a United win but I'm not sure if it's going to be two one or two nil," Roger said.

"I definitely think United will score two, it seems to be their popular tally per game and, I do think Shearer will score one, so two one for me," said Dennis.

"I agree, I can't see United losing this, but what I think is *most* important is they get through today with no injuries to the key players for Wednesday,"

Before Dennis could respond to Johnny, Peter Jones, the referee, blew the whistle and the 1998/1999 FA Cup Final got underway.

CHAPTER FIVE

Newcastle United started at a fast pace and within minutes a Ketsbaia foul on Johnsen resulted in a free kick *and* a ball change.

"They changed the ball!" Alf scribbled this fact to his list of cons about the game.

Eric raised his eyebrows but kept silent. Tom Jackson leant forward to peer over Alf's shoulders and read the list; the capital letters evidence of his displeasure.

David laughed and pointed to the screen. "There's another first and last just happened right there."

"What?" Mark asked. "What did I miss?"

"Gary Speed; he's just tackled Keane."

"He knows he's not going to meet Keane again until next season." Mark gave credit where it was due. "He got the ball though, it was a well-timed tackle."

"Yeah, he doesn't seem to realise Keane is like an elephant, he never forgets a tackle."

His forehead furrowed, Tommy said. "He's limping a bit."

"He'll be fine he just needs to run it off." Mark was sure Roy Keane had muscles of steel.

"I hope so, especially after last season."

Walter swung his arm around Bert's shoulders. "This is going to be an end to end game I reckon; Newcastle are not going to lie down and just defend."

"There's not much point in *just* defending. Someone has to win today."

"Audacious shot by the first Peruvian in an FA Cup Final." David hoped Bert had heard his comment; he turned to him and was met by a full display of Bert's teeth and a thumbs-up followed by a dig in the ribs from Duncan.

"Yeah, Schmeichel had it covered. Fortunately," said Duncan.

He nodded to the image of Keane and said to Sir Matt. "It doesn't look like he can run that injury off."

"He could still be suffering from that ankle injury he got a few weeks ago."

"It's not like him to let a niggling injury get in the way of a game, it must be serious."

"You're right; he's not the type of player to malinger so if he's still limping, it looks like it could be serious." Sir Matt put his pipe to his mouth and frowned at the image of the hobbling Keane.

"He'll be okay." Duncan crossed his arms but quickly shook out his posture and sat up straight, his feet on the ball. "If adrenaline doesn't get him through this then..." He left the sentence unfinished. "It's his last game this season."

Nolberto Solano took a clever shot at goal but it was saved, at the second attempt, by Schmeichel.

All focus was on Keane as he kicked the ball out and bent over with his hands on his knees; he squatted, fists on the pitch, head bowed. Alex Ferguson wildly gestured to those around Keane. His teammates circled the wagons, hands on hips.

They knew, in their heart of hearts that this was the end of the season for Keane. A medic ran onto the pitch as Keane placed his hands around his left ankle. Alex Ferguson and Steve MacLaren were deep in hurried, unplanned discussion about who would replace him.

"They've got the stretcher guys on." Jimmy could not disguise his disappointment; not for the sight of Sheringham readying himself for substitution but the fact Keane's season was over.

Keane waved away the stretcher and stood. His face a barometer of how much his ankle caused him discomfort but his demeanour was proof of how he would try to soldier on. The roar of *Keano, Keano, Keano,* grew louder around Wembley.

Tom Curry's shoulders slumped. "I can't believe it. He's our warrior."

Dietmar Hamann played a sliding tackle into Phil Neville as he tried to keep the ball in play and was given a yellow card by the referee.

"He didn't even get the ball." Geoff began to tap his foot and quickly stopped; it was too early to experience nerves.

"If Newcastle continue like this there's going to be a serious injury to another United player," Roger said.

"Maybe that's what Newcastle want, you know, by any means necessary."

"I hope not. It's not sportsmanlike is it?"

"Newcastle have *tackled* Scholes, Keane and Phil Neville, with some serious intent." Jimmy crossed his legs, his elbow on the back of the booth. "If the referee didn't take control by showing Hamann a yellow all hell could break loose."

"They're not allowing them anytime on the ball at all. It's disrupting their usual flow of play." Sir Matt knew United would settle down and hoped it would be before Newcastle did any serious damage.

Roger said. "Well, I don't know if the game has changed that much. Remember the Villa game at Old Trafford, September 1957?" They experienced their own visuals of the game. Roger's mouth twitched and his eyes sparkled. "Stan Crowther was giving our Billy a hard time. I had a word with him."

Most tried to stifle a smile at the memory.

"I said he needed to chill out, as they say these days. I couldn't imagine how or why he was still on the pitch. I can't say it was my proudest moment but in the end, I let him have it full throttle. He got the message, don't mess with United." Roger crossed his arms and sat back.

Billy could not hide the delight he felt at the memory. He stretched over and touched Roger on his arm. "Crowther knew then; if *you* asked him something then he had better take notice and oblige." Dennis, Johnny and Jackie exchanged knowing glances.

"The potential was always there but now, with TV and different camera angles, and everything, players should be less inclined to take it too far," Willie said.

Teddy Sheringham received instructions to warm up. Alex Ferguson may have preferred to preserve him for the Bayern Munich game but it was not to be; a decision needed to be made before Keane caused himself further injury.

Ryan Giggs picked up the ball on the halfway line and made a run down the wing; he slid a diagonal ball, anticipating a run by Cole into midfield. On the edge of the eighteen-yard box, Domi thwarted Giggs' intent as he edged ahead and squared the ball to Charvet who almost caused embarrassment by taking too much time. Harper kicked the ball away before Cole could pounce.

"They're not giving them a chance to get settled." Jackie's nostrils flared. "United know Keane needs to be substituted, you can see nerves are becoming jangled."

Willie stood and applauded as the ball went out of play. "It's the last seconds of the warrior's season. That's a real shame."

United supporter escorted one of their favourite gladiators off the pitch. *La la la la, la la la la Keano.*

Mark nudged Tommy. "How do you think Sheringham's going to fit in?"

"It looks like Solskjaer's going out to the right." Tommy pondered the rejig and shook his head. "I don't know; I suppose it could release Beckham to play alongside Scholes. They'll miss his crossing ability from out wide though."

"It's a position Beckham's comfortable in, but I get your point."

It was quiet in the Bar. Each reflected on the impact Keane's injury would have on the team but no-one dared to give credence to their worried thoughts by verbalising them.

Manchester United had a free kick. Beckham sized up his options and sent a diagonal ball to Scholes in the centre circle. Scholes played it back to his fellow redheaded colleague, David May. A long forward pass by May to Cole and the fluidity of play between United increased.

"Nice touch by Cole," David said.

Andy Cole faced and passed the ball to Sheringham. He skipped around two Newcastle defenders and, with his first touch of the ball, flicked into the space where he knew Scholes would soon enter. Scholes continued his run and thread the ball forward to Sheringham now on his way into Newcastle's penalty area.

Sheringham had no time to think but, with a striker's intuition, saw Harper move forward and, with his right foot made contact. The ball sailed through the advancing Harper's legs and hit the back of the net.

The back of the net billowed and an energy wave swept through the Bar. It launched people up like rockets, arms stretched to the ceiling, heads back and the word, *yesss* expelled. A champagne cork flying out of a shaken bottle could not have exploded more effervescently. It was the same in the Stadium.

The arched double doors swung open as souls and archangels rushed into the Bar to watch the replay and join in the celebrations.

Tommy, with a smile wider than the goal scorer's, jumped up and copied Sheringham's celebration. The other Babes, arms around each other's shoulders, ran around the booths, up to the bar and along the screen, smiles so bright the sunlight streaming through the stained glass windows reflected off them, a sight that mesmerised.

Sir Matt watched them, his pipe halfway to his mouth. He brought himself back to the present and used his pipe to point to the screen. Alex Ferguson was celebrating the goal the same way, arms up in the air. "Look at your man's face there."

David, hands pressed to his cheeks, flopped back into the booth. "What an entrance!"

The excited conversations, the laughter, the giggles of the archangels vibrated in the air of the Bar, the suspended shirts fluttered their approval.

"How many minutes has he been on the pitch?"

"It's seconds."

"Incredible."

"I can't imagine Schmeichel letting in a goal like that," Duncan said.

Sir Matt nodded. "Harper's inexperienced in comparison but, he should have done better." He liked Harper and did not want to overly criticise the man. Sir Matt saw the replay and nodded. "He should have stayed on his line."

"It was still a well-worked goal by United." Willie walked back to the booth, his hands almost sore from the celebratory applause.

"You're right; Scholes and Sheringham worked a great combination. You know, I think Newcastle knew what they were doing with Keane on the pitch but, when he came off and Sheringham came on, the Solskjaer position change threw them a curve ball."

"Yeah, it threw them out of formation."

We shall not, we shall not be moved. We shall not, we shall not be moved. Just like a team that's gonna win the FA Cup, again; we shall not be moved.

Willie looked at the screen; Alex Ferguson beamed. "That's a happy man."

Cheer up Alan Shearer, oh what can it mean to a sad Geordie bastard and a shite football team.

The screen gave a close-up of Shearer as he attached himself to a long ball from Speed. Johnsen harried him enough that the only option was for him to pass the ball back, towards Lee.

Patient passing play by Newcastle ensued and Lee crossed the ball into the box only for the ball to be headed wide by Shearer. A semi-derisive *aaah* escaped from the mouths of the United contingent at Wembley.

"Good defensive play there by Gary Neville," Geoff said.

Roger knew, given half the chance, Geoff would be Down Below following Neville around the pitch. "Yeah, he read it well; he knows what Shearer can *and* will do given the opportunity."

"For his age, Sheringham's quite nimble, you know," Johnny added. "At the age of thirty-one, to go to a top club like United; Alex Ferguson must have had faith he'd get a couple more years out of him."

"And he replaced Eric Cantona! Some pressure," responded Jackie, he put his arm along the back of the booth. "Think of the age we started, in most clubs, we wouldn't have been given a chance, it was *such* a big deal they called us Babes."

He shrugged and glanced back at the screen. "I don't know maybe it's because the lifespan of a footballer has stretched further than it did in the fifties. These days you could actually have a playing career spanning twenty years or more."

Dennis laid his head on the back of the booth and looked at the ceiling. "That's just unbelievable, isn't it?"

He positioned his body to mirror Jackie's. "Look at that eighteen-year-old, Michael Owen; last year he became England's youngest player and youngest goalscorer in a World Cup final tournament," Dennis spoke with wonderment. "It took over forty years to take Duncan's record; that's a long time. But times are definitely changing. I bet Owen will still be playing in twenty years *and* I wonder what other records and achievements he's going to pick up along the way."

Johnny asked. "If you had the chance to experience a year playing football Down Below, in this era I mean, would you take it?"

The shake of the head came without hesitation. "No." Dennis was adamant. "We played in the era we did and I wouldn't change a thing."

Jackie smiled and turned back to the screen. "Me neither Dennis, me neither.

Duncan had overheard the conversation. He rolled the ball away from him several inches, flicked the ball up with his right foot, caught it, spun it around and said. "I would; *but,* with this ball."

***

David Beckham clattered into Dabisaz; the referee's whistle summoned him back to be reprimanded. It was obvious it had been perpetrated in retaliation for Griffin's tackle on Giggs a few seconds earlier.

Willie shook his head. "You've got to stand up for your teammates but you've also got to be careful. One wrong move could mean a serious injury or a card."

We are the pride of all Europe, the cock of the north. We all hate Scousers and Cockneys of course and Leeds. We are United without any doubt; we are the Manchester boys, la, la, la.

Tommy started to laugh. "United are starting to rough things up a bit now; even Solskjaer's getting in on the act."

Ole Gunnar Solskjaer would be the first to admit tackling was not a strong element of his game and when he tackled Speed in the twentieth minute, most people thought: *that's for Keane.*

"Excellent dive and triple roll by Speed; I give him eight out of ten."

Eddie crinkled his nose. "Come on Billy, that's only a seven out of ten; there was no clutching of his ankle *and* he's back on his feet within seconds."

"I suppose you're right; let's split the difference and give him a seven point five."

"You're on." Eddie sat back and grinned. "Eight out of ten! You're losing it Billy boy."

A free kick was the result of Solskjaer's rash but understandable challenge; it was a fair distance but goals have been scored from similar positions.

"He's not going to score from there," Mark predicted as Solano lined up the free kick. It skimmed the top of the net, much closer than Shearer's headed attempt.

***

George turned to Eric. "I like Solano. How do you think he would fit into a United team?"

"He's good but I don't think he's the type of player United need." Eric pointed to his United squad list. "Look. There's an embarrassment of riches in midfield right now, he'd just be warming the bench."

Crystal bells rang out across the Bar; Roger stood and made his way to pick up the ballot slips for the FA Cup goal of the season. He hid his amusement at the number of archangels behind the bar; *working*.

The Bar doors resembled a Wild West saloon as souls and archangels came in to watch the rest of the match. Everyone was relaxed and, although the game was only midway into the first half there was a belief this was Manchester United's game and Newcastle could do nothing to stop the march forward to.

Manchester, Manchester United, a bunch of bouncing Busby Babes they deserve to be knighted.

Mark was lost in thought as he focussed on his new Nike trainers. Although Sir Matt had requested suits for finals he had not expressed a preference for formal footwear. David startled him when he said. "They look great; much better than those Air Flights you've been wearing for decades."

"I liked my Air Flights and, for your information, I wasn't wearing them for decades, only eight years or so, no time at all."

Tommy slipped his feet under the booth but David, eyes on the screen said. "Don't bother Tommy, I noticed back in the cinema you were wearing those tired old New Balance."

"I like you and Eddie being our *fashion gurus*," Tommy chuckled as he used air quotes, "but to be honest when it comes to trainers I get lost; especially when they become more ridiculous." Tommy appeased David by adding. "But I love those baggy jeans you had on before." He didn't. David sat back, content with the progress they were making in improving fashion Up Above.

Duncan decided to change the subject before David said anything about his football boots. "I hate to say this, but Sheringham seems to be in total control of the midfield right now."

"I know what you mean. They're not too dissimilar in play but I think Sheringham just edges it in terms of control and poise." Sir Matt looked as he flicked *ash* from his tie. "Keane's more of an *assertive* player."

Duncan looked at Sir Matt and laughed out loud. "Assertive? Okay, we'll call it that."

Yip Jaap Stam is a big Dutchman, get past him if you * can. Try a little trick and he'll make you look a prick, Yip Yap Jaap Stam.

"Did you hear that?" Tommy said.

"What?" Mark and David asked, in unison.

"Solskjaer's got seventeen goals from sixteen starts this season! That's incredible."

David started to chuckle. "And he got four of those in ten minutes."

Mark recalled the memory. "He looked embarrassed. Jim Ryan told him to go on and hold up the midfield, nothing more."

"I remember Steve Stone's face; it was the epitome of shell-shocked."

"He's a United legend in the making that one. That tackle he did on Speed a little earlier reminds me of the tackle he made on Rob Lee last season." Tommy stroked his chin and smiled. "He knew it was a rash tackle, but he knew he had to stop him heading for goal, by any means necessary. The red card was a certainty. He got up and started to walk towards the tunnel, even before the referee got the card out. A United player who knows what he has to do for the cause."

"He put the team first; that and his crucial goals. He's a legend in the making. Remember how he turned down the *done deal* move to Spurs last season," Tom Curry said.

A Griffin tackle on Giggs left Griffin the worse for wear with blood streaming down his nose; first blood to Manchester United.

"That looked like a wrestling body slam by Giggs," Billy said.

Eddie laughed. "I was just thinking the same. He must have taken a few lessons watching WWF."

"You're not still watching WWF, are you?"

"No." Eddie hoped his face had not reddened. "I just remember a few moves; that's all." He flicked Billy's ear. "Don't pretend you didn't get all excited when it first came out."

"It's contrived, that's what I think."

Johnny moved forward, his head between Eddie and Billy. "That's the way the world of sport is going at the moment." They mirrored each other as they turned to Johnny. "A lot is for theatrical effect, for television. You only have to see the way some players roll around like they've been hit by a bullet when the opposition brushes past them."

"It's become acceptable," Jackie interjected. "The more people see it on TV, the more they think it's acceptable, the more players do it. It's a vicious circle that will only get worse for the game."

David Beckham's free kick sailed into the box over the heads of May, Cole, Johnsen *and* Sheringham; out for a goal kick. The replay, seen from a different angle showed just how close Sheringham had been for his second and possibly winning goal.

"That was close," Willie whispered.

"That's where the money has been spent in football I suppose; all the cameras, the ability to see a shot from several different angles, within seconds." Johnny had his head back against the edge of the booth, his eyes on the screen. "It's certainly helped the armchair supporter become more of an *expert*."

Dennis shrugged. "I suppose it's brought the game to a wider audience but it doesn't change the game. It's played by two teams of eleven men, a referee and a couple of linesmen."

The atmosphere was relaxed, the men slouched; the archangels were quiet. Walter said. "I hate feeling this relaxed; there's no real tension in the air at all for this game."

"I was *just* going to say the same thing! I wonder why that is."

"Could be confidence in their ability to score more goals; I don't know."

"In the grand scheme of things how we feel is not important. *We* can relax and not experience nerves, they can't," replied Bert.

"That's it!" Willie pointed at the screen. "Look! Domi fights for the ball, he stays on his feet, they're in the box but there's something missing. They don't look in the least bit threatening, do they?"

Tom Curry began to fidget. "I don't think it's their fault, United have that edge today, plain and simple. You can see it, it's almost telepathic play." He wondered if Roger would hand out the ballot slips early today; his mind was on his top three FA Cup goals.

"Remember last Saturday's game?" Sir Matt said. "Spurs didn't look threatening and then Ferdinand popped up out of nowhere and scored."

Jimmy laughed. "There was tension in the air that day; they were nervous. The fact that results with Arsenal could have changed things didn't help."

Willie loosened his tie. "I suppose you're right. For me, I can't escape the fact this game seems to be, inevitably, Manchester United's."

Alan Shearer backed into Johnsen and was immediately reprimanded, accompanied by catcalls from the United fans in the Stadium. The awarded free kick was taken by Schmeichel and although the ball landed in Newcastle's box it didn't reach Cole or Sheringham. Although Cole kept the ball in play he hit it straight into the appreciative arms of Harper.

Tom Jackson shook himself out of his jacket and an archangel appeared to whisk it away. The game on the screen commanded only half of his attention; the rest of his thoughts were on the top three goals of this FA Cup season.

"There's any number of United players who could score another goal but will it be a classic?" Tom was warming to the subject. "Cole's goal against Spurs flew into our lists after we'd written them up but they don't all happen like that." He stretched his arms wide, stood and made his way over to Roger to collect the ballot slips for the journalists' booth. "Okay; I'm ready to write down my top three."

Archie's eyes followed Tom through the screen to the Busby booth but his auditory attention was on the match. "Sheringham's been close to getting his second, Cole has looked dangerous in the box and of course, you've got the ginger prince who's playing in his last game this season. I don't think they'll sit back on their laurels, they'll want to score more; they usually do."

"Well, Newcastle could spoil that particular scenario; they're stringing together a good couple of passes between them now." The moment Henry's comment left his lips Speed delivered a pass to Shearer which caught him offside.

Roger raised an eyebrow. "I take it the vote for the number one goal this FA Cup season is Giggs' in the Arsenal replay?"

"It would be hard-pressed to find another goal that delivered so much; it's my number one." Willie looked down at the ballot slip in his lap and began to write.

"Can I have a show of hands please?" The vote was unanimous.

"It's not even halftime and we're voting for best FA Cup goal of the season! We really should concentrate on the game; we're still in the first half!" Willie flashed a guilty smile as he resumed writing down his goals for second and third place.

Geoff pointed his chin towards the screen. "That's proving to be an important battle, Johnsen and Shearer."

Roger agreed. "Johnsen is really thwarting Shearer's play today."

"He's a great central defender who's hardly put a foot wrong this season."

***

Paul Scholes slotted a ball to Sheringham who had his pass to Solskjaer intercepted by Domi. Gary Neville took the throw-in, aiming for Beckham; he passed it back to Gary who crossed it into the box.

The ball eluded Solskjaer in front of goal but it reached Giggs on the left who hit the ball back into Newcastle's penalty box.

"Solskjaer's opportunity to get on the score sheet; and he knows it," Tommy said.

"He'll kick himself when he sees the replay; so near, yet so far."

"Sometimes, it's those missed opportunities you look back on and think, what if, maybe, you know?"

Mark agreed. "I know. If only I'd scored that goal against X then we would be three points in ahead, that kind of thing."

"Yeah, it's what makes the game so beautiful one minute and so soul destroying the next."

"He'll get another chance."

In that moment, Beckham kicked the ball to Solskjaer who, selflessly, headed it down to Cole. It had *goal* written all over it when the ball left Cole's right foot. However, Dabisaz rescued the blushes of Harper by deflecting the ball from the intended target.

Duncan was on his feet; he pressed his hair back with his hands. "Oh I can't believe it, how did that not result in a goal?

"Harper off his line again! He should buy Dabisaz a pint or two tonight." David could not stop shaking his head.

"Yep, Manchester United, I reckon, will score at least two more." Duncan sat with both feet on the ball, but his posture showed he was ready to jump up the second it looked like the Newcastle net would bulge.

"Well, if this past half hour is anything to go by then I think you're right. Johnsen is stopping everything going Shearer's way and I had to check who else was up front because I don't think he's had a look in yet."

Newcastle United played their part in dissipating the cloud of complacency that hovered over Red Cloud Bar; they were not out, they still had their part to play in the match. On their way towards United's goal, Ketsbaia held up play and waited for reinforcement in the guise of Hamann.

His attempt, before it could become valid was blocked by Johnsen. The ball fell to Speed, whose shot, well over the net, was not worthy of the work Ketsbaia had put into setting it up. Speed probably felt frustrated at himself, judging by the subsequent challenge he made on Gary Neville.

"Speed needs to watch himself. That was a late challenge on Gary Neville there." Geoff became almost protective of the older Neville brother.

Eddie held his hands in the air and squinted. "The headline for this section of the movie will be, *The Clash of the Garys*." He cast his eyes around the booth. "You know; a play on the Clash of the Titans? Nobody?" Eddie looked to the journalists and received blank stares. "Seriously?" Eddie was disappointed.

Ketsbaia was at the crux of any relevant play by Newcastle. His next opportunity came with nine minutes of the first half left. He held up play and passed to Domi who moved up the pitch and gave the ball back. Ketsbaia spread play to Hamann. The blistering shot caused Schmeichel to dive and hit the ball out for a corner.

Willie took in a sharp breath. "Fantastic save! We're going to miss him."

"Don't remind me," said Dennis.

"I think David needs to keep quiet for the rest of the game." Johnny joked. "Hamann had his first real shot at goal just as you mentioned he'd been quiet!"

David laughed. "It would be the first time my words have influenced play in any meaningful way." And hand over his heart area said, "I'm touched."

"Is this their first corner?" Jackie queried.

"I think it's their second, but it's the first time Schmeichel has been tested; and" Johnny glanced at the clock. "We've got five minutes left."

A long ball into United's box by Lee and Dabisaz went to ground.

"He's looking for a penalty!" Willie pointed to the screen; sure he was the only one who had witnessed the dive.

"I give him seven out of ten for acrobatic performance and minus seven out of ten for sportsmanship." Sir Matt said.

"I'm surprised; he's not usually that type of player."

"Frustration I expect, but that's when they will start making mistakes."

The disgruntled Newcastle players were matched by the determination of the United players; evident when Cole saw off challenges by three separate players to retain the ball and pass to Scholes. The run was cut short when Beckham was dispossessed. Never one for letting a challenge go unanswered, he ran back for the ball, challenged Ketsbaia and gave away a free kick.

"You can't disguise the fact the lad loves playing for United. But, to be honest, I think some referees are going to want to make a name for themselves and red card him because of who he is and who he plays for rather than the tackle itself." Sir Matt reflected on how much influence the media had on football these days.

"He'll have to be careful." Willie straightened his back and made eye contact with Eric. "I believe Alex Ferguson told the press to go forth and multiply after Beckham's *scapegoattery* in the World Cup."

Eric stood, mimed taking off a top-hat and made a bow: "Use it as you wish."

The archangels giggled and scrambled to make a note of the use of the word.

"Hamann will be disappointed he didn't make more of that," Tommy said.

"Where's Shearer?" David said; his eyes roamed about the screen. "I've not heard his name for the past few minutes."

"He's trying to escape Johnsen." Roger, felt a semblance of pity when a camera panned to show the disappointed face of Shearer.

Duncan clutched David's forearm. "Please, please David, stop mentioning names."

Gary Neville sent a well-timed cross in the box for Sheringham. His head connected but he shot inches wide of the target. Alex Ferguson had risen from his seat, his body twisted, almost urging the ball over the goal line; he thought it was their second goal.

"Gary Neville's supplied some wonderful crosses into the box, hasn't he?" Geoff was delighted to see everyone nodding in agreement.

Billy said. "He's getting into areas Newcastle can only dream of, he's a passionate player."

"I wonder if Ruud Gullit is happy with Newcastle's performance so far," Jimmy asked, rhetorically.

Sir Matt looked into the bowl of his pipe and thought for a second. "It's difficult. Most people *think* they can do better. It's hard to walk in another man's shoes. The Newcastle players are doing okay, but they've created, what, two credible goal-scoring opportunities? United have created six or seven, that's going to make the difference at the final whistle. The law of probabilities says United are more than likely to score again. Add that to the fact, I *believe* they want it more than Newcastle."

A brief silence followed as the journalists formulated possible phrases to quote.

The last five minutes saw United, yet again, put pressure on Newcastle's midfield and defence.

George dropped his pad and pen to the floor and stretched his legs in front of him, his arms stretched in the air. "That's the third or fourth time Shearer's been caught offside."

"The pervasiveness of Johnsen's play is stopping Shearer from even *touching* the ball," Swifty remarked.

"And long may that continue."

The souls in the Bar spent the remaining seconds of the first half in their own private thoughts, listening to the supporters sing *their* love for the team, past and present.

Mark broke into the private reverie and inquired. "When do you think we'll hear another one of the Busby chants?"

"If…" Walter shook himself. "Sorry, I mean, when they score a second I bet you'll hear them, raise the roof with one."

Peter Jones lifted the whistle, checked his watch and blew for the end of the first half; the sound met with satisfaction. The twenty-five moved around the Bar as though to stretch their legs, conversations broke out in small groups and archangels flittered from one group to another.

***

"Alex Ferguson should be happy with that," Billy said as stood with Duncan in front of the screen. "What do you think? There's not a lot he can say to the lads when they get in the dressing room, except make more of your chances."

Duncan caught the ball in his solo game of keepy-uppy; he traced the leather panels and said. "But that's one of the crucial parts of the game. You can play like champions but if you don't put the ball in the back of the next you're the runner-up." They exchanged knowing smiles; Duncan dropped the ball and they played gentle one-touch football.

"It's possible he'll make some changes up front." Jackie moved to the front row to watch Duncan and Billy. "United's defence and midfield are having a great game so far; I just think up front we need to change it up a bit."

Billy trapped the ball under his foot, hands on hips and looked to Duncan and then Jackie. "Who would you take off and for who?"

Without hesitation, Jackie responded. "I'd take Solskjaer off and put Yorkie on, a straight swap." He looked up at Duncan. "What do you think?"

"I'd do the same but, what do we know."

Billy nudged the ball forward and Duncan stretched to keep it in *play*. "If it was me," his hand on his chest, "I'd keep the formation the same, at least for the first few minutes of the second half, you know, counteract any changes Newcastle might make."

"Do you think they will make any changes?"

"Well, I don't believe Gullit is a knee-jerk manager and he will want to keep faith in the team he picked but, to be honest, I think he should take Shearer off. You need to take sentimentality out of it. I know he went to Newcastle to *win trophies*, but…"

"He's had about three offside calls as far as I can recall and that's unusual for him."

"There's a fair bit riding on this game. The second cup in a possible Double, the second cup in a possible historic Treble but it feels like fa…"

Please remember, there is no fate.

The smile on David's face sparkled as he turned and looked to the rainbow orb hovering over the bar. "There is no fate but what we make."

Everyone sensed The Omnipotent One's smile. The Omnipotent One had a quark sized soft spot for David.

***

Alf, Donny and Henry remained in the booth poring over their first-half reports.

"Well, it's a beautiful poetic article so far, if I may say so myself." Alf got to his feet and straightened his tie in a self-congratulatory manner.

Henry chuckled. "Well Alf, I suppose someone has to." He looked up and laughed out loud at Alf rubbing his middle finger up and down his cheek.

"Sorry guys remind me of who's on the bench for Newcastle." Donny's head was hunkered over his article and a whisper of a frown creased his forehead.

Henry glanced down at his laptop. "They've got Shay Given, Warren Barton, Silvio Marić, Stephen Glass and Duncan Ferguson."

"So, it's likely big Dunc will get a run out; there's not really many other options up-front are there?"

Before the possible substitution options were dissected and scrutinised Roger stood, his cough was accompanied by the peal of crystal bells. "Okay, thank you. We've got ten minutes to select our top three goals of this season's FA Cup run."

Sir Matt raised his pipe. "Well, we've all voted for Ryan Giggs' goal against Arsenal in the semi-final replay as number one. Of course, if something out of this world happens in the second half, I will reconsider."

"One of the great things about that game is how they never gave up; and to score a goal like that as well." David rubbed his forearms as though his hairs were on end.

Willie looked up to Roger. "Can I say something?" Roger nodded and Willie continued as he got to his feet to face everyone. "Okay, there's a goal that I'm sure is the next highest on the list of everyone and, if so, then maybe we only need to write down one nomination for third place."

Sir Matt smiled and waved his pipe. "Let me guess? Is it Solskjaer's goal against Liverpool?" The response was gesticulated hands, foam balls thrown into the air, laughter and a sprinkling of applause. Roger turned to the bar; he opened his mouth to speak and saw one of the archangels waving a sheet of paper with Ryan Giggs at number one, Ole Gunnar Solskjaer at two and a blank next to the number three.

"Well, that's a first time. We've got some time so, who wants to say which goal they've got for number three?"

"It's got to be Beckham's goal against Arsenal in the semi-final replay. I mean, if it wasn't for the goal Giggs scored later it would definitely be in the top two." Tommy handed his slip to Roger.

Mark agreed. "You're right mate; it was an amazing strike from open play."

David glanced at Duncan's slip. "Which one have you gone for?"

"Well, not many games to choose from, in comparison to the Premiership and Champions League, but I've gone for Yorke's second goal against Chelsea back in March."

Dennis nodded. "Yeah, there's not an embarrassment of riches to choose from like the other two trophies but for me, it was a toss-up between Beckham's and Yorke's." Peeking over the shoulders of Roger and Geoff he saw that they too had the same dilemma.

"Okay, I suggest we put both in joint third place." Roger was met with nods and thumbs up. "Good, okay." Roger smiled when he turned to the bar and saw the archangels jigging around holding aloft the sheet of paper with the top four FA Cup goals written on it. "Of course, if there's a wonder goal we're going to have to revisit this."

Everyone sat back in their booths and watched the highlights of all four goals.

CHAPTER SIX

Both teams ran onto the pitch. Newcastle had replaced Hamann with Ferguson, a player who had started the season wearing the blue of Everton. A camera panned and followed the fast walk of Alex Ferguson as he made his way to his seat.

"He's got to be happy with the match so far," Eddie said, half his attention on Sheringham and Cole waiting to kick-off and the other on his new trick, rolling a coin across his knuckles.

Geoff shrugged. "I'm not sure. Yeah, they're one nil up but they should be at least four nil up. I hope those wasted opportunities don't come and bite them on the proverbial come full-time."

"I'm not sure that's the right substitution Gullit should be making. If it was me, I would have taken off Shearer but I think he's not brave enough to do that." Johnny wanted the game to be more of a gladiatorial match.

"Shearer hasn't threatened United's defence at all but I'm not sure Duncan Ferguson is a nippier player than Hamann. He's solid, I'll give him that."

Johnny was persistent. "Shearer should be subbed at some point."

"You're not his greatest fan, are you?" Billy said.

"It's not that, well it is but, a team is more than one man; a team is greater than sentimentality, do you know what I mean?"

"Sure I do." Billy nodded over to the journalists. "I imagine they're writing the same thing."

"Hamann picked up a knock, apparently, that's why he's off. He was their biggest threat, in my opinion." Jackie decided a change of subject was in order. "So, how do you think Ferguson will change the style of play?"

"He'll play up front and it looks like Dabisaz will slot into midfield, replace Hamann." Johnny half shrugged. "They'll hoof it up to Ferguson and Shearer and hope for the best."

"He'll be more of a threat in the air." Jackie was excited to see how Ferguson would fit into the Newcastle side after his move from Everton. "He's not the most disciplined of players but having someone like him, the opposite, I suppose, of Shearer could be a magic combination or it could blow up in their faces. Who knows?"

"No cards for United's defence in the first half; so although he may test them, they still have a bit of wiggle room."

At Wembley, the teams started the way the first half had ended, with gusto. The extra pace in midfield was noticeable and an unequal battle of Ferguson and Phil Neville brought a wry smile to the faces of some.

Ketsbaia had placed himself outside the penalty box and waited for delivery of the ball; he took a couple of steps to his left. It was clear he was ratcheting his left hip; this did not translate into his left foot. The connection was weak and belied his hip action, the shot at goal skimmed over the pitch like a pebble over water, wide of the net.

"They're certainly more active, aren't they? They've got into United's box more times in this first five minutes than they did for the whole of the first half." Geoff took off his suit jacket and now loosened his tie.

Roger lay his arm along the back of the booth. "That can't all be about one substitution though. They're probably realising they've got forty minutes to produce something or they're going home to yet another loser's parade."

Geoff paused. "How many turned up?"

"Twenty-five thousand lined the streets to welcome them home, *without* a trophy."

Dennis sat on the edge of his seat and tapped Roger on the shoulder. "Is that true? Newcastle had a loser's parade?"

"I kid you not." Roger turned to Dennis. "It's nice and everything but you can't be doing that two years in a row."

Geoff felt the need to play devil's advocate. "Technically I don't think they set out for it to be a parade but twenty-five thousand did turn up to see them back into the city."

"Their morale seems to have been lifted having Ferguson on the pitch. Let's hope it comes to nothing." Eddie laughed.

"I'm not sure May's going to be up for the job of containing Ferguson for the full forty-five minutes." Billy paused for a second. "Without getting himself a yellow card, that is."

Jimmy rubbed his hands together. "Game on here now. Newcastle have had most possession this half, and United's midfield are still in the dressing room."

No sooner had Jimmy finished speaking when Beckham tackled Domi. He slipped the ball short to Solskjaer who slotted the ball forward to Cole. Chavet prevented him from laying it back to Solskjaer; Newcastle were in possession again but not for long. Giggs dispossessed Ketsbaia and the Newcastle midfield fought hard to win it back.

Willie sat forward. "It's possible Newcastle could equalise here; they're dominating play."

The Newcastle supporters raised their volume several decibels; they sensed they had the upper hand. A ball from Griffin destined for United's box was intercepted by the head of Phil Neville and retrieved by Giggs.

"And, has been the case on many occasion this season, United are hitting them on the break." Bert's belief and anticipation of the outcome of the duel was short-lived; Newcastle won the parry.

"Newcastle fans are drowning out the United fans." Walter was not happy.

"That's probably because the United fans are still making their way back to their seats."

Walter laughed: "Yeah, it's a well-known fact United fans take longer to down their pints than other supporters."

"That's because they like to savour all things of quality; no rush." Tom Curry said.

Just above the laughter, Eddie started to sing and within the first few bars, everyone in the Busby booth raised their voices to join Eddie. The archangels swayed to the chant; the new ones eager to learn.

We'll never die, we'll never die. We'll never die, we'll never die. We'll keep the red flag flying high cos Man United will never die.

"Blimey, that nearly worked then," Mark said as he nudged Tommy.

A perfectly placed pass from Giggs found Cole, who captured the ball, spun on a sixpence and lost Chavet. He headed towards the Newcastle net, closely followed by the Newcastle defence.

The synchronised move of those in the Bar, as they raised a couple of inches off their seats, ready to spring upright, confident a goal was coming. However, the Newcastle defence did their job and Dabisaz cleared. Newcastle were on the march again and bottoms slowly eased back into the booths.

David leant closer to Duncan. "The half is proving to be great for neutrals."

"You're right chief, five minutes in and there's some real end-to-end stuff."

At Wembley, a miscommunication between Phil Neville and Schmeichel resulted in Schmeichel expressing his irritation. "That's not good."

"Yeah but deserved; Neville should have dealt with it earlier or at least left it for Schmeichel at the first attempt."

"They had a *disagreement* in the first half too."

"They need to calm down a bit." Duncan loosened his tie. "Duncan Ferguson has woken them up but they have to be careful they don't make any mistakes."

Ketsbaia played a ball to Domi that was in a dangerous position but was dealt with by Gary Neville; the ball went out for a Newcastle corner. Silence descended on the Bar. Newcastle were running along the touchline, intent on trying to find Ferguson and, yet again, Gary Neville was there to protect and serve.

"Have they cloned him?" Tommy said, in wonder. "Gary Neville seems to be single-handedly defending."

Visual attention was on the action at Wembley, part of the soundtrack was the ever-increasing giggles of the archangels. The souls were unaware this was due to the dancing orbs of individual memories over the heads of more than one or two of the Babes.

The vision of Ryan Giggs as he accelerated down the wing caused the orbs to dissipate. Dabisaz caught up with Giggs and made the decision to play the ball upfield rather than out. Solskjaer intercepted and, played it forward, passing to Sheringham. He held up play for a fraction of a second and spotted the run of Scholes,

Sheringham laid the ball off to him. Scholes raced forward and, just outside the Newcastle eighteen-yard box he didn't hesitate; like a pebble skimmed on a pond, the ball bounced a couple of times on its journey to the back of the net.

Twenty-five voices roared in unison. "Gooall!" The vibration of the cheer rose and the suspended shirts danced in the air.

Billy, with his arms aloft, became inundated by hugs and pats from the rest of the Babes as they mirrored the mobbing of Scholes by his teammates. Snippets of excited conversation filled the Bar.

"The SSS squad strike again."

"It was completely against the run of play but what a fantastic goal by Scholesy."

"Sublime."

"He scores goals for fun that kid."

He scores goals galore, he scores goals; he scores goals galore, he scores goals; he scores goals galore, he scores goals; Paul Scholes, he scores goals.

Sir Matt said as he clapped his appreciation. "What a player."

The excited Babes made their way back to their seats. Eddie's smile was broad; he believed Scholes would be an integral part of any top-flight team.

The journalists let their pens and fingers do the talking, heads bowed over notepads and laptops; they selected a flurry of superlatives to describe the goal.

"I can't remember the last time that lad had an injury."

"He's a real workhorse." Jimmy placed his elbow on the back of the booth and half-turned to Bert. "He would have been amazing to work with, a bit like Jonesy here, I reckon. What do you think Tom?"

"He's a one-off. There'll be others wanting to be a Paul Scholes but, from what I've seen so far, there's only ever gonna be one like that."

"You start to feel that maybe if…"

Bert interrupted Jimmy. "You know the word *if* is banned here." Jimmy chuckled and decided not to continue with his thought.

"The quality of that shot, if it is to be the winning goal; well, it's a fitting goal to win the FA Cup; a fitting goal to end the century at Wembley," Donny noted.

"A legend in the making, mark my words," said Henry.

"Gullit's going to have to lift the spirits of his team. It's a blow but, you never know, they could get something out of this."

Nonplussed everyone turned to Donny and asked, without words, if he was watching a different game.

"I'm just saying there's a possibility."

"A possibility that Manchester United are going to give up a two-goal lead?" Swifty looked confused.

"Well…"

"Okay, c'mon lads. There's still half an hour to be played."

The journalists became fully absorbed in the energy from the opposite booth and the atmosphere at Wembley. The United supporters could be heard chanting, behind the bar the archangels whistled.

We shall not, we shall not be moved. We shall not, we shall not be moved. Just like a team that's gonna win the FA Cup (again); we shall not be moved.

"What's happened to Beckham?"

"I'm not sure. He's probably gone all in for a tackle judging by the fact that Newcastle have a free kick."

Charvet took the free kick in his own half and launched it into United's box. He could only watch as it was blocked and kicked clear by Gary Neville to Cole. Giggs made a run forward and Cole laid it off to him. Giggs hit an optimistic ball as he anticipated Solskjaer and Cole would press forward, to the edge of the Newcastle box. They didn't; Harper collected.

Willie exploded with laughter. "I can't help but laugh each time I see Yorke's face. He's like a kid with all his Christmases and birthdays at once when he pulls on that shirt."

No sooner were the words spoken and the screen was covered by the infectious smiling face of Yorke as he readied himself to make an entrance on the Wembley turf.

"His first season and he's scored twenty-nine goals; phenomenal," David said; the smile on his face matched the smile on Yorke's face.

"I can't even begin to imagine the goal tally he and Cole will amass next season." Duncan thought the partnership would break all records put before them if they maintained this current form.

Smiles slid when Schmeichel came for a ball hit by Robert Lee into the box. He punched the ball out and away from Shearer, almost to the feet of Ketsbaia. On the edge of the box, Ketsbaia took aim and all twenty-five men clasped their heads as the ball connected with the boot of a prone David May.

"Was that May, or the post? My word, he deserves a medal for that."

"What was Schmeichel thinking?"

"Why is he panicking?"

"I don't think he has 100% confidence in Phil Neville and maybe that's making him a little nervy."

"I told you. The fat lady's not singing yet."

United were on the break again as, so many times this season, a near miss invariably met with them charging up the opposite end of the pitch.

Tommy pointed at the screen. "Giggs is going for an Arsenal run again."

Unfortunately, Newcastle foiled Giggs' intended smash and grab and took possession of the ball; they regrouped.

"So who do you reckon Yorke's going to replace?" Mark asked.

"Well, if it was me I'd take Sheringham off and save him for Wednesday."

"Peggy! You can't substitute a substitute!"

"There are no rules against it. Remember Dominguez was subbed after being subbed for Ginola." David turned to Bert. "Is there Bert?"

"No lads, there are no rules against it but I can't see it happening."

David felt vindicated. "He'll probably take off Cole. The game *should* be safe now so give Yorke a runout and save Cole for Wednesday night."

"If Alex Ferguson puts Yorke and Cole up front then, I think the Newcastle defence will start making mistakes."

"True, but that need only happen if they were losing; he needs to keep one eye on Wednesday night and not do anything unnecessary."

"We're open to making mistakes too." David reminded Mark. "Don't forget Phil Neville and Schmeichel have already had a bit of a kerfuffle and May saved the Great Dane's blushes not five minutes since. Game's a long way from being over."

"That was really beautiful play by Giggs there."

Ryan Giggs held off Dabisaz and slid the ball forward onto the run of Beckham. He sent in a cross intended to fall to Gary Neville; however, Newcastle had other plans.

"What do you say Johnny, is that passion or anger on Beckham's face?"

"I was just thinking the same myself," Jackie said. "*My sources* told me Alex Ferguson *and* the United supporters closed ranks around Beckham after the…"

In unison, they all finished the sentence. "Scapegoattery."

"Well done lads, you've done me proud," Eric said with a huge smile. His new word had been used twice today; a hat-trick of uses was his aim.

Sir Matt brought the conversation back to its start. "If there was even a sliver of anger that could cost United Alex Ferguson would have had words with him. It's passion, lads, pure passion. He wants to show those, I'm not sure what to call them, anyway; he's out there showing them he plays for a winning team; he plays for Manchester United."

Willie was bemused. "I can't imagine how it is, to play for your country and supporters want you *dead* for making a mistake."

"And the media; don't forget the media put petrol on the fire of that one."

"I know the game's changed since our day but there's something wrong when an England player is booed by England supporters because he plays for Manchester United."

"I remember playing for Scotland against Wales, back in 1933. It was an unbelievable feeling to put on that shirt."

"I remember that game too Boss. What was the score again?" Jimmy, who had played for Wales in that game, of course, knew the score-line. He returned Sir Matt's smile.

"He'll continue playing for them I reckon but it's tainted for him; only my humble opinion, of course."

"That's strange Willie." Jimmy sat back in his seat. "I would never have called you humble."

The United supporters in Wembley acknowledged Yorke's entry onto the pitch. Sir Matt leant closer, his forehead furrowed.

"I can't quite make out the words. I thought they said pornography." He laughed and slapped his thigh.

"Err, Boss, they did." An abashed Dennis Dwight Yorke's terrace chant for Sir Matt.

Dwight Yorke wherever you may be, you are the king of pornography. You stuck two fingers up at Gregory, now you play for MUFC.

Sir Matt could not stop laughing; he stopped to wipe his cheeks. "I don't know how they come up with them."

"There's a guy called Pete Boyle and he comes up with a lot of them." Dennis was happy he had made Sir Matt laugh so hard.

"I won't embarrass you by asking what he did to deserve that chant."

***

Down Below a United throw-in saw Alex Ferguson and Gary Neville play one-touch football. The United half of the crowd stood and cheered and the smile on Alex Ferguson's face was a joy to behold.

"Ay, he's relaxed and enjoying himself now." Sir Matt knew this game would not disappear from under Alex Ferguson.

David added. "I just wish he'd stop chewing gum like that."

"If that's the only negative you have against him then I'm sure he'll take that."

"What about that singer you like, he's always chewing gum, isn't he?" Swifty winked at George.

"Which singer?"

"Elvis Presley."

"You need to move with the times Swifty! My musical tastes have developed."

"And not for the better, I may add." Eddie never understood why David locked himself into the fifties.

David smiled. "The fifties were a precursor of what the sixties had to offer. I could have embraced that era with a flower in my hair and a smile on my face."

A United corner was dealt with by Newcastle, but only as far as Scholes who delivered a pass to the left onto the chest of Giggs. He shimmied to the left, then right and sent a cross into the box. Yorke, a lonely figure in front of goal, rose up in the air; his head made contact. If you asked Yorke to stand in front of goal, no defenders and hit a perfectly weighted cross into the back of the net he would do it blindfolded, nine times out of ten. Today the ball sailed over the net.

Billy gasped. "How was that *not* his thirtieth goal?"

"He didn't hit it as cleanly as he would have liked."

"He's only been on the pitch a couple of minutes; give him a chance."

The confidence of United grew unabated and a period of exhibition football followed. The string of passes, the quality, the accuracy and the fluidity was proof of the total belief that had settled on the team.

A Scholes attempt at goal was the finale of twenty passes between the team. It was deflected off Charvet for a corner. Beckham crossed into the box; the ball was cleared by Newcastle but only as far as Giggs' right foot; his shot went wide for a goal kick.

Tommy applauded. "That was a great strike."

"Beautiful."

"Look at the smile on his face, Peggy."

"I know; he's incredible."

Giggs, Giggs will tear you apart again. Giggs, Giggs will tear you apart again.

Dwight Yorke capitalised on Sloppy defending by Newcastle and raced into the Newcastle box with the ball glued to his feet. He passed to Giggs who saw Solskjaer apart from the crowd. Solskjaer could not control the ball and his shot was deflected straight at Harper. He spilt the ball; Newcastle shielded him and the ball was collected for a goal kick.

Duncan said. "I'm starting to feel sorry for Newcastle."

Mark could not suppress his urge to be sarcastic. "Don't be. They'll get a losers welcome and ticker tape parade when they get back to Newcastle."

"How long have we got before the referee puts them out of their misery?" Duncan rolled the ball between his feet, keen to hear the final whistle, eager to have a kick about.

Bert squinted at the clock out of habit. "Sixty-five minutes played. Newcastle need to make a change or this could easily end up being a rout."

"However, by the same token Manchester United need to start putting away more of their chances. This should be about six or seven nil by now." Jimmy said.

Walter shrugged. "I can't see them capitulating in the next twenty-five minutes; their confidence is too high but another goal would relax me and finish the game off."

We shall not, we shall not be moved. We shall not, we shall not be moved. Just like a team, that wins the FA Cup, (again,) we shall not be moved.

An attempt by Griffin sailed over the United net and was met by disdainful whistles by United supporters *and* a substitution by Newcastle. Gullit felt Solano was not being effective and replaced him with Marić.

Roger asked. "What do you think of the substitution Boss?"

"Well, he's not made a great impact on the game but then again nor has Shearer. I don't know too much about the man Marić but, a change is as good as a rest, so they say."

"Maybe the tactic is to hoof the ball upfield to the big man."

"Possibly; I don't think Ruud Gullit wants to concede another; that would be too humiliating. He's got to salvage some pride and throw the kitchen sink at it."

Eddie's face blossomed from deep concentration into a smile, he nudged Billy. "Listen. The Shearer chant just got louder."

"Well, they're never going to let him forget about the choice he made."

"Sheringham said much the same thing, but made the right choice; Shearer chose the wrong team."

Cheer up Alan Shearer, oh, what can it mean to a sad Geordie bastard and a shite football team.

Geoff pointed to the screen. "Ketsbaia seems to be the most threatening in terms of getting one past Schmeichel."

"He's certainly not afraid to go for it, that's for sure, but two golden opportunities and still no goal." Roger shrugged.

"It's just not their turn mate."

"You're right. I'm not one to call a game before the final whistle but this game makes United treble Double winners in my book."

"There's still over twenty minutes to play." Geoff was aware anything could happen in a minute, never mind twenty.

"This should be where the lads relax; don't take unnecessary risks and conserve their energy for Wednesday night."

"Wow. What's he playing at?"

Duncan Ferguson, in possession of the ball in United's half, had passed the ball to Griffin who delivered it straight to Phil Neville.

"As I said, it's just not their game today."

"Who's your man of the match?"

"I don't want to jinx it but I'm going to say, Giggs. You?"

"Part of me wants to say Beckham. He's been a terrier, nipping at the heels of every Newcastle player with the ball, losing it, winning it back. But I'm going to wait for the final whistle to say for definite."

"True, but I think Teddy Sheringham should get it. He came on for the captain and within seconds got a goal."

Geoff opened up the debate. "What do you lads think?"

Without hesitation Billy said. "The goal poacher Scholes gets my vote."

The words left Billy's lips at the same time Scholes raced towards the Newcastle net.

Eddie laughed. "That sight has to put the fear into any defender."

"I know it would me," said Roger.

"It's difficult to pick one man of the match especially because of the charmed life of the Newcastle goal," Duncan said. "I'll wait until the final whistle to say who gets my man of the match." He went back to rolling the ball between his feet, his eyes fixed on the screen.

The run of Scholes led to a corner. Ronny Johnsen made contact with Beckham's ball but hit it over the net. Everyone read his mind, *I should have done better.* Harper's goal kick reached Phil Neville who fumbled the ball and saw Shearer pounce.

Mark shook his head. "If Phil Neville doesn't want to feel the wrath of Schmeichel he'd better get that ball back; like now."

Phil Neville was doing exactly that, he harried Shearer to the touchline and the ball went out of play, touched over the line by Neville. A goal kick was given to United.

Jimmy, hands aloft and smile on his face said. "What did I tell you, when it's not your game, it's not your game."

Alan Shearer was furious with the linesman's call which delighted the United supporters.

The play between the United players was almost flawless. Up Above they sat back in the booths, minds raced to the final whistle, to savour the vicarious feeling of lifting the Cup.

The Bar was *alive* with whistling archangels; it seemed to start a second or two before the chant Down Below. "There you go."

"They took their time!" Jackie said with mock indignation. "I expected it after the second goal."

"You know they don't usually sing this one unless they're on the home stretch and sure of the win, so I guess now is the best time."

Forever and ever, we'll follow the boys; Of Manchester United, the Busby Babes; for we made a promise, to defend our faith, in Manchester United, the Busby Babes. We've all sworn allegiance, to fight till we die, to stand by United, and the Red flag we fly. There'll be no surrender, we'll fight to the last, to defeat all before us, as we did in the past.

"I get a lump in my throat when I hear this one. Sometimes I think they may forget about us."

"You've got to be kidding Johnny. You and the lads are imprinted on the fabric of the club, in every brick at Old Trafford, in every stitch of every shirt worn by players and supporters alike, on every blade of grass, everywhere. You will never be forgotten."

"Hear, hear Willie," George said.

A broad smile and eyes gleaming Mark rubbed his hands. "As if things weren't bad enough for Newcastle Yip Jaap Stam is warming up."

"Good call." Tom Curry said. "United have no problems up front, they look threatening but they need to shut up shop before Shearer and Ferguson come a-knocking."

After watching Scholes tackle Speed Billy shook his head. "I love Scholesy but the lad can't tackle for toffee."

Eddie laughed, "True, but he gives it a go and, sometimes he gets away with it."

Roger rose and made his way to the far corner of the bar. It happened without words being spoken; the rest of the Babes stood and joined him.

Walter, eyed them suspiciously, "What are they up to?"

Swifty laughed. "If it's anything untoward we'll hear from The Omnipotent One, so don't worry."

Potential pranks by the Babes, especially David and Eddie, were usually curbed by the sound of The Omnipotent One. Early on in their time Up Above the sound could be heard almost daily but now, not so much. The advent of new things to occupy their minds, the arrival of family and friends, meant mischievous minds dwelled on more productive activities.

The journalists had their heads bent over their articles, however, one ear listened to the game and one ear tried to catch what was being said in the corner.

Sir Matt had his full attention on the game. "They're playing such beautiful football. Alex Ferguson should be proud of them."

The exhibition football culminated in a shot by Beckham, deflected out for a corner. It gave Alex Ferguson the opportunity to make the substitution he wanted. Scholes, to tumultuous applause, was replaced by Stam.

Archie got up. "Yeah, I don't think I can watch this anymore. Sloppy play by Newcastle at this stage of the game *and* they're two nil down. Terrible." He made his way over to the bar.

The Babes broke their rugby style huddle, the smiles on their faces ranged from self-assured to shy.

Jimmy scrutinised the Babes as they walked back and shook his head. "That's not a good sign."

Roger walked to the edge of the booth and ran his index finger down his Adam's apple. "Excuse me. Can I interrupt for a minute?" All eyes turned to Roger, intrigued. "Walter, Tom, I know we said we'd have a four-a-side before Wednesday's game but we've decided against it now. It is a big occasion and I don't think any of us will be able to concentrate knowing what's happening in Barcelona."

Tommy added. "The build-up to Wednesday's game is going to be phenomenal, and we don't want to miss any of the coverage."

Walter and Tom acknowledged they had been hard-pressed to keep their concentration on the game before the Spurs match so nodded their approval.

"Sounds like a good idea lads." Sir Matt said, his eyes still glued to the screen.

"What's happening? What've we missed?" David exaggerated a wiggle to get comfortable in his seat, knowing they had missed nothing of import.

Willie nodded towards the screen. "Ferguson's going to replace Scholes with Stam."

"Okay; that's good."

"Is he injured?" Mark said.

"No. I think Alex Ferguson just wants to give Stam a runout and shore up the defence a little."

Paul Scholes ran off the pitch and those in Wembley and Up Above, and many watching around the world, stood and applauded. His job done for the season and his impact on it was recognised.

Geoff crossed his legs and placed his arms along the back of the booth, relaxed. "The defence is a brick wall now; it will give the rest the chance to forge ahead and hit Newcastle on the break. There are more goals in this United team."

A Yorke tackle gifted the ball to Giggs who, in his all too familiar run for goal, shimmied turned his back to goal and slid the ball to his left, to the feet of Sheringham. A carefully delivered chip made contact with the crossbar.

"See that's what I mean," Geoff said, preaching to the already converted.

Ruud Gullit took the opportunity of making his own substitution and replaced Ketsbaia with Glass. Eddie pounced on the opportunity and began to sing into a microphone that appeared from nowhere.

Once I had a love and it was a gas. Soon turned out it had a heart of glass. Seemed like the real thing, only to find; mucho mistrust, love's gone behind.

Sir Matt put his pipe to his mouth to disguise his smile as Eddie's singing was met with wolf-whistles, catcalls and foam balls. Eddie blew kisses to his audience and curtsied. As he made to sit down, his face towards the screen, he was hit on the back of the head by a foam ball. The giggles gave away the culprit.

Jimmy shrugged. "Well, I suppose he knows what he's doing."

"Ketsbaia didn't put away any of the chances he had," Jackie said. "But at least he's had chances, more than can be said for Shearer."

"Throwing Glass on now with fifteen minutes to go…" Jimmy left the rest of the sentence unsaid and shrugged again.

Willie whispered to Sir Matt. "It's beautiful, isn't it?" Sir Matt nodded; he was confident he knew what Willie meant. It was beautiful to watch United games Down Below with those in the Bar.

Manchester United dominated possession and played with confidence and belief. Every cell in their bodies exuded the knowledge they would add another piece of silverware to the trophy cabinet at Old Trafford.

Giggs' pass was meant for Yorke but it was intercepted and cleared away by the head of Dabisaz.

David stretched his legs, his hands behind his head. "He's put in a good shift today, shame he's on the losing side."

"They're throwing everything but the kitchen sink at Newcastle." Duncan kicked the ball up, caught it in his hands and put it to rest on his lap; he was eager for the final whistle.

"If this was a boxing match the referee would pull Newcastle to one side and ask them to count fingers."

David's analogy caused everyone to laugh; a party atmosphere began to envelop Red Cloud Bar.

"I suppose the fat lady is clearing her throat now," Dennis asked.

Jimmy chuckled. "She's going through her musical scales as we speak."

They could hear glasses being filled and placed on trays and then Newcastle reminded United supporters not to slip into congratulatory mode too early.

Griffin crossed the ball into the centre, just outside United's box. Ferguson rose to meet it but missed, and it fell to Marić. He took aim and with only Schmeichel to beat, hit just wide of the post.

"Oops. That was an opportunity to take the fizz out of the champagne." Billy said as he turned to the archangels behind the bar.

"Look at the faces of the Newcastle supporters, they know it too." Eddie, aware the celebrations had begun too early also knew the tables were unlikely to be turned at this late stage.

"That will deflate them even more." Johnny sat on the edge of his seat, his forearms on the seats in front. Geoff felt a draught on his head and began to lift his arm before he realised it was Johnny's breath playing with his hair.

Eddie frowned and put his left hand to his ear. "Can you hear that?"

The Bar grew quiet, everyone strained to hear what Eddie had heard, even the archangels. Billy and Geoff were confused and asked. "What? What did you hear?"

Eddie started to sing opera, badly. When the foam balls began to fly through the Bar, Eddie ducked behind the booth still singing; catcalls and whistles drowned him out. After the last ball was thrown he stood, straightened his tie, smiled and bowed "I thank you", and took his seat.

La la la la, la la la la Keano. La la la la, la la la la Keano. La la la la, la la la la Keano.

Jaap Stam gave Newcastle a lesson in how to defend and foiled Ferguson twice in quick succession.

A comfortable silence descended. "So if there's no pre-match match on Wednesday, what are you guys up to?" Willie knew his question would not be answered with the truth but asked anyway.

Roger avoided eye contact as he scrutinised his fingernails. "Nowt, really, you know, watch the build-up and then come in here; nothing special."

There wasn't a single soul in the Bar that believed him but they decided not to push it further. It was obvious their plans involved nothing untoward because of the lack of intervention by The Omnipotent One. They relaxed and decided to let the Babes have their fun.

Happy to have a diversion away from Roger's untruth Geoff hid a chuckle in his hand and nodded at the screen. "Oh, look May is giving Duncan Ferguson a big old hug."

"Yeah, and Ferguson doesn't look too pleased about it.

Manchester United supporters were singing their commiserations to Alan Shearer, loud and clear. Duncan dropped the ball back to the floor and placed his left foot on top. "That has to hurt, to hear your name being sung so loud by the opposition fans."

David understood the desire of opposition fans to highlight comments made by any player that fell short of actual delivery. "Shearer's used to it, or he should be." He knew it could so easily have been opposition supporters making chants about Sheringham.

"Do you think Alex Ferguson should make another substitution, you know, try and save legs?"

"No. There are only five minutes left to play and they're passing comfortably. I feel he'll ride out the clock with those on the pitch."

Mark agreed. "I think you're right. Shearer and Ferguson have had the wind taken out of their sails; they're on the ropes, to use David's metaphor."

"The boxing officials have started the countdown," Tommy said.

Over in the other booth, Donny contributed. "The umpire's taken off the bails."

David looked around the Bar. "Anyone else?"

"United have scored a touchdown!" Dennis said.

"Anyone else?"

Duncan put his arm around David. "No. I think we're done."

You are my Solskjaer, my only Solskjaer. You make me happy when skies are grey. Though Alan Shearer was so much dearer, please don't take my Solskjaer away.

And then the final whistle.

Alex Ferguson rose; his arms in the air; he turned to his right and grabbed Roy Keane. The embrace and shoulder pats said more than a thousand words. On the pitch, the squad hugged and danced and smiled and sang. The Busby Babes copied them, jumping up and down as though on pogo sticks.

On the screen, everyone saw Schmeichel take off the captain's armband and put it back on Keane's arm. Sir Matt exclaimed. "I knew he'd do that. Keane will collect the trophy as captain. Marvellous."

We're gonna win the lot, we're gonna win the lot, and now you're gonna believe us, and now you're gonna believe us.

The enormous arched doors swung open, the suspended shirts danced in the air. Shouts of congratulations filled the Bar.

Willie had his arm around Sir Matt. "I have to be honest and say I really hope the Newcastle supporters don't have another loser's parade for them. That kind of stuff shouldn't become the norm."

"You're right. Their defending was woeful and shouldn't be celebrated. But, then again, United dominated and when you meet a dominant United side there's not a lot you can do."

"You can pray they don't humiliate you and end the game with a cricket score."

The fizzing from the champagne, the pipe and cigarette smoke and fireworks; Red Cloud Bar was noisy with chatter, chanting and singing.

***

Manchester United's captain, Roy Keane, led his team up the stairs followed by Peter Schmeichel. So many Manchester United supporters around the globe and beyond rubbed their forearms as the hairs stood to attention.

"Unbelievable. They've already made history and if they win on Wednesday night they could accomplish another historical achievement. It's incredible."

Willie nudged Jimmy; Jimmy turned to Tom Curry and made a gesture for him to stand alongside the screen; Bert and Walter quickly cottoned on and joined them. The archangels started to whistle and the men started to sing.

Manchester, Manchester United, a bunch of bouncing Busby Babes, they deserve to be knighted; When they're playing in your town, get yourself to that football ground, where you will see football taught by Matt Busby.

The journalists joined in and Eddie and the rest of the Busby Babes danced the conga around the Bar. Sir Matt sat, smiled and clapped along. A celebration of what had been and what was, all happening at the same time. The moment was punctuated when Roy Keane held the 1999 FA Cup trophy in the air.

***

Sir Matt stood and cleared his throat but it took two attempts before he could be heard over the partying. "I'm away lads; I'll see you all on Wednesday night."

The Babes walked him to the door and watched until he turned the corner, homeward bound.

As they walked to the bar to continue watching the celebrations Archie said; "Two down, one to go."

Glory, glory Man United. Glory, glory Man United. Glory, glory Man United. And the reds go marching on, on, on.

CHAPTER SEVEN

The evening of the 1999 Champions League Final arrived and Red Cloud Bar was busy, very busy. Although there had never been restrictions on family members, friends and supporters visiting the Bar not many did. Tonight was different.

The *working* archangels, and several non-working archangels, were mingling in the bar; the orchestra of crystal bells evidence of their excitement.

Without exception, everyone looked to the rainbow orb hovering above the arched doors. The Omnipotent One made it known, *you're welcome* before the thank you was uttered; the person said it anyway, *thank you.*

The journalists and their families found seats close to the halfway line. It didn't matter where they sat they were able to see every part of the pitch. The match would be in the eyes of the beholder.

Tom Jackson's dad took in his surroundings. "This is incredible. I can see why you spend time here."

"Actually Dad, I've never seen it like this before. This is beyond anything I expected." He turned around; his arms out wide. "This has rendered me speechless."

"Well, make sure you put that as the headline to your article. *'Journalist speechless'.*

Charged energy circulated through the air, each suspended shirt appeared to be dancing to separate rhythms. First timers to the Bar would tell others they were sure the shirts appeared to be worn, not empty; they *saw* the contours of the body underneath.

A large number of vocal supporters in Estadio Nou Camp created a small vibration; the loud flares startled a few, the red smoke choked many. Manchester United fans were now pouring into the Nou Camp having sampled the Spanish hospitality along Las Ramblas until a mixture of nerves and excitement propelled them into the stadium.

In Red Cloud Bar they tasted the *cerveza* bubbles as they mingled with the tingle of chillies in *the albondigas*. The archangels giggled when a soul stuck out their tongue to taste the flavours in the air.

George made his way to sit in front of Frank; he turned and shook his hand.

"How's it going Swifty? You okay?"

"I'm grand George, just soaking up the atmosphere." He paused and, with a sigh. "It's like I'm there, I can almost feel all the sensations."

"I know, it's incredible, isn't it?"

"I never imagined The Omnipotent One would do something like this, you know, for them."

"It's definitely a special evening Frank."

They sat in companionable silence and drank in the sights before them. The other journalists joined them. They knew if United won they would write of bravery, solidarity, heart, passion, a never-say-die attitude, but also the build-up to the event.

After several minutes, Swifty broke the meditative aura. "They're going to miss Keane tonight."

"I know. It's a huge blow, having him *and* Scholes suspended. The midfield has lost its Rolls Royce engine."

"Who's in the line-up to replace them?"

Henry took his time to respond, stuck his legs out leant back and let out a long slow breath. "Butt and Beckham are in central midfield." He paused. "Blomqvist is out on the left and Giggs on the right, and obviously, Yorke and Cole up front."

Donny spun his head around. "What? Giggs is on the right?"

Henry felt defensive. "Blomqvist will be okay. I don't think it's his dream team but what can you do when you have the two powerhouses suspended?"

"This is a big match for Blomqvist, first season at Manchester United, one goal and two medals." Donny played with his earlobe. "How many games has he had this season?"

"Thirty-seven, thirty-eight with this game. There must be a method in his thinking to put Giggs out on the right. I just hope it doesn't come and bite him on the backside later."

Alf made his way to the booth, keen to add his opinion to the midfield debate. "To be honest, I don't think it would have happened if Hitzfeld hadn't announced his team a couple of days ago. And I think, don't quote me on this, but I *think* Ferguson didn't want a Babel and Giggs battle in midfield and that's why he switched him. He knows the damage Babel can do."

"Didn't Ferguson try to buy him after Euro 96?" Archie asked.

"Yeah, he did," Alf replied.

Before the conversation could be derailed Swifty took it back to its beginning. "The loss of both Keane *and* Scholes is going to make more of an impact than we realise. Their displays in midfield, over the past few games, in particular, meant the likelihood one of them would pick up a suspension for this game was high. I don't think anyone reckoned on *both* of them losing out. *And*, don't forget, as much as United will miss them tonight; think of how they must be feeling."

"Gutted probably; I know I would be."

"I can't imagine it. They've pulled out some pivotal performances this season." George smiled as his mind flicked through the achievements of Keane and Scholes during the season; a season that would be over in three hours.

Tom Jackson strolled to the booth and paused next to Swifty and George. "The Scholesy goal against Inter in Italy and Keano's goal against Juventus are the two games that spring easily to my mind." He glanced up at the ceiling; his brown eyes had a sparkle to them.

"Me too Tom, me too."

Swifty diverted the conversation back to the match soon to take place. "Who's in defence?"

"Denny Irwin, Yip Jaap, Johnsen and Gary." Henry then read out the players on the bench. "Van de Gouw, May, Solskjaer, Neville, Sheringham, Brown and Greening are all on the bench."

"Yeah, I suppose it makes sense now, Giggs on the right."

"I feel Sheringham will make an appearance at some point."

"Oh definitely; he's put in a shift for United this season. He's not a fan favourite yet, but you can't deny he's given his all for the team.

"I think he's won them over this season. I'm not sure why it took time but…

Henry looked at the door. "It feels strange."

Donny laughed. "I was just about to say the same. They'll be here soon."

The journalists felt relaxed. They answered questions posed by their families and friends. Although some had resided Up Above for a long time they had not met the Busby Babes. Many were excited and spun around each time the door opened.

***

Roger knocked on the glossy red door and waited. As he heard footsteps, he stepped back. The door opened and Sir Matt's wife, Jean, gasped and covered her mouth with both hands. Her eyes shone as she turned and said. "Matt? There are some people at the door for you."

"Really? Who on earth? Today of all days."

Sir Matt opened the door fully and stepped out next to Jean. He saw the eleven Busby Babes flanking the path outside his residence. Sir Matt gulped, Jean took his arm.

Roger stepped forward. "Hey Boss. We thought we'd walk you to the Bar."

Sir Matt tried to form words but his emotions clogged his throat. Jean squeezed his elbow and he was able to gather himself. His voice choked. "You look grand lads."

The silent walk to Red Cloud Bar spoke volumes. Pride was an emotion that didn't exist Up Above but, the tingle that ran through his body told Sir Matt he was proud.

At the doorway, he paused for a second, took a deep breath and the doors opened; Sir Matt and the Busby Babes entered Red Cloud Bar. Roger had organised for every soul to stand and sing *Happy Birthday* to Sir Matt. Roger had not informed them the Babes would be wearing the kit they had last worn against Red Star Belgrade.

The collective intake of breath was held for three seconds before Jimmy, the first to break the trance, started to sing; the rest followed.

Happy birthday to you; happy birthday to you. Happy birthday dear Boss/Matt/Sir Matt; happy birthday to you.

Sir Matt raised his arm in acknowledgement of their good wishes. They noticed the change at the same time.

Estadio Nou Camp *was* in the middle of the Bar. Jaws dropped; they were there. They could reach out and touch the supporters, feel the blades of grass and smell the smoke from the red flares that swirled around them.

Eddie clutched at Duncan's arm, lost for words, syllables were stuttered, then finally, a coherent sentence. "We're in the Nou Camp."

Sir Matt looked up at the rainbow orb and said, "I can't thank you enough."

You're more than welcome.

The Babes, unspoken words loud and clear, ran towards the *pitch*. Jimmy swallowed hard and thought back to the last time he had seen some of them in *those* shirts run towards a pitch as a squad. He believed tonight *belonged* to United, it was Ferguson's team playing the game but the Busby Babes would be there in spirit.

Roger, hands on his hips, made to step over the hoarding; he turned to the rest of the Babes. "Who's up for a kick about then?"

Laughter broke the trance. It was a historic moment but it didn't stop the moment from being tinged with sadness. Although another Busby Babes team had won the European Championship in 1968; tonight was different. Tonight they were there watching the Final with the Boss.

A different feeling enveloped them than those they had been aware of before. A glance between them was enough for them to realise each was experiencing the same.

George strolled over to Duncan and nudged him. "Solskjaer will come on and nick the winner I reckon."

Duncan threw his hands in the air. "Well that's just put the kybosh on that then, a journalist predicting a correct score."

"Schmeichel as captain, playing his last game for United, lifts the Champion League trophy. It's the stuff of movies." Willie was alongside the pitch staring up at the stands.

"Some say reality is stranger than fiction."

"I don't know; there's something that makes me think it's written in the stars, so to speak."

The silence that blanketed the Bar was broken.

Just to reiterate…

In unison, the regulars in the Bar said. "You have no influence over events Down Below."

***

"What's the Bayern Munich line-up?" Billy focussed on the United players warming up, his body mirrored their movements.

"I know who's going to be on the pitch but the actual formation," Archie shrugged. "I'm not sure."

Eric interjected. "Jancker, Zickler *and* Basler are up front."

Sir Matt lowered his pipe, still mesmerised at the changes in the Bar. "Hitzfeld's gone for a three, four, three, of sorts. They mean business."

"It's going to be a historic match whoever wins. A Treble for both teams is at stake."

"You're right Jimmy." Sir Matt's voice dropped slightly. "They're favourites I think."

"And the rest of their line-up?" Willie asked.

"Tarnat, Effenberg, Jeremies, Babbel are in midfield with Kuffour, Matthäus and Linke in defence."

"He's not pulling any punches with that team."

"This goes beyond football, *apparently*. The whole England vs Germany thing has got under the skin of some of the journalists Down Below."

"Well, you can't escape the fact that an English team is playing a German team. Manchester United will rise above the other nonsense."

"I agree. Anyway, let's change the subject." Donny said. "What information do you have on the referee?"

"Pierluigi Collina?" Eric looked down. "I've done a search and, to be honest, there's not that much. He's Italian and he refereed a couple of games last year in the World Cup but not much else."

"This is his first major European final game." Henry volunteered.

"I saw him in a couple of games at the World Cup. He was sound. One of the papers said he was 'quietly imposing'. He made fair decisions none of which appeared influenced by crowd noise." Swifty knew United were in safe hands.

Donny nodded. "It's a good referee that doesn't look to make the headlines."

"True."

"It's only the second final in ten years no Italian team has taken part. It's great he's got the nod for this."

"Both the linesmen are Italian too."

Bert laughed. "If you were Down Below you'd have to call them referee's assistants."

Henry shook his head. "I despair for the game, I really do."

The noise in Estadio Nou Camp rose to a deafening level; it became the noise in Red Cloud Bar. A connective energy that can only be felt in a loud pulsating football stadium encased everyone. Some of the archangels became struck by the enormity of the event; they took *seats* around the Busby booth.

"Okay, lads, it's nearly time." Roger reluctantly left the touchline and made his way to the booth, the others followed.

"Any idea of the numbers who've travelled?"

"I have no idea but as you can see." Walter swept his arm around the stadium, with a grin from ear to ear. "Barcelona is awash with red, black and white."

"I bet there's a lot there who've just gone for the craic," Billy said.

Willie rubbed his arms. "If I could experience goosebumps, I'd experience them right about now."

"It's being televised live in over 200 countries," Bert was impressed.

Jimmy moved forward, his hands on the shoulders of Duncan in front of him. "Pound for pound, inch for inch, Bayern Munich dominate in weight and height. United are going to have to be wily. They're David and Bayern Munich Goliath and you know what happened there."

***

The excitement was palpable as the twenty-five took their seats. Their eyes twinkled as the image of Freddie Mercury appeared on the big screen in the stadium and his duet of Barcelona, with Montserrat Caballè began. Others in the Bar watched those in the Busby booth.

"Wonderful." Sir Matt whispered.

The auditory delights continued as the teams lined up for the Champions League anthem accompanied by the crystal bell giggles of the archangels. The view panned along the focussed players on the pitch; some in the booths sat forward as they looked into the faces of the Manchester United team.

Everyone applauded amongst the shouts for *Come on United* as the music reached its conclusion. In the Bar, they settled into their seats for the next hour and forty-five minutes.

***

Both teams readied themselves for their biggest football match to date and Pierluigi Collina blew the whistle to start the last Champions League Final of the century.

Roger slid to the edge of his seat. "That was a great pass from Beckham."

"Yeah, pity Giggs couldn't get it to Cole but, it's less than a minute gone so…"

His body language belied his relaxed, confident words. Geoff was as far forward as Roger, his elbows on his thighs.

Willie was the epitome of relaxation, his legs outstretched, crossed at the ankles. "They're just finding their feet nothing's going to happen for twenty minutes or so I reckon. They're sizing each other up."

"He should have done better with that tackle."

"*That* was ambitious from Tarnat."

"Schmeichel had his goal covered anyway."

Everyone talked, no-one listened; a tried and tested mechanism to dissipate nerves.

Four minutes into the game; souls were still making their way into seats when Manchester United conceded a free kick just outside the box. Jancker appeared to swerve into Johnsen.

Dennis grimaced. "The lads are going to have to be careful."

"Aye and the referee will need to keep a clear head on him. Pun intended." Jimmy received recognition of the joke in the shape of a foam ball to the back of his head.

Peter Schmeichel, face etched with concentration, lined up his defensive wall and noted the infiltration of Babbel. Basler complained the wall wasn't back enough but took it anyway. In the Bar, not a sound was made as all eyes followed Basler's free-kick. The ball bounced on the six-yard line and, left Schmeichel wrong-footed; it flew past him into the back of the net.

Less than half of the Estadio Nou Camp went wild. The celebrations of the Bayern Munich team on the pitch *and* on the bench proved how much this game meant to them.

Sir Matt broke the stunned silence that had befallen the Bar. "We've got a hurdle to climb but we've done that before."

"The wall didn't get their positioning right." Jackie exhaled sharply. "That goal was our fault but we can rectify this. We've got plenty of time."

Johnny nodded. "You're right the wall should have covered that corner but, sorry to say, it was a good goal."

The men in the Busby booth sat forward in their seats, synchronised, and silently hoped Bayern Munich would not shut up shop.

Willie and Sir Matt were the exceptions, their backs straight, bodies relaxed. Sir Matt tapped his pipe on his thigh. "We've got to remain calm. There are more than eighty-five minutes to play."

It was what they needed to hear; they adopted a similar stance to Willie and Sir Matt, as they realised drooping heads now would be foolish; they were too close.

The energy in the Bar became refreshed when the sound of the thousands of United supporters in the stadium grew.

Manchester United pushed forward, a whipped in cross into the Bayern Munich box, meant for Yorke, caused a collision between Yorke and Kuffour. Yorke got to his feet, ready to get back in the fight. Kuffour required assistance from the referee, who received a stroke of his head as a thank you.

Tom Curry wrung his hands. "The team need to settle down; we can't afford to make any more mistakes."

"I think they will try and hit them on the…"

Mark leapt to his feet and interrupted Walter. "*What's he doing?*"

Non-communication between Irwin and Schmeichel resulted in the Great Dane flexing his vocal chords. Fortunately, United's blushes were spared as the ball deflected off a Bayern Munich player to go out for a throw-in.

Donny rubbed his solar plexus. "They really need to stop doing that."

"I know there are only seven minutes on the clock but to go behind so early on is not the best way to take control of the game." Swifty rubbed the back of his neck. "If they're going to be chasing the game they need to be a bit more disciplined and cohesive."

"They'll get it together," Alf said. "It will happen, trust me, it will happen."

"I just hope it happens before the final whistle," Henry added.

George shook his head and smiled. "Oh, ye of little faith."

A Beckham long ball, like a heat-seeking missile, picked out Giggs on a foray into Bayern Munich's eighteen-yard box. The potentiality was heeded by Bayern Munich and the ball was kicked out for a corner.

Beckham placed the ball, looked up and around, wanting to take advantage. The ball travelled past the near post but was deflected out of Bayern Munich's penalty box and they were now racing up the pitch on the break. They crossed the halfway line but further progress was halted by a well-timed tackle by Blomqvist.

David started it, a hum under his breath, picked up by Tommy and gradually spread through the Busby booth, then the families and soon it was being sung like a mantra throughout the Bar.

"We'll never die, we'll never die. We'll never die, we'll never die. We'll keep the red flag flying high cos Man United will never die."

Some were able to shake the negative feeling off, others increased their positive emotions; the singing had helped to relax nerves that, even at this early stage had become frayed. By the eleventh minute calm rational heads prevailed and all settled back in their seats.

"He's been phenomenal, there's no getting away from it."

Willie knew who Sir Matt was talking about. "He's had his fair share of critics of his system but he's proven them wrong. You had your critics too."

"Yeah, but they weren't as vociferous as they are these days."

"True. This game, win or lose will declare him on a par with you, in my humble opinion of course."

Jimmy placed his forearms on the top of the booth behind Sir Matt. "You won five Championships and four League Cups. Your thirteenth year you won the Champions League. Fergie's won five Championships and four League Cups and this is his thirteenth year in charge. It's a mirror Boss. They're gonna win this."

"I would say something about *writing* and *stars* but I don't want to interrupt The Omnipotent One's enjoyment of the game." Eddie's eyes sparkled as he tried hard to keep his face serious.

Billy nudged Eddie in the ribs; they *felt* The Omnipotent One smile and the archangels giggled.

Basler, now deep in United's half, crossed the ball into the eighteen-yard box, his target, Zickler. The confident tackle by Stam stopped Bayern Munich's progress and Schmeichel placed the ball for a goal kick.

"He's got the right kind of face for a defender, hasn't he?"

"You mean etched with determination?" Mark knew exactly what David meant but did not want to get into a banter session with him about Stam. Tommy hid his smile and kept silent.

"It's a face chiselled out of granite, you know?"

"He's an old-school kind of defender. Alex Ferguson needed someone of his ilk after Pallister. Can you imagine coming up against him as a forward?"

David turned to Jimmy. "It would definitely be a challenge, that's for sure."

On the pitch, discord played out between Yorke and Beckham about the delivery of the latter's free kick.

"I know I'm preaching to the converted here but they really need to settle themselves before Bayern slip in and double their goal tally." Tommy's shoulders were hunched as he sat forward.

Duncan inched forward and made eye contact with Tommy. "Who's your player of the season?"

"Wow." Tommy sat back, his fingers tapped his mouth. "There's so many to choose from. You've got Schmeichel for some of the blinding saves he's made, you've got Yorkie, firing in from every angle and you've got to add Cole to that too. Actually, think of all the forwards, up there for a shout. It's difficult."

Tommy slipped away into his own memory to try and ascertain if one player stood head and shoulders above the rest. Duncan bit his lower lip, happy his deflection technique had worked.

The doors to the ever-expanding Bar remained open as many souls poured in to watch the match. It took them a few minutes to acclimatise themselves and note the sheer size of it and marvel at how it did not lose the close intimate feel they had heard about.

Bert looked behind and was astonished at the number of archangels who had developed a love of United; he turned his attention back to the pitch.

"Have you had a chance to have a gander at John O'Shea?"

Billy smiled at Jimmy's question. "I saw his debut against Villa; he shows tremendous promise. I only hope he delivers."

"I feel if he keeps on the straight and narrow, and injury-free, of course, then he's likely to be a United defender for a long time."

"I caught one of his games for Waterford Bohemians before he signed for United, he was good; definitely Manchester United material." Billy gave a half-shrug and turned to Jimmy. "But, you know I don't have to mention names, you can have the best talent in the world but if things off the field are not as they should be then things go south quickly."

Willie and Sir Matt glanced at each other and smiled. It was a conversation that they had had earlier, the impact off-pitch activities could have on a great footballer's career.

A long throw-in by Neville reached Bayern Munich's penalty spot. Cole was in the right place but he was not alone; he found himself surrounded by Bayern's defence and his attempt was deflected out for a goal-kick.

Lubricated larynxes of the United supporters urged their players on. The sound of *United, United, United* rang out across Barcelona, not just the Estadio Nou Camp.

"I hope it's not going to be one of those days for him and Yorkie."

Sir Matt placed his hand on Duncan's forearm. "They've scored fifty-two goals between them this season. I trust there's at least another goal left in one of them."

An undaunted Johnsen slid into a tackle with Jancker as the latter made his way down the wing. Although Johnsen was adamant he got the ball he was penalised by Collina.

Roger shook his head. "That was a bit harsh, he did get the ball."

"It'll even itself out, and look," Geoff said as Basler's free kick sailed over the United crossbar. "They didn't profit from it."

Manchester United's goal kick flew halfway into the Bayern Munich half but could only reach the head of a Bayern defender; back to the halfway line then progress was halted for a United offside. Bayern Munich, as can be expected of a team on a one-goal lead, appeared comfortable on the ball.

The free kick found Zickler who played a one-two with Effenberg outside the eighteen-yard box before racing towards Manchester United's goal. Schmeichel made himself big, added to that the pressure from Johnsen meant Zickler's header, as he went to ground, was saved by Schmeichel.

"This is where they're really missing Keane. I feel inspirational leadership can gain a team points."

Jackie considered Johnny's observation for a second. "You're right, the team on the pitch are doing okay but there isn't a team leader, like Keane. He can grab a game by the scruff of the neck and make it beg for mercy!"

"Maybe Beckham will take on the mantle," Dennis suggested.

"Schmeichel's the captain so he should, but it's difficult to captain a team from between the sticks; not impossible but difficult."

"Both goalkeepers are captain today so it should be interesting to see how it pans out at the final whistle."

"We still haven't settled yet. We're making silly mistakes; fortunately, Collina is being more than fair and not looking to make headlines."

"I don't know about you but I've never been able to settle watching the first twenty minutes of a game. It's like, I suddenly remember I have to breathe and relax but it doesn't kick in for twenty minutes."

Eddie swivelled to look behind him; he flashed his teeth. "You're a funny one Dennis, there's no denying it and not in the amusing sense of the word."

Dennis stretched and gently clipped Eddie across the top of the head. Eyes were on the pitch but light-hearted banter, borne out of close friendship, followed.

Swifty looked over at the Busby booth and thought, *laughter is good medicine when your team is one nil down and you have seventy minutes to play.*

***

George looked up from his notepad. "Bayern have been caught offside several times."

"I think that's their third." Donny turned to Henry for confirmation.

Henry glanced down at his laptop, at the statistics spreadsheet he had open alongside the article he was writing. "Yeah, it's their third."

"Not all of them correct shouts mind you," Eric said. "Bayern were onside with that one."

"Collina's been the busiest man on the pitch so far."

"And Kahn has been the least busy."

"You're not wrong."

Manchester United felt the pressure from the tackles meted out to them by Bayern Munich. The *ole* choruses from the Bayern Munich supporters seemed to stiffen United's resolve; their purpose began to solidify.

"I know we've got plenty of time but I feel that if we don't get a goal soon Bayern may shut up shop for the rest of the match."

Bert held up his palms and responded. "I feel the same Walter, but look at the Juventus game, we were two goals down! In ten minutes! Everyone wrote us off at that moment and look where we are now; the final."

"They have to tap into the belief that drove them forward that day." Tom Curry bobbed his head and sat back. "I know they can do this."

Resolute defending by Bayern Munich continued to foil advances made by Manchester United; stymied by the German midfield and defence as they worked as a pack. Johnsen intercepted Kahn's goal kick and launched the ball back into the Bayern Munich half; it was retrieved by Giggs after over confident play by Tarnat.

Giggs, aware of Beckham's advancing run, slid the ball forward. Beckham's cross, the Bayern Munich six-yard box the target, was deflected out for a corner. The United supporters in the Estadio Nou Camp roared their approval of the extra effort their team displayed.

David Beckham whipped in a corner that seemed to hover before Jeremies sprang up to head the ball over the net; another corner kick. This time, Beckham took it short, to Giggs; Jeremies interrupted the intended one-two between Giggs and Beckham and the ball went out for a United throw-in.

United had assessed the game and realised they needed to take control; fluid play between them began to develop.

Ryan Giggs, the target of Beckham's throw-in, passed the ball back. Beckham crossed the ball into the six-yard box, close to the upright, where it was met by Yorke. Yorke turned and his right foot connected with the ball in one fluid movement; the ball sailed towards the Bayern Munich goal.

Kahn was more aware of Cole and punched the ball away to prevent Cole from equalising from a backspin laden shot. The determination of the Bayern defence hardened against the barrage of attempts by United. Matthäus, as he faced his own goal, reverse headed the ball away to Effenberg; another United throw-in.

Jimmy stood and applauded. "This is more like it." His hands felt hot. "The Bayern defence are standing strong but United have to keep on chiselling away."

"Well, there's no problem with that Jimmy. There'll keep chiselling, no doubt about it." Dennis felt the spark had now been ignited in United and he believed a goal for them was inevitable.

***

"Look at their faces; I mean both teams," Swifty spoke as though he was commentating. "One is going to be the loser of this game, no-one can sustain this pressure for a full match. It's only twenty-five minutes in and each team is playing at one hundred percent."

Archie nodded. "One won't sustain it. I hope it will be Bayern Munich."

"You'd be thrown out and barred if you thought otherwise."

Peter Schmeichel barked instructions to his team; he could not allow Bayern to go two-nil up in the first half of the first half. Games like the semi-final against Juventus only come about once in a lifetime.

The Tarnat throw-in sailed to the edge of United's six-yard box; Neville was there to clear it away. Yorke brought the ball down and played it square to Irwin who launched the ball towards the centre circle and United surged forward again.

Sing your heart out, sing your heart out, sing your heart out for the lads; sing your heart out for the lads.

Jesper Blomqvist passed to Beckham midway in Bayern Munich's half and almost saw United dispossessed by Effenberg. The ball was squared to Yorke who saw Giggs to his right, on the edge of Bayern's eighteen-yard box. Giggs shimmied himself into the centre, ratcheted up his left leg and fired a shot, only for it to be blocked.

"They're figuring out a way through. It will happen. They *will* come back from this." Mark spoke confidently.

"Imagine if Giggs, playing out of position, got the equaliser?" David had a wide dreamy smile on his face; in his mind's eye, he saw it could be a possibility.

"I don't care who scores it, the quality or where it comes from, it could be an own goal, anything as long as they get one; soon." Tommy sat back in his seat.

The confidence brought about by the win against Spurs had lifted them and saw them through the game against Newcastle. Today was different. No English team had ever been in this position before.

Some people Down Below felt United should be happy with their lot; a treble Double was still a historic achievement, maybe the European Champions League was one cup too far. Up Above tension was high but the belief was even higher.

Bayern Munich's move forward was foiled by a horizontal Irwin, into the path of Beckham. A Beckham and Butt midfield combination brought the ball under control and a second later, Neville delivered a precise ball to the edge of Bayern's eighteen-yard box, onto the run of Cole.

The dangerousness of Cole in that position required two Bayern defenders to block his shot from reaching his intended target, Yorke, stood close to the penalty spot. The defended ball made its way back to United who duly sent it back into Bayern Munich's half.

"Their height domination is proving to be a bit of a problem for us," Bert said to himself. "They're winning all the aerial balls."

Jimmy countered. "Well, we're just going to have to deal with it. It's not like they can sprout a couple of inches in the next hour or so."

Sir Matt smiled; the bluntness of Jimmy's words direct and true. "Possession-wise, United are doing okay, they can't let up the assault though. They can't afford to take off the pressure."

"They've got to be relentless." Jimmy clapped his hands together as though ready to perform a flamenco. "They'll be no fat lady singing early tonight lads. Tonight; tonight we will dance to something a little bit more passionate."

A clash of heads by Yorke and Kuffour and the Busby booth erupted into laughter, whistles and slow claps.

"He deserves an extra mark for the writhing on the pitch. What do you think lads?" Geoff looked around as he continued to slow clap.

Eddie chuckled. "You should get a mark for using the word writhing."

"For me, he gets an extra point, not for his *writhing* but for his acting as though his hand is hanging on by a tendon," Billy said.

"Great. So that's seven points to Kuffour." Roger turned to the bar to confirm they had heard and was startled, at how many archangels were behind the bar. A light-hearted tussle between several archangels was swiftly curtailed and they all assisted in making a note of Kuffour's points.

While Kuffour was off the pitch receiving treatment United set up their free kick. The screamed commands from Kahn could be heard by around the Stadium. Yet again, Beckham's cross, into Bayern's box, was cleared out for a corner.

"They're chipping away, chipping away." Duncan rolled the ball between his feet, a movement that mesmerised those sat behind the journalists' booth.

Sir Matt agreed. "They're putting pressure on the defenders and Kahn."

Beckham placed the ball in the corner, looked for his options, decided and delivered the ball into the box. Kahn, confident in his ability and the cohesiveness of his defence, punched the ball out.

Unfortunately, Kahn also caught Kuffour who received a blow to the back of his head; those in Red Cloud Bar noted how quickly Kuffour got to his feet, no writhing around this time.

Duncan turned to Sir Matt. "I hope they can keep up this pressure; they've been relentless the last five or six minutes."

"Relentless is right. They will keep on, keeping on until the final whistle."

"They need to capitalise on a corner; get a head on it or find Giggs." The *butterflies* continued to flit around Duncan's stomach as he settled into a conversation with Sir Matt. The first game after Sir Matt's arrival the Babes had decided to accommodate his preference for where he wished to sit. When he had taken his seat and gestured Duncan to sit beside him, the lads jokingly called him teacher's pet.

David Beckham appeared to have had the ball for the majority of the last ten minutes as he took yet another free kick.

"It doesn't look like Bayern have many answers going forward. They're an all-out defending force at the moment." The unspoken in Johnny's words almost a prayer, the desire to see United do the opposite.

"I hope they don't make any silly mistakes," said Dennis. He gave himself a little shake to disperse the tension taking a hold within.

Willie was pragmatic. "Beckham seems to be everywhere at the moment. He's had the most touches of anyone out there so far."

"He needs to be careful; Bayern Munich will try to draw him in for a foul. They're not above taunting play for the sake of it."

"They're not even attempting to get close to the box. Hit it long and hopefully find Schmeichel off his line." Tommy's frustration was evident.

It took three Bayern Munich players to dispossess Beckham of the ball and, for the first time, in what seemed to be an age, Bayern were pressing forward towards United's eighteen-yard box.

Zickler hurried the low shot, went for glory rather than team play and the ball went wide of the mark and a diving Schmeichel; he expressed his displeasure to his defenders.

"That's what he needs to do, stamp his authority on the game." Geoff's left hand cupped his right fist as though to punctuate the point. "In my opinion, a problem could be between Schmeichel and his defence."

Roger nodded towards the pitch. "Well, it's half an hour in and we've seen May warming up and now Greening and Brown. Not exactly the attacking force we should be looking at when we're one-nil down."

"Maybe he's just letting the lads have a bit of a warm-up."

"There's the attack force of Sheringham and Solskjaer on the bench if he needs to change things up."

"It's fine lads." Jackie leant forward, his arm around the shoulders of Geoff and Roger. "They've got plenty of time; there's no need to make snap decisions."

The souls in the Bar leant towards the *pitch* and urged the United players on.

"This set up The Omnipotent One has done is unreal." Eddie's head slowly turned as he took in the decor inside the Bar; he looked back at the pitch. "I could reach out and touch Giggs," he turned to smile at Billy. "Just pick him up from the pitch."

Billy chuckled. "You're off your head Eddie."

Red Cloud Bar continued to expand. The suspended shirts appeared, to those who could drag their attention from the match, like a chattering of starlings. Souls and archangels from several other clouds continued to pour in to see why every soul on Red Cloud, and several other clouds too, were all in one place.

"I'm optimistic for the outcome of the game but if the worse should happen then to watch the match like this has been an amazing experience. You know? Watching it like this."

Johnny's words struck a chord with those in the booths and surrounding seats, the pause of reflection did not last long; United were on the march again, relentless, determined.

Peter Schmeichel delivered a long ball, collected by Giggs, who although he slipped on the pitch, bounced back up and dribbled his way to the edge of Bayern's penalty box, sending the ball square to Yorke.

"Yorke will be disappointed he didn't make better contact with that." Tom Curry eased himself back into the booth after he had mirrored Yorke's move.

"I know; he can't let his head drop though."

"Do you know…?"

Walter clapped his hand to his cheek. "Oh dear, I can feel a stat coming on."

Tom laughed. "No, listen; anyway that's Bert's job." He shuffled in his seat, his body language an indication he was about to launch into information-giving mode. "There have been forty-four Champions League finals and of those forty-four matches, eleven teams have come back from a one-nil deficit to win. Real Madrid did it four times, Benfica twice, Milan, Celtic, Feyenoord, Bayern Munich and Porto."

"Great Tom; so United have a one in four chance of winning tonight, is that it?"

"In a nutshell, yes."

Willie took his eyes off the pitch and was ecstatic so many souls had decided to join in the occasion. There was an electrical atmosphere he had not experienced before.

He looked around and recognised Bela Miklos and waved to him and his family. Ken Rayment and Tom Cable sensed Willie's glance and waved; he returned the wave with a smile that stretched from ear to ear.

Sir Matt nudged Willie and said. "If Celtic can do it then United can do it."

The souls relaxed a little and leant back in their seats. There was plenty of time for Manchester United to pick the pockets of Bayern Munich.

A few seconds ticked by before Kahn finally took the goal kick. Hitzfeld was on his feet and urged his team forward while shaking his head.

"What's his problem?" asked Tom Curry.

"He's probably thinking his defensive line should be back a bit more, I don't know". Walter sat with his head back against the booth as he twirling his thumbs; he soaked up the full atmosphere, the excitement in the air.

Ryan Giggs ran onto the ball from Kahn, lost it and battled to gain it back. Beckham was there to assist, his eyes focussed on the Bayern Munich goal. He distributed a cross to Yorke who squared it to Cole just outside the Bayern Munich box.

Cole had a huge task before him, his back to goal with Kuffour breathing down his neck. He stood his ground, looked up and saw Beckham had made a run; Cole slid the ball to Beckham who made a cross that could only find the head of Kuffour.

Bayern Munich took advantage of their height advantage and the ball remained in the air until they could get themselves back into position. The difficult work of going forward by United was faultless, however, confusion spread across the faces of everyone watching when Matthäus ran towards United's goal, unchallenged, and hit over the bar.

Roger flung his arms in the air. "Why are they standing back?"

"He made a forty yard run and no-one attempted to tackle him." The surprise in Dennis' voice was a reflection of the overall feeling in the Bar.

Willie grimaced; his fingers tapped an unknown tune on his thigh. "There's no wonder Schmeichel isn't happy."

"Beckham and Butt are at fault there." Geoff crossed his arms and slipped further down his seat. "I'm surprised at Butt. And Beckham seems to forget he has a defensive role to play, not just attacking."

"They're lucky Matthäus had his selfish head on and went for the goal because that could have cost them."

"Do you know…?" Bert was about to launch into a statistic.

The collective cry came; "No Bert, we don't."

Some archangels, in a reflection of what they had seen the souls do, bit their bottom lip and looked upwards in a nonchalant way in an attempt to stop the smile. One turned towards the mirror on the back of the bar and made eye contact with Swifty. His eyes sparkled with merriment and he winked at the archangel who worked even harder to prevent the smile.

A foul on Johnsen by Jancker resulted in a United free kick, taken by Schmeichel. He hit a long pass towards Bayern Munich's goal. Giggs played it back to Beckham who settled the ball and chipped it inside but Bayern Munich read the play.

United recovered and turned back towards their target, the back of Bayern Munich's net. A ball by Blomqvist was picked off by Bayern Munich but United's midfield stood strong and the direction of play quickly returned towards the Bayern Munich goal but the Beckham pass had too much on it; it went out for a Bayern Munich goal kick.

"He's getting animated now," said Sir Matt at the sight of Alex Ferguson on the edge of the pitch, as he urged his players to be careful.

Willie nodded. "And so are the United supporters in the crowd."

United, United, United, United, United, United. The word, like a mantra, echoed around the Nou Camp

Jancker received the Kahn ball, deep in United's half and crossed the ball to the wing. Alex Ferguson's remonstrations had hit home. Beckham tackled and played the ball out to the left but a hasty pass back to Schmeichel saw Jancker on the edge of the eighteen-yard box, ready to pounce. Schmeichel saw it and made a clearance, right back to Bayern Munich.

Basler, confident after his goal, weaved his way towards United's penalty box. Irwin shadowed Basler every step of the way and the ball became too hot for Basler to handle; he slid the ball to Effenberg, who saw Matthäus on the wing. Matthäus took a shot at United's goal, more in hope than good judgement; it was safely collected by Schmeichel.

"He's a bit of a selfish so-and-so, isn't he?" said Eddie. "That's two woeful attempts he's made that could have been played closer to goal, to a Bayern Munich player in a better position."

"Long may it continue, I say." Billy crossed his ankles and stretched his legs in front of him. "I'd like to see United's midfield harry them a bit more."

Peter Schmeichel rolled the ball out to Giggs who began his usual maze-like run down the wing. Over the halfway line he was abruptly cut off by Jeremies; level with the Bayern penalty box.

"He should have a free kick for that." Bert was peeved.

"That's as maybe but he didn't. More importantly, he's back up and running again." A smile danced over Jimmy's lips as he continued. "He's a marvellous winger that lad. Can you imagine what the England team would have achieved if he'd decided to play for them instead of Wales?" He enjoyed the banter and at times just lit the firework for the sake of it.

"It was his decision to make and I'm sure he's *not* unhappy with it," Johnny said.

"The Welsh team don't have the talents of the English team." Jackie had taken the bait.

"We're in a similar position to you guys over in Northern Ireland. I reckon it's because we have our own national sports that we're good at." Jimmy sat back and placed his arm along the back of the booth behind Dennis.

He tapped Jackie's shoulder. "Tough sports like hurling, Gaelic football, rugby and you have…" He brought his arm around Dennis. "Remind me again? Ah, that's it cricket for four months of the year."

In mock defence Bert said. "It's nearly five months actually."

Jimmy gasped, touched his heart space with his hand. "I stand corrected."

"Aye, it is what it is."

David Beckham hit a long ball forward which found Giggs, in the Bayern Munich box, Kuffour on his tail. The linesman blew offside.

David said. "The lad's right to be miffed, he was never offside."

"I think it was blown for Cole." Mark proffered.

"Yeah, but he wasn't interfering with the play was he?"

Mark held his hands up. "Messenger only."

"No, I tell you; the rules and regulations these days have me baffled."

"They're playing with more confidence though, aren't they?"

Tommy fought hard to keep the pleading from his voice. "So long as they don't become overconfident, they should breach the wall."

His forearms on his knees, his feet on the ball Duncan agreed. "If they can make it to halftime without conceding another goal, I'm sure they can regroup for the second half."

"How long's left of this half?" asked David.

Duncan glanced at the clock. "Just under ten minutes."

"So why didn't Babel join Manchester United after Euro 96?" Mark wanted to change the subject; to take it away from clock watching.

Tommy responded. "Apparently they couldn't come to an agreement on the personal terms."

"How do you think he would have fit in with the team Alex Ferguson has built now?" Mark asked.

"It's difficult to say; you know the way *marvels* in European and World competitions have come to England and failed to deliver. It's the luck of the draw, I mean, look at Karel Poborsky."

"To be fair that that was more to do with how brilliant Beckham was playing, no slight on Poborsky and his lobs."

Tommy nodded, his eyes centre on the pitch. Johnsen had just made an unusual mistake and had headed the ball to Bayern Munich instead of a man in red.

"They're making a few unforced errors. Alex Ferguson will be praying for the half-time whistle." George's words were spoken, a fraction above a whisper, only those in his immediate surroundings could hear.

"He's not the only one." Henry had envisioned more of an attacking flurry by United.

"I don't think I can bear to watch anymore," Donny said it but still couldn't drag his eyes away from the action on the pitch.

"It's like they're playing rugby down there." Archie felt compelled to say the words but could not eradicate the feeling of unease.

"Zickler could have gone down and played for the penalty there. There are many that would."

"I know, so many United players around him, it would be difficult for the referee or linesmen to say otherwise."

"Butt got the ball from Basler cleanly but I'm not sure what the hell was happening in the box."

Swifty put his hands together. "Please referee, just blow the whistle."

"In saying all that, this is Bayern Munich's first corner kick."

"Is it? Are you sure?" Alf frowned and peered over at Eric's laptop to check.

Eric pointed to the screen, to his statistics page. "Yeah; Manchester United have had six, this is definitely Bayern Munich's first."

"If they play a set piece like they did for the goal then there's going to be a two-goal deficit going into halftime."

"They really should have done better but I think they're playing as individuals and not as a team. They're going for self-glory rather than team glory." Tom Jackson made a note to use that phrase in his article.

"I think you're right."

"I hope that's their undoing."

"Jancker and Zickler keep switching and I feel that's causing problems for United."

"And Basler's playing a little bit deeper than a striker."

"Aye, you're right they've been loose on a number of occasions, no-one's picking them up."

United, United, United, United, United, United, United, United.

Willie scratched his head. "United have had a lot of possession but they've not done a lot with it."

"It's not what you do; it's the way that you do it, that's what gets results."

It was to the chagrin of some that Eddie had the ability to have a song to fit almost every conversation. He felt relaxed in the knowledge that most references would not register with everyone as a song lyric.

"I liked that one." Sir Matt turned to Eddie and tried to keep his face straight. "They were a lovely group of girls." Eddie's cheeks reddened as Billy sniggered.

Dwight Yorke made progress towards Bayern Munich's goal and hit the ball square to Giggs. He directed a bending cross into Bayern Munich's six-yard box, to the far post. It bounced out to the eighteen-yard box, chased by Blomqvist.

Although harried by Babbel, Blomqvist brought the ball under control and calmly played it back to Butt. The ball was sliced forward, back into the penalty box, towards Yorke, Cole and an advancing Beckham.

Bayern Munich were quick to defend, they pounced and hit the ball out. Manchester United quickly regained possession, still in Bayern Munich's half, trying to breach the defensive line. Giggs delivered another cross into Bayern Munich's six-yard box, to the far post but it was too far for Blomqvist to make contact with; out for a goal kick.

"Bayern Munich are clinical getting their players back behind the ball in the box. United can't seem to penetrate that fifteen-yard line Bayern Munich have drawn." Dennis sat further forward; elbows on his thighs and chin on his clasped hands.

"It's frustrating but at least they're having a go."

"You can't expect anything less."

"Alex Ferguson wants more from them." Jackie pointed to the touchline, to an animated Alex Ferguson.

Glory, glory Man United. Glory, glory Man United. Glory, glory Man United, as the Reds go marching on, on, on.

Manchester United again tried to pick the Bayern Munich lock. Beckham lined up a free-kick, thirty yards out, almost in direct line with the centre of Bayern Munich's goal; it bent around the Bayern Munich wall but went wide of its target.

The Bayern Munich supporters in Estadio Nou Camp became louder and their whistles drowned out the chanting of the United supporters. Kahn lined up the goal kick.

"They're one-nil up going into half-time so it's understandable that they're more vocal," David said of the *celebrating* Bayern Munich supporters.

Duncan slapped his hands on his cheeks, eyes wide, almost lost for words. "What on earth?"

Sir Matt gave Duncan a nudge. "I think Peter Schmeichel is one of the best goalkeepers in the world but I hold my breath when he comes out like that."

"Maybe he should have cleared it out, but he was calmness personified." Under his breath, Duncan added, "Fortunately."

He returned his hands to his lap and hesitated over his heart area, in an instinctive gesture.

Peter Schmeichel's cleared ball went out for a Bayern Munich throw-in, deep in their half. They didn't retain possession long before the ball was back with Schmeichel for another launch towards the Bayern Munich goal. The ball dropped onto the chest of Yorke as Kuffour shadowed his every move. Yorke brought the ball down and spread play to Irwin down the wing.

Irwin passed the ball forward to Blomqvist who looked up to assess his options. He saw Beckham just outside the centre circle and passed the ball into midfield, with pinpoint precision Beckham played a diagonal cross to the feet of Yorke who touched it onto Cole just outside the penalty box.

The run on, towards the penalty spot, saw Giggs in a dangerous position but Kahn put his body on the line, smothered the ball, millimetres from Giggs' right foot.

"That was wonderful link-up play by United." Willie was on his feet applauding, so were many others.

"Kahn nicked the ball from the tip of Giggs' boot then!" Roger said.

"He reacted a bit slow to Cole's ball though."

"Yeah, but he had Tarnat on him as well."

"If Giggs had reacted a second quicker that could have been the equaliser."

"Ifs and buts..."

The United supporters in Estadio Nou Camp regained control of the volume in the stadium.

We'll never die, we'll never die, we'll never die, we'll never die; We'll keep the red flag flying high because Man United will never die.

"What's the possession statistics Statman?" asked Walter

Bert laughed. "Manchester United have had fifty-seven percent and Bayern Munich forty-three percent."

"Really?" Tom Curry was surprised. "I thought we had more than that."

Denis Irwin took a free-kick; it reached Bayern's eighteen-yard box onto the head of Kuffour, as he piggy-backed Yorke. United regained possession; Giggs steadied the ball and hit it back to the edge of the penalty box, to the feet of Yorke.

Kuffour made sure Yorke had no opportunity to turn and shoot. Wisely, Yorke tapped it to Giggs as he advanced towards the target. Giggs took the shot with his left foot; it was deflected and out; another United corner.

Beckham's sweeping ball was smothered by the midriff of Kahn. United seemed unable to find a way through; Bayern Munich were happy to put every man behind the ball until the halftime whistle. Dominant in midfield, United collected Kahn's goal kick and tried to find another way to breach the Bayern goal.

A United long ball was chased down by Irwin but Babbel had read it well and he shepherded it into the grateful arms of Kahn. Alex Ferguson stood on the touchline, his body moved and swayed with every kick of the ball.

La, la, la, la, la, la, la, la Keano. La, la, la, la, la, la, la, la Keano. La, la, la, la, la, la, la, la Keano.

"We're in the final minute." Tom Curry knew everyone was aware of the time but said it anyway.

"They're actually not doing that much wrong are they?" Billy said as he turned to Eddie. "They're working hard, shots into the Bayern Munich box; they just need to persevere."

"They'll not give in; they'll keep going."

"If they can last out the next minute or so and regroup over halftime, they could do it."

"I'm just a little worried Bayern have locked up for the night; it's for United to chase the game now and I feel that's where the potential is to make mistakes *and* for Bayern to hit them on the break."

Jancker and Zickler had made a foray into United's box and everyone tensed. Jancker dropped to the pitch in the presence of Stam who held his hands up and away. Collina was convinced there was no foul and play continued.

A Blomqvist long diagonal cross found the right foot of Cole, positioned outside Bayern's penalty box. Cole steadied himself and weaved his way into the box, progress was blocked by two defenders; his pass to Giggs deflected. Giggs was unable to make strong contact with the deflected shot and the ball dropped into the hands of Kahn.

We shall not, we shall not be moved. We shall not, we shall not be moved. Just like a team that wins the European Cup, we shall not be moved.

"Oh, come on, blow the whistle already." Tom Jackson said, under his breath.

Eric heard and tilted his head, eyes glued to the pitch. "There's going to be about two minutes of stoppage time I reckon."

The archangels were busy behind the bar drawing straws for who would take the ballot slips to Roger. The Omnipotent One had kept quiet over the number of archangels congregated in the Bar so they tried to keep roaming down to a minimum.

We love United, we do; we love United, we do; we love United, we do. Oh, United we love you.

Geoff stood and stretched. "In an hour one of these two teams will lift that Champions League trophy. It's incredible." He sighed as he placed his forearms on his head. "There's some part of this that seems so surreal."

"Can you imagine how it feels for them Down Below?" Roger said.

***

Collina blew the whistle to end the first half.

Souls rose to move around. When they had first entered the Bar they had been too awe-struck to take in some of the details. They inspected the trophies, shirts, posters and pennants.

"Hey look, the Newton Heath shirt from 1878!"

"Have you seen Ernest Mangnall? He's here somewhere with James Gibson."

"Shall we try and speak to Matt Busby?"

"Do you think they can do it?"

"This is my new favourite place."

"The atmosphere is awesome."

Inside the Bar swirls of pearlescent rainbow colours interspersed with conversations and the ethereal; it gave a shimmering glow to Red Cloud akin to a beacon.

CHAPTER EIGHT

Roger made his way to the bar to collect the ballot slips for the Champions League goal of the season. Sir Matt and Jean were already there.

He combed his hair with his fingers. "What do you think so far Boss? If you were in the dressing room, what would you be saying?"

Sir Matt thought for a second. "It's a difficult one, son. I don't know." He glanced around the Bar. "I'd probably tell them, if they believe they are giving the game their all, then that's all I can expect."

Roger turned to distribute the slips. Sir Matt touched him on his arm. "But, I would also say that at the final whistle they will walk up those stairs, pass the trophy and collect the runner-up medals. *And*, if that was good enough for them I would speak to them in my office on Friday."

"Yeah Boss; that would do it."

***

The twenty-five felt self-conscious as the rest of the souls in the Bar gathered around; this was their first ballot in front of such a big audience. The tiers of seats seemed to stretch until the eye could barely see. Conversations dropped to a whisper and giggles from the archangels took on a reverential tone.

"I feel like we're on Mastermind!"

"I don't think Magnus Magnusson would allow a practical joker category."

Eddie made a song and dance of laughing and holding his ribs. "Oh, oh, very funny, Jimmy. Anyway, it's not Magnus Magnusson anymore it's someone else."

Roger cleared his throat, twice, and went through the instructions, more so for the audience than the voters.

Wanting to take the pressure off Roger, Jimmy spoke first. "I'd like to talk about the honorary goals, you know, the ones that were magnificent, and or crucial but didn't make my top three. And they are," he leant forward and tapped the top of David's head, "drumroll please maestro."

David, joined by Tommy and Mark and countless archangels, provided the requested drumroll.

"All the goals United scored against Brondy back in October, in particular, Cole's and Keane's."

Jimmy grinned as he sat down and looked around for recognition. Bert turned to him, paused and said. "Not sure they are worth a drumroll."

Sir Matt, the Brondby game in his mind's eye, said. "That game gave them so much confidence, they played with such fluidity; it was a beautiful game."

The six Manchester United goals were replayed to the gasps and wide eyes of the newcomers to the Bar. It quickly segued into Old Trafford, where the five goals scored two weeks later, against the same opposition, were replayed.

"Eleven goals in two games; and," Mark held up a finger to emphasise his point. "Not a single tap-in."

"I'd be proud to kiss the badge for any one of them; great goals," Tommy said.

David warmed up to having an audience and placed his hand on his heart space and said. "For me, the month after, November, seemed to be the pivotal month. Peter Schmeichel announced his retirement and Kiddo left."

"I agree, but we're talking about goals." Eddie winked as David wrinkled his nose at him.

"It's usually a difficult period, you know, the winter season," Duncan said as he looked down at the ball under his feet.

Willie broke the silence and brought the conversation back to the task at hand. "What about the Cole/Yorke combination against Barcelona?"

Geoff thought back to the combination of Yorke and Cole. "The Cole and Yorke axis for so many of United's goals has been incredible. I've just had a look at them now; so fluid, so psychically created." He continued. "Some of them were impossible to defend. I'd hate to have faced them in the form they're in right now."

"For me, the three goals against Barcelona in September were all peaches but I've already picked out my one, two and three." Jackie handed his slip to Roger.

"I want to mention the goals against Juventus and, in particular, Keane's against them last month." Johnny sat back and crossed his legs. "I don't want you guys to forget."

Dennis laughed and said. "Not a chance we'd forget that one. It's my number two."

"I don't mind saying who and what's on my list," said Walter. He felt the eyes of the crowd on him; the audience silenced their whispered conversations. "Okay, I've got the Cole/Yorke combination for number three, Scholes against Milan in March and, of course, Keane's against Juventus as number one."

"Same here." Tom Curry waved his completed slip at Walter.

"Me too," Willie said as he stood and handed his slip to Roger; he was ready to circulate and soak in the experiences of some of the first-timers to the Bar.

Roger looked around to gauge the reaction. "Okay, it looks like we've got the three goals so, short of a wonder goal being scored this second half then, I think, we're done."

"I found that difficult. When you see the goals in isolation you get to see how fantastic they all were." Sir Matt, considerate of the new souls in the Bar, turned to the bar and the many, many archangels congregated there. "Maybe we could have a reminder of all the goals."

The *pitch* switched with ease from Estadio Nou Camp to all the stadiums that witnessed the might of United's strike force; newcomers revelled in the seamless transition as much as the goals.

Some last minute changes and cheeky annotations for the archangels were made before Roger handed the twenty-five slips in at the bar.

The noise level in the Bar increased as people milled about, as they tried to stand close to Sir Matt, the Babes, the pitch; taking in every nuance, word and vibration. It was an occasion, even for those who had been Up Above for many decades, which brought out a sensation of awe.

Sir Matt circulated to thank various people he knew had come to watch their first United game, certainly since he had arrived. Birthday wishes from some, brainstorming potential second-half tactics with others, he also made his way over to the bar to thank the archangels. He smothered a smile at their giggles which had revered fever pitch.

***

"Okay lads," said Jimmy as he took his seat. "Any substitutions?"

"No." Swifty shook his head. "They're keeping the faith with the teams they picked at the start."

In a wistful voice, Mark said. "It's electric down there."

Eddie, who had only just sat down, jumped to his feet, his face etched with passion as he shouted to the pitch. "Come on United."

Billy exploded with laughter at Eddie's exuberance and turned to Johnny, his leg tucked under him. He wasn't as tightly coiled as Eddie. "If United equalise then it goes to extra time. I don't think any team wants that."

"United will just have to score two goals then." Johnny was unaware he had crossed his fingers.

Jackie made his way past Johnny. "It's not impossible."

"True. However, if Bayern Munich score *another* it could be all over for United."

Eddie spun round to Jackie and Johnny. "They can, and will do this." He turned back to the pitch. "We need to believe."

Dennis nodded. "Yeah, I'm with Snake Hips; they can and will do this."

"What do you reckon Boss?" Duncan queried.

The noise level dropped, heads inclined towards the Busby booth, eager to hear what Sir Matt would say. "They can do this. We need to believe."

Eddie smiled.

Pierluigi Collina blew the whistle and Bayern Munich kicked off.

***

"I'd think about switching Giggs to the left but it looks like he's going to keep the same formation." George upper body was slumped forward as if he was one step away from approaching Alex Ferguson to give his opinion.

"They've created opportunities but Bayern Munich are so cohesive in defence." Donny knew missed chances were the ones to keep you awake at night.

"True." After a brief pause, Archie continued. "I'd definitely think of throwing Solskjaer into the mix."

"It's likely Bayern Munich will look to play defensive and protect their one-goal lead, but it could be the unmaking of them if they do."

"You're right Henry. This season United have *always* scored when it was needed."

"This game will produce another goal, you mark my words," Henry added. "But it will be for United." Tonight was a time when Down Below superstitions felt comforting to prevent a *jinx*.

"They've had more of the possession in the first half and they're quick off the mark now." Alf bent his head to scribble down his thoughts, interspersed with his wishes.

Peter Schmeichel launched a goal kick deep into Bayern Munich's half, it found the head of Tarnat who knocked it back towards United's goal. A sliding pass reached Jancker, sandwiched between Johnsen and Irwin.

The pincer movement narrowed Jancker's options and he aimed for goal, however, with no opportunity to angle it correctly Schmeichel touched the ball out for a Bayern Munich corner.

Eric shook his head and tutted. "Jancker got the better of Johnsen *and* Irwin."

"United shouldn't concede another goal so early in this half or Bayern Munich are *definitely* going to shut up shop!" Tom Jackson put his pen down and, with less than one minute played, discovered he was perched on the edge of his seat. He slid back and rolled his shoulders.

Willie squinted, laughed and pointed at the screen. "Is that Solskjaer at the corner *intimidating* Basler?"

"No, it's Teddy Sheringham!" Sir Matt said as he glanced at the touchline

"Good. Keep the pressure on and off the pitch."

"He's not trying to intimidate anyone. He's just doing some stretches."

"And that's the only place he can do them." Willie winked at Sir Matt. "I understand."

The corner was taken by Basler and driven out by David Beckham for yet another corner and the *dance* repeated - a Basler corner intercepted by Beckham.

Blomqvist seized a sliver of opportunity and ran upfield, hoping to release Giggs. His thought was read by Basler who made his way back to defend; he intercepted Blomqvist's pass and the ball went out for a throw-in to United.

"Kuffour's having a heck of a game. He's like Andy Cole's shadow."

Mark stroked his chin. "He can't keep it up Tommy, not till the final whistle anyway. So I'd, if I was Alex Ferguson of course, consider bringing on the fresh legs of Solskjaer."

"It's a possibility but he'll let the second half settle and make a decision in the last twenty minutes or so."

"Is there anyone who can come on for Kuffour?" David asked.

"I suppose Thomas Helmer could but, I don't know; I don't think Hitzfeld would want to mess with the Kuffour and Linke combination. If he doesn't pick up a yellow card he should stay on as long as he can." Duncan quickly added. "Of course, I'm speaking from an objective point of view."

"Good observation Duncan." Sir Matt said.

Duncan felt confident to continue. "Kuffour looks determined to go the full game. I don't think Hitzfeld will sub him. Look he's even taking on Giggs now."

Eyes were on the tableau before them. Kuffour was able to hold Giggs off the ball and pass to Zickler. However, Beckham was there to impede progress.

"Beckham needs to dial it back a bit. His challenges are looking a bit rash." Walter's looked at both Tom Curry and Bert, hoping for a confirmation from either of them.

Bert did not hide the smile that danced across his lips and, in a raised voice said. "You're just nervous about Beckham after the…"

And, as expected, everyone in the Bar said, in unison: "*Scapegoattery.*"

The multitude of archangels giggled; Eric stood and took a bow accompanied by a rotating hand, finger pointed. "I thank you."

Attention was brought back to the pitch as Beckham crossed the halfway line and raced towards the goal. He slid the ball forward and hoped it and Cole would connect.

In a one-on-one race, Cole and Kuffour ran forward, both determined to get to the ball first; Kuffour won.

Some thought of what it would be like to have Kuffour playing for United. No-one needed to ask who he was talking about when David said. "He's everywhere! He's their best player on the pitch tonight."

"He's definitely thwarting and frustrating the strikers."

Eddie nudged Geoff and frowned, in an attempt to look serious. "Word of the day – thwarting?"

"Yeah; I like it, the sound is comforting, in a weird sort of way."

Before Eddie could think of a witty response all eyes were on Pierluigi Collina, as he jogged over to Sheringham, on the touchline and asked him to step back.

"I suppose it was a bit off-putting," Geoff said.

"Maybe he's whispering sweet nothings into his ears," Eddie replied as he grasped Geoff's shoulders in an attempt to demonstrate.

Roger, unaware of the good-natured grappling between Geoff and Eddie, assumed. "He could be passing on tactics from Alex Ferguson."

"I'll go along with Roger's idea. He's giving tactics from Ferguson rather than the sweet nothings, sorry." Billy ducked in an effort to avoid Eddie's wet whisper into his ear.

"By rights, the linesman should have had a word before Collina got involved," Dennis said.

"Well, the advantage, if ever there was one, has been lost now. He'll just have to get..."

Johnny was unable to finish his sentence; his jaw dropped as he watched Schmeichel make a slow clearance in the penalty area. A fast-moving Jancker, unable to control his run the deflected ball; it fell to Jaap Stam to clear.

Cole took advantage and held up play midway in Bayern's half and waited for support in the guise of Yorke. Down Below heartbeats calmed as Yorke took the game down a notch.

"There's an element to the back four and Schmeichel that's making me hold my breath each time the ball goes back there." Swifty smoothed his hair back and began to rub the back of his neck.

George put his pen down. "We should do more to stabilise the midfield, to protect the back line. I think, maybe switch Giggs back to the left and bring on Sheringham for Blomqvist."

"Well, Giggs has earned a corner. I know they're creating chances. But, the potential problem is at the other end." His eyes left the pitch for a second as he checked the screen in front of him; Swifty saw no mistakes in his copy, his full attention returned to the pitch.

David Beckham whipped in a corner. It reached the edge of Bayern Munich's six-yard box where a gathering of Bayern and United players mingled together. Johnsen, unable to control contact, headed over the bar. His disappointment mirrored by every Manchester United player and supporter.

Oliver Kahn placed the ball and searched for a target. It skimmed the head of a leaping Jancker and fell to United just outside their own eighteen-yard box. The ball travelled back across the halfway line onto the chest of Cole who brought it down but progress was halted by Bayern Munich.

Frustrated, Jackie said. "The last three minutes has been throw-in after throw-in."

"It's only six minutes in." Jimmy felt it was too early to become despondent. "That's a lovely ball in from Beckham." He applauded, not because it was a great ball, but to rally the troops.

"They've come out of the traps fighting, that's for sure." Willie wriggled in his seat.

"They have; but I think maybe a substitution could shake things up a bit, you know, throw Bayern off guard a little." Sir Matt felt Willie's nervousness and nudged him. "United will do what they need to do, don't worry. If it's one step too far for them then…" His shrug punctuated his sentence.

Collina awarded a free kick to United, after a collision between Irwin and Jeremies. It was intercepted by Kuffour on the penalty spot and fell to Cole. He slotted the ball onto the forward run of Butt; unfortunately, Butt could not reach it.

The ball was picked up by Bayern Munich and taken to the halfway line by Jeremies. Neville read Jeremies' intent and cut him off; Jeremies concluded a tactical retreat was in order. An Effenberg flick and the ball made its way to Basler who attempted a cross into United's eighteen-yard box; it was blocked by Blomqvist.

"How many corners is that for Bayern Munich?"

Bert turned to Walter. "Four. United have had almost double that."

Basler strolled to take the corner as if he had all the time in the world. He readied himself, glanced up and hit the ball into United's box; it was flicked away, but only as far as Effenberg on the touchline.

A long cross found Kuffour in United's box, unmarked and his diving header sliced the ball wide of the goal.

Tom Curry said. "Nobody picked him up." He sounded shocked.

"To be fair, I don't think anyone expected him to be there."

"That's not the point David."

The archangels felt tension in the air and began to giggle; the effect on the souls was like a gentle massage. Everyone sat back, shoulders relaxed and a calmer aura blanketed the Bar.

Peter Schmeichel's goal kick sailed over the halfway line and a leaping Matthäus made contact. Kuffour appeared to climb on the back of Yorke to reach it and headed the ball into the path of Giggs as he chased up the flank, with Tarnat as his companion.

Giggs, level with the penalty spot, paused, looked up and delivered the ball into the six-yard box. Tarnat tried to block the cross but failed. It travelled towards Yorke who, closely marked by Linke, was unable to make contact.

The ball pinged on the heads of a couple of Bayern Munich players before it fell to Yorke again. He took control this time and sent it to Giggs who in his indomitable way dribbled the ball into Bayern Munich's box where it was kicked out for a corner.

United, United, United, United, United, United, United, United

"He's like a magician with those runs of his," Tommy said, his hands mimicked the twirling baton of an old-time magician, complete with imaginary top hat.

"He's an amazing player, beautiful to watch." David's appreciation of Giggs was clear.

"The roar of the United fans will help in this second half, behind Bayern Munich's goal."

Mark agreed. "Yeah, it will give them an added incentive."

"They're doing well chief." Duncan's belief was unshaken. "It's just a matter of time."

Manchester United were pushed back to the halfway line but, before long, they were on the march forward again. Cole and Giggs played one-two as they moved along the touchline, looking for an opportunity to breach the Bayern Munich defensive line.

Giggs crossed the ball towards the six-yard box, to Blomqvist,

"What an opportunity!" David, his arms in the air, dropped his hands onto his head; he had been ready to celebrate a goal. "That's the first time he's been in a position like that."

"Kahn off his line *and* an empty goal." Tommy shook his head.

"He should have buried that," David said as he scratched the top of his head.

"Opportunities are knocking for them." Jimmy rubbed his hands together in anticipation; able to see the positivity in the movement.

Willie turned to Jimmy. "It was a brilliant ball in by Giggs."

"Superb," Mark said.

"Shame it was over the bar but, like you said Jimmy, opportunities are coming." Willie turned back to the pitch and continued. "It's just a matter of time."

Tommy was lost in the missed chance. "He could have been the hero."

"It's okay lads, there's over half an hour to play," Duncan said. "Come on, keep the faith."

Oliver Kahn's goal kick, again, found the head of a United player, this time, Yorke. He was unable to control the direction of the ball and it fell to Bayern Munich on the wing. Effenberg took stock of the situation before he moved towards the halfway line.

His stray pass eventually fell to Neville who although blocked by Jeremies was able to tease the ball to Butt. A midfield scramble ensued; Effenberg was the loser and Beckham eyed up the free kick.

"For the last five minutes, the game's being played in one-third of the field," Willie said.

"Ryan Giggs. He's the key." Sir Matt surmised as his eyes swept over the pitch.

"True. He's getting in some delicious crosses but the final execution in the box is lacking."

"Remember what Tom said earlier about teams that have come back from one-nil down at half-time to win this trophy?" When Willie nodded Sir Matt continued. "Benfica did it in 1961/62, Inter Milan in 1962/63, Celtic in 1966/67 and Porto in 1986/87. If there's going to be one in the 90's then Manchester United *should* come back to win this."

"Of course they'll come back and win this."

"I *feel* they will. Everything is set up for this to be a historic night for United." The tone of Sir Matt's voice left the audience with little doubt he believed it was possible.

David Beckham took the corner quickly and Bayern Munich dealt with it, all their players back defending. Basler now had the ball at his feet outside United's penalty box. He tried to cut it back but was denied access, so made his way back to the halfway line.

Eddie nodded to the pitch. "That's not something you see often."

"I know. First, he's knocking on the door then he takes it back over the halfway line." Billy shook his head, confused.

"Yeah, that's because most of his teammates are still back there."

"They're leading one-nil so he has no need to try and score," Geoff said.

"Of course he does." Billy slid forward. "You get in a position like that and you at least make an attempt either by driving yourself forward into the box or crossing it."

"They're happy with the one goal. They're not even trying to score a second." Geoff believed this would be Bayern Munich's undoing.

"Teams should know by now that you can't let United have the slightest whiff at goal," Eddie remarked.

"A one nil lead is not sufficient to be sitting back on your laurels." Jackie counselled.

"United, to be fair, are not giving them many opportunities to do that."

"And here he goes again."

A stray ball by Matthäus found Giggs; in a déjà vu moment he ran down the wing and crossed the ball to Cole just outside the box. United fans behind the goal brought it to the attention of the referee, with derisory whistles, that Cole had been fouled by Matthäus.

Collina did not blow *his* whistle however and play continued; the ball made it as far as the head of Jaap Stam.

"Stam's header back to Schmeichel was almost delicate."

Roger laughed and turned to Dennis. "The idea of the word delicate being used in the same sentence as Stam *and* Schmeichel is funny but I know what you mean; after the earlier confusion between the two."

"He didn't need to put any pace on it so I suppose delicate is a good a word as any," Johnny said, his attention reverted back to the action on the pitch.

"Yeah, especially after he practically throws it across the halfway line to Giggs."

Tom Curry leant forward to join in the conversation. "Delicate or not Schmeichel needs to keep himself alert to danger in every second. If, like Kahn, possession is almost entirely in your half then your adrenaline levels are on high all the time. Schmeichel, even though United are one nil down has had very little to do."

Duncan turned to Tom Curry. "Do you mean switching off?"

"Yeah; I know he's not likely to do that, I'm just saying."

"Blathering you mean?" Bert added.

"Yeah, blathering."

Walter recognised the game and raised the stakes. "Spouting nonsense?"

"Yeah, spouting nonsense."

"Uttering…"

Tom Curry interrupted Jimmy and sat back. "Okay, enough."

Glory, glory Man United. Glory, glory Man United. Glory, glory Man United; as the Reds go marching on, on, on.

Manchester United looked for a way to gain parity. A rare foul by Giggs on Tarnat saw Collina blow his whistle. The result was a free kick that appeared to ping-pong between the players. It finally fell to Babbel who, unable to turn towards United's goal, was dispossessed by Johnsen for a Bayern throw-in.

Willie sat bolt upright. "Have you seen the time? Where's the time gone? They've only got half an hour!" His relaxed persona now vibrated with a sense of urgency.

Roger raised his eyebrows and sighed. "I know; the last fifteen minutes have just flown by."

"Giggs is having a blinder of a game on the right. It was a great decision by Alex Ferguson to switch it up that way." Geoff said.

"If it pays off, it will be seen as a great decision. If not…" Willie crossed his arms and his shrug finished his sentence.

Pierluigi Collina gave a yellow card to Effenberg for a sliding tackle on Giggs.

"He did get the ball," Mark noted but continued. "However, I'm not complaining."

A free kick close to the halfway line; Beckham looked for the right teammate and decided on Yorke. Out on the wing, Yorke delivered the ball back to Beckham on a forward run. Beckham distributed a long ball into Bayern Munich's box and, as Kahn knocked it down with both hands, he collided with one of his own players.

"Oops, a bit of a communication problem there," Billy said.

Eddie agreed. "Yeah, unfortunately, we couldn't capitalise on it."

"Bayern Munich are defending for all their worth."

"You're right. It's going to cause us problems; you know how much we're the kings of counter attacks."

"They're going to have to be clever and keep pecking away at that lock."

"Bayern Munich are capable of making mistakes. I know it's not huge but you've just seen Kahn collide with his own player."

"Every little counts."

Roger moved forward, elbows on his thighs. "Now Effenberg's on a yellow card maybe that could be utilised, you know?"

"He may start to play more cautious." Geoff contributed to the uncertainty of how United would breach the clinical defending of Bayern Munich.

The journalists' booth noted the tension that emanated from the Busby booth. Many of the general onlookers in the Bar had started conversations, albeit whispered, about other topics; minds on other things after realising the task before United.

Alf felt the odds were against United but would never say the words. He looked over at Eric's laptop. "This is United's last game of the season but Bayern Munich have another game still to play for their treble. Is that right? What's their media saying about their chances?"

Eric's sigh was long. "They were optimistic before kick-off and," he bounced his chin towards the pitch. "I can't see that attitude changing much now."

Archie looked up; a deep frown between his sharp eyes. He had just finished skimming an article in a redtop British newspaper; he stabbed at the keyboard with his finger, closing the page, "Some people are getting their knickers in a twist over this game; it's England against Germany in the eyes of some."

"It's an English team against a German team, of course." Henry pursed his lips; he knew the article that had riled Archie. "United have been hijacked by some neutrals but I expect they'll slink away *if* they lose."

"They've not progressed much, have they?"

"Down Below? Not so much, Tom, not so much."

Meanwhile, back in Barcelona, Kahn did his part to take seconds off the clock; his clearance fell to United. Neville brought the ball down and hit it long, down the wing.

After a weak effort by Bayern Munich to dispossess United, Giggs attempted a dummy and gifted the ball back to Bayern Munich. They retained possession for five seconds before a clinical interception by Stam saw United switch play into midfield.

"Most of our possession has been on that right side with Giggs. They should try switching it up a bit and use Blomqvist more."

David glanced up at Mark. "Don't forget Alex Ferguson switched Giggs so he didn't have to face Babel but…" He crossed his legs. "The fact Giggs is giving Bayern Munich such a torrid time I think he should stick with this formation."

"You're right although I'd like to see either Sheringham or Solskjaer make an appearance soon. You know; fresh legs and all that."

David agreed with Duncan's assessment. "Killer instincts too. Don't get me wrong Cole and Yorke have been great but it's just not happening for either of them tonight."

Jeremies crossed the ball to Basler and, as he inched forward, just inside United's half he saw Schmeichel off his line; he made an audacious attempt at goal. The ball took its time sailing over the crossbar but it did, much to the relief of Schmeichel, his teammates, and Alex Ferguson, to name a few.

"Which goalkeeper let one in like that?" Dennis asked after breathing a sigh of relief.

"I remember that; it wasn't a pretty sight for a goalkeeper." Jackie shook his head and smiled. "Who scored it? I can't remember."

"It was Nayim for Zaragoza in 1995, against Arsenal," Eddie said.

"Yeah right. Nayim was closer to goal though."

"There have been some crackers over the years."

Dennis smiled. "Beckham's against Wimbledon in 1996."

The replay of that goal flashed quickly through Jackie's mind's eye. "That is definitely up there in my top five best goals ever."

"It looks like Alex Ferguson heard you Duncan." Sir Matt pointed to the pitch. "I think Sheringham is coming on."

"Who's he going to take off?" Although Duncan spoke rhetorically, everyone thought of whose role had now finished for the season.

"Beckham took a bit of a knock early on in this half and he's not been in the game much since then." Jimmy knew this would be the substitution he would consider but he was all too aware he was *not* Alex Ferguson.

"No." Dennis laughed. "Beckham would probably sit down and refuse to come off if Alex Ferguson tried to sub him."

"True; he's got the ball now." Bert leant forward to pay close attention to Beckham's movement on and off the ball. "Let's see if he's struggling."

"Alex Ferguson won't allow sentimentality to cloud his judgement of who to substitute and when." Tom Curry crossed his arms and sat further down in the booth, unsure why he felt so off-kilter.

Oh Teddy, Teddy; Teddy, Teddy, Teddy, Teddy Sheringham. Oh Teddy, Teddy; Teddy, Teddy, Teddy, Teddy Sheringham.

Denis Irwin held the ball aloft, ready to launch a throw-in; Butt made himself available, took delivery and tapped it back. Irwin launched the ball forward, onto the run of Blomqvist. He was hotly pursued by Babbel who, although he tapped the ball out, Blomqvist was adjudged to have had the last touch by the only person who matters in those decisions, the referee.

Kahn launched a ball that saw Bayern Munich move towards the United penalty box. United's defence worked hard to prevent Jancker connecting with the ball on the edge of the eighteen-yard box.

Tommy glanced at the clock. "Twenty-five minutes." He clenched his fists and his jaw. "Come on, United; we can do this."

Gary Neville and Zickler leapt into the air; both intent on making contact; neither did. It fell to a gazelle-like Stam who played the ball to the feet of Beckham. He considered a cross but thought better of it and played it to the wing, hoping it would find Giggs.

Unfortunately, United were divested and Bayern Munich made their way back to the halfway line to regroup. Effenberg wanted to press forward. The ball reached Tarnat and his cross into United's eighteen-yard box, towards two of his teammates, found Jancker offside.

Donny massaged his neck. "They've been more attacking this second half." He felt traitorous for feeling that United should be grateful for the two trophies already won this season; his belief had started to ebb. He closed his laptop and decided to put his concentration into the match.

Peter Schmeichel urged his players forward as he looked for a beneficiary of his goal kick. Sheringham, on the touchline, had stripped down to his strip, eager to join the fray. United were now in Bayern Munich's half, determined to find a way to nirvana. A Beckham cross into the Bayern Munich box was intercepted and the ball went out of a corner.

"Blomqvist's making way for Sheringham." Willie applauded Alex Ferguson's decision.

"I'm not surprised really." Sir Matt turned to Willie. "Sheringham is taller and more physical than Blomqvist. It allows them more opportunity to switch up play from the right to the left now."

"He'll go centre midfield and maybe Beckham out to the right and Giggs back to the left. It's a shame Blomqvist didn't make the desired impact." Willie brought his hands together that started as a clap and morphed into the prayer position. "Let's see what oh, Teddy, Teddy can do."

The corner kick connected with the domed head of Stam who headed way over the crossbar; his face showed frustration and disappointment but he was quick to shake off those emotions.

A trilby hat appeared on Jimmy's head and as he took it off he said. "You've got to take your hat off to Alex Ferguson for his Giggs Blomqvist tactic."

Dennis ignored Jimmy's attempt at humour. "It was a brave decision to make, so let's see what happens now."

Kahn's long clearance fell into the path of Basler; he scanned the pitch for a teammate. Confident he'd found the best man for the job Basler hit a long ball towards the United goal, Zickler his intended target. The linesman's flag flew up and the whistle was blown; offside.

"Beckham's gone to the right and Giggs to the left." Billy nodded his approval of Alex Ferguson's decision.

"That's more like it," Eddie wriggled in his seat like an over-excited child.

The battle of the European giants continued in the middle third of the pitch as Tarnat intercepted a Neville ball to Beckham and kicked it out for a throw-in just inside Bayern Munich's half.

Johnny chuckled and nudged Jackie. "Neville's developed selective blindness with where the throw-in should *actually* have been taken."

"Good lad."

The customary long throw-in by Neville travelled over the edge of Bayern Munich's eighteen-yard box and found the head of Yorke. His flick to his right found his striking partner, close to the penalty spot. Cole, with his back towards goal, tried an overhead kick.

The movement saw Tommy lift off his seat, ready to make a celebratory leap into the air. "That would have been a spectacular goal if he'd connected with more power *and* it would have gone anywhere near the goal." He slumped back down and flung his arm around Mark's shoulders.

"Ifs and buts," said Mark. "He'll be disappointed, that's for sure."

"United have had so much possession." David shook his head as he looked at the clock. "Twenty minutes left. Twenty minutes to score at least one goal." He heard the pleading in his own voice.

"They've not lost this year." Duncan could not tear his eyes from the pitch; he leant his body sideways, towards David. "Trust me, they'll score, I can feel it."

Oliver Kahn, as was now common practice, took his time with the goal kick; the ball travelled as far as United's defence, whistling over the head of Jancker, Kahn's intended target.

Tom Curry jerked his head towards the Bayern Munich bench. "It looks like Hitzfeld is going to react to the Sheringham substitution."

Walter brought his attention back to the pitch. "Okay, yeah; Mehmet Scholl for Zickler." He had been distracted by the droves of souls leaving the Bar.

"Zickler looks exhausted."

"Scholl's fresh legs could be a problem for United but Bayern also have Sheringham to contend with."

"What they're going to do is have Babbel drop back into the right full-back position and Scholl will go in midfield." Bert sat back with a huge smile. "But's that just my opinion."

Jimmy rolled his shoulders back and moved his head from side to side. "Bayern have been more attacking this second half. United are going to have to be careful they don't get hit on the break."

Bayern Munich retained possession in midfield and seemed to grow in confidence; evidenced by an ambitious attempt at goal by Effenberg, twenty-five yards out.

Roger noted Bayern had been happy to hoof and hope rather than make any real attempt to pick apart United's defence. He ran his fingers over the studs on his boot. "The change in formation will give them a bit more confidence to be daring and go for goal rather than just sitting back."

"Thankfully, Effenberg was a little greedy. He had other options than to make such a long-range attempt at goal." Geoff sat upright, his elbows on the back of the booth. "If he'd been on target I don't think Schmeichel would have been able to save it."

"Matthäus looks exhausted." Willie was secretly impressed a man of Matthäus' age could continue to perform at this level. "I bet Hitzfeld makes another substitution soon."

A training ground move saw Yorke, on the edge of Bayern Munich's penalty box, feed the ball to Giggs, close to the wing. Unfortunately, Giggs passed the ball to where he assumed another United player would be but wasn't. Bayern Munich made a break.

David's hands covered his open mouth, his eyes wide. "He switched off."

Tarnat delivered a ball to the only Bayern Munich player in a forward position, Jancker. Twenty yards out, facing the centre of United's goal Jancker slid the ball to his left to Effenberg, who evaded Irwin and Stam and took a shot that required Schmeichel to make a finger-tip save.

Several souls in the Busby booth jumped up and wildly applauded the save and chose not to dwell on what led to it.

In the journalists' booth, George turned to Henry and grimaced who could only shrug in response. Nervous chatter broke out; everyone talked, no-one listened.

"That was an amazing save."

"You could almost see every sinew and muscle of his body stretch to make that save."

Basler wasted seconds as he arrived to take the corner. He cast his eyes around his teammates; the Bayern Munich supporters sensed blood and encouraged their team to go in for the kill. The corner kick was taken short to Tarnat; he and Basler played a one-two and Basler aimed for Scholl, in the centre of United's half. United pounced on the stray ball and raced towards the halfway line.

The roar from the United supporters in the Nou Camp were testament to the fact that they were not giving up on their team. Excitement in the Bar grew, it was palpable. Souls started to speak at once and moved closer to the pitch.

"This could be a game changer if Manchester United can capitalise on it."

"That's the second time Beckham has hit a ball to Sheringham and it's been too long."

"Hey, it looks Solskjaer is going to come on."

"That wasn't Beckham's fault. It looked like Teddy took his eye off the ball."

"He looks frustrated at Beckham."

"Well, it wasn't Beckham's fault."

The ball was back with Kahn and his clearance produced a Giggs foul on Scholl. Effenberg hovered over the ball, the seconds ticked down as he watched his teammates get into position.

His scrutiny over, he played a long ball that bounced ten yards from goal, a point where none of his teammates thought he would play it. The ball safely crossed the line for a Schmeichel goal-kick.

Duncan raised his eyebrows. "He'll kick himself for that wasted opportunity."

"Yeah, I've no idea who that was intended for." Sir Matt said. "Let's see what United can do with it now."

Schmeichel launched the ball over the halfway line where it eventually fell to Giggs who made his way into the penalty box; surrounded by three Bayern players. He lost possession.

The ball remained with Bayern Munich for a couple of seconds, when they crossed the halfway line United again retrieved the ball; they knew they had fifteen minutes to score and take the game to extra time.

"That's better," Willie spoke for everyone in the Bar.

For some of those who had come to watch the match as neutrals, time of death on the game was pronounced. Conversations unrelated to football could be heard, souls moved to look at the memorabilia, archangels giggled and pointed out certain match programmes and shirts, others had seen enough and left.

"I'm glad some of the neutrals have left." Swifty dropped his voice to just above a whisper. "They were making me a bit nervous."

George laughed. "It's the game that's making me nervous."

"We've got to keep the belief that they'll score."

Eddie started to sing and the chant was picked up by everyone.

We'll never die, we'll never die. We'll never die, we'll never die. We'll keep the Red Flag flying high, cos Man United will never die.

The nervousness that had, once again descended, almost visible, rose and disappeared into the ether and belief became the prominent emotion.

Eric caught the eye of Sir Matt, smiled and winked. "It's right Matt."

David Beckham tackled Matthäus on the halfway line. He caught him high and Matthäus dropped to the ground and, a helpful Beckham assisted him to his feet.

"That was a bit rash." Roger broke out a broad grin. "I imagine he'll feel that in the morning. He's no spring chicken is he?"

"He's thirty-eight; a bit old for a player these days."

"They're really controlling play here but Bayern are not letting them get at goal at all; frustrating, to say the least."

"Like I said earlier, they're going to sit back and defend for all their worth." Geoff's gaze took in the activity in front of United's bench and he liked what he saw. "It's going to take something extra special to get through that defensive wall."

"I think Alex Ferguson should think about bringing on Solskjaer now." Tommy's words were spoken, as though his words could travel Down Below and find the ear of the United manager.

Mark agreed. "Well, he's warmed up so I think it's only a matter of time."

Manchester United had possession and settled to move forward. Stam passed the ball to Neville on the wing; he found Yorke who appeared to be confused as to which direction he should face.

Yorke repositioned himself and the onward march continued as far as Butt who intended to cut it across into space, just outside Bayern's eighteen-yard box. Effenberg knew this and pounced on the gift and touched the ball into the path of Basler.

Billy's voice was high. "Wow. He's really running at United." A frown deepened, he sounded shocked. "They allowed him to cut into midfield."

Basler was still going; no United player deemed it prudent to halt his run.

Willie jumped to his feet and shouted. "Where's his man?"

Basler, having run almost the entire length of the pitch unchallenged, faced the United's net, on the edge of the eighteen-yard box; he now had backup and after all his hard work he left the ball for Scholl.

A collective gasp Down Below mirrored the gasp in Red Cloud Bar as Scholl's chip, from twenty yards out, seemed to fly in slow motion, hit the post and fall into the grateful hands of Schmeichel. A second of impenetrable silence followed.

"That was incredible." Donny dropped back down, stunned.

Tom Jackson shook his head. "Alex Ferguson needs to throw Solskjaer on and go for broke."

"Fink is coming on for Matthäus." Archie typed the words as he spoke but his mind was still on the lack of challenges made on Basler.

"I'm not surprised, it's been a high octave game and he's run himself ragged." Henry talked of Matthäus but his mind was on United's midfield. "Look at his face, he's exhausted."

Personal and private thoughts edged towards this match being one step too far for United but the words were not uttered. They knew ten minutes was sufficient time to change a game.

United continued to press forward and Butt kept alive a ball that was destined to go out and played it back across the front of Bayern Munich's goal. Attempts by Cole and Sheringham to reach it resulted in Bayern Munich stretching to defend. The golden opportunity had resulted in a corner.

Johnny rubbed his hands up and down his cheeks; he started to feel anxious. "I only hope they don't live to regret that."

"They've got a corner out of it." Eddie stood, his fists clenched and shouted. "Come on United, come on."

"Solskjaer's coming on. Who's he taking off; oh, it's Cole." Dennis was disappointed. He had envisaged both Cole and Yorke would add to their tally of goals for the season. Then he thought about it and realised the incisiveness of Solskjaer's play, especially from the bench, could be the secret ingredient United needed.

Jackie was more pragmatic. "I can't say I'm surprised. He's not had as much of a sniff of the ball in this second half."

"Fresh legs will help." Sir Matt, eyes affixed to the pitch, tilted his head back to speak to those behind him. "Even though they're young lads it's been a hard season and a tough ten days."

You are my Solskjaer, my only Solskjaer. You make me happy when skies are grey. Though Alan Shearer was so much dearer; please don't take my Solskjaer away.

Ole Gunnar Solskjaer ran onto the pitch in the eighty-first minute, in time for a corner. As the ball sailed towards the far post, Kuffour was there to head it away from the six-yard box.

It fell to United and they brought the ball back to the edge of the eighteen-yard box. A cross was delivered towards goal and Solskjaer appeared to twist his body around a defender to head the ball towards the net. It was gathered and smothered by Kahn.

"Kuffour, there again." Geoff was exasperated. "I reckon they should drug test the guy!"

Roger laughed. "I know; he's been phenomenal tonight."

Kahn's goal kick was returned to Bayern Munich's half by Schmeichel, with a bounce, it almost reached the eighteen-yard box. The ball remained in midfield and Bayern Munich kept possession, back to the halfway line to regroup and work out a way to put the game out of reach for United.

Effenberg slid the ball forward to Scholl who ran towards United's box and, twenty-yards out, fired a blistering shot at goal which was saved by the fingertips of a diving Schmeichel. He was livid with his defence.

Tommy dropped back down after jumping up to applaud Schmeichel's athleticism. "They shouldn't have allowed him to get that close." He turned to Mark then quickly returned his attention back to the pitch.

"Stam should have closed him down." Mark's body was folded over his thighs, his chin on his fists; his disappointment was evident to all.

The Bayern Munich supporters celebrated their corner as it was taken but it fell straight into the hands of Schmeichel. He didn't pause; he threw the ball out to Yorke on the left.

Yorke held up play and waited for his teammates to get into position, then switched play to Beckham, close to the centre circle.

Beckham noticed his psychic twin, Neville and brought him into the mix. Unfortunately, the ball was intercepted by Bayern Munich and United were on the retreat. Effenberg delivered a ball, from the centre of United's half of the pitch to Scholl, out on the right, who shimmied his way to the goal line, dogged by Irwin. The ball rebounded off Irwin; out for a corner.

"Scholl got what he wanted out of that; a corner and a chance to regroup." David slumped down in the booth and looked around at the now thinning crowd. His thought of not giving United his complete belief made him sit up straight.

Duncan nodded towards Schmeichel as he jabbed at his wrist. "He's not happy with Bayern Munich's time-wasting."

"Their fans are getting louder."

"They sense this is it."

Basler took the corner. It eventually bounced close to the penalty spot and a header by Scholl reached Jancker, his back to goal. Not to be deterred Jancker performed a bicycle kick; the ball ricocheted off the crossbar.

The air seemed to be sucked out of the Bar and back in, imperceptible to most except the archangels. United scrambled to get the ball away.

"I don't believe it." Willie looked about him and back to the pitch. "They've got six minutes and stoppage time to turn this around."

A pulsating energetic wave not seen but felt touched the United supporters in the Nou Camp. It rippled through the screens of every television screen of every United supporter watching. In the face of what was happening now, and what had happened over the last eighty-five minutes, conviction increased rather than decreased.

Belief in United did not transmute to Bayern Munich; they sensed the game was theirs. They were in the lead and were making more opportunities than United could handle.

Jancker was back in United's eighteen-yard box, trying to single-handedly go for glory but his progress was blocked by five defending United players. His attempt was not rewarded when Collina blew his whistle for a United free kick.

Peter Schmeichel made his way out with the ball and urged his teammates forward. He sent the ball long and to the right. Progress was denied when Collina, again, used his whistle to signal a foul. Kuffour took his time but the eventual free-kick fell to United, out on the wing.

"Settle down lads, settle down." Sir Matt whispered.

Gary Neville delivered a ball to the edge of Bayern Munich's eighteen-yard box where four Manchester United players waited, so was Kuffour who headed the ball clear. Bayern Munich had possession.

They crossed the halfway line and spread play to the wing; Giggs intercepted and paused for a split second to assess his best option forward. His best option was to pass back to Irwin and run into space.

"I think they've done an exceptional job this season but," Tom Curry whispered to Walter. "This is one game too many."

"I'm not sure. Those goalpost saves, as well as the couple from Schmeichel, must be frustrating for them; they've given a sliver of hope to United."

"There's still five minutes left on the clock. They've scored loads of last minutes goals and, you know." Bert shrugged. "Well, the last time they didn't score a goal was back in December. The odds are definitely in their favour to get one back."

"You've got to keep the faith, lads." Jimmy had overheard their conversation. "I know, let's have a little sing-song, to get the spirits up. Any requests?"

"How about, you say it best when you say nothing at all."

"I'm hurt Eddie, wounded in fact."

Stam, on the halfway line, drove the ball forward to Bayern's penalty box where Kuffour leapt on the back of Sheringham. It fell to Solskjaer and he backheeled the ball to Sheringham but he was unable to get any real purchase on it and Kahn threw his body on top.

David could only whisper. "With a little more power."

The twenty-five men, family, close friends and archangels were the only ones left in the Bar.

Possession was back with United. They were relentless in trying to forge a way through but every attempt in the eighteen-yard box seemed to lack something. Heads dropped when a golden opportunity fell to Yorke and he was unable to convert it into a goal.

A cloud of sadness wafted over the journalists' booth, not for them but for the booth opposite. The archangels giggled and the cloud disappeared.

"We can't get despondent guys, they've still got a couple of minutes," Alf said.

"It's not the time that's the factor here, I mean, look at Yorke just then. When have you seen him with two left feet? He had an open goal." George raked his fingers through his hair. "I'm not despondent, I'm just being realistic."

"Well, don't let them hear you," Swifty said as he nodded towards the Busby booth.

Duncan shivered. "Wow. Did you feel that?"

"You mean that *electricity*?" David felt it too.

"Me too." Sir Matt said quietly.

"Something's happening, something's going to happen. I can't sit still." Willie got to his feet and walked to the bar; he stood, looked at the pitch and then returned to his seat.

Down Below people felt the hairs on their arms stand to attention, stomachs rose and fell like tidal waves rising high into the air and crashing back down.

In the Nou Camp Jancker was in United's box penalty box; he tried to fight his way towards goal and glory, he smelt blood. The Bayern Munich supporters smelt it too. He was denied access by United's defence and as Schmeichel's clearance fell to Bayern Munich Collina blew for a United free kick.

Tommy shook his head and expelled his held breath. "We need this breathing space." He rubbed his chin vigorously. "That was pretty tense."

"Time's ticking away and it seems all of the chances are falling to Bayern," Mark said.

David was hunched forward, his chin on his fists. "Yeah, but they're not going in. They're not going in."

"This has got to be our year, it just has to be." Duncan's words were confident but hesitant.

"Nothing *has* to be son." Sir Matt turned to Duncan. "Don't worry Duncan everything will work out the way it should. If it's one step too far for Manchester United then it's one step too far. If this game doesn't come out in their favour then they will bounce back and try again."

"I know Boss, thanks."

Swifty shook his head in astonishment. "They are relentless."

"They've got to throw caution to the wind," Henry said.

"The danger then is that Bayern Munich could hit them on the counter-attack."

"Two minutes left on the clock."

Johnny stood up, for some reason he felt the need to stand and shake his legs and arms loose. "Kuffour's tired. They need to take advantage of that."

Jackie, in total contrast to Johnny, was sat with his chest on his thighs and his hands on his feet. "Yeah. But the chances we've had…"

No-one needed the sentence to be finished, they knew.

"Having Solskjaer on has made a huge difference, let's just see how much stoppage time there is. The fat lady's not singing yet." Jimmy leant forward and patted Sir Matt on the shoulder.

***

Hitzfeld, in the eighty-eighth minute, felt Basler should exit the field and revel in applause from half of the Nou Camp. Basler acknowledged the recognition and made way for Salihamidzic.

The journalists looked to the Busby booth and noted the rainbow orb had reappeared; it hovered over the booth and took on an iridescent glow. They were able to drag their attention back to the Nou Camp as United had a throw-in in Bayern Munich's half, in the ninetieth minute.

The fourth official held up a board; the game had three extra minutes to be played; unless United scored.

"It's been a great season; it really has." Willie linked arms with Sir Matt.

The throw-in reached Bayern's penalty box, it was defended but Beckham turned it back towards goal. Effenberg threw himself at the cross headed for the six-yard box and Manchester United had a corner.

Wide surprised eyes, open mouths and clasped heads greeted the sight of Schmeichel in Bayern Munich's penalty box.

"Please, please," Roger said.

The corner looked as though it was meant for Schmeichel as he rose to make contact but it was too high. It was loose, Bayern Munich, tried to clear. Yorke, on the edge of the six-yard box, tried to make clear contact.

Finke tried again to clear the ball. It fell to Giggs. Giggs, with his right foot, took a shot at goal; it was weak but it bounced.

Sheringham made contact and the ball rolled into the bottom left-hand corner of the net. He paused, turned, checked; no flag.

Screams, hugs, clenched fists punched the air, heads were thrown back as a roar escaped; pandemonium ensued. There were no giggles from the archangels, they were awe-struck. United supporters in the Nou Camp raised their roar to a deafening level.

"Yes, yes, oh yes."

"This is it. We can do it, come on."

"Come on United, come on United."

For the first time ever none of the Babes replicated the goal celebration.

The Bar became full again. The twenty-five men did not notice.

Bayern Munich looked shocked. Schmeichel made his way back to his net. The possibility of extra time was now on the cards.

The twenty-five instinctively placed their hands on their heart space, unsure where the pulsating feeling was coming from. They took their seats again and immediately got back up.

"It's not the prettiest goal they'll ever score but who cares, eh? Bring on extra time I say." Jimmy appeared to be the only one who could speak.

Ninety seconds remained. Bayern kicked off. The red smoke from the flares filled the Bar. Everyone stood and screamed encouragement as Solskjaer won a corner off Kuffour.

David Beckham swung the corner in, on ninety-two minutes and fifteen seconds. Sheringham got a head to it as it reached the six-yard box.

It dropped to Solskjaer. He stuck his foot out and the ball hit the roof of Bayern Munich's goal.

The archangels watched as the Bar erupted. They had not experienced anything like it.

For the first time, tears began to flow down cheeks. Tears of happiness as hugs followed on from the long drawn out word – yes.

The noise from Red Cloud Bar mirrored the noise from the Nou Camp.

Tommy, Mark and David held each other, unable to speak. Wide smiles and tears said more than words.

Sir Matt had his arms around Duncan and Billy. "They never gave up, did they?"

Eddie spoke. "Is this a dream?" He looked around. "No, it isn't." He slid along the floor as Solskjaer had just done and then replicated Schmeichel's cartwheel. He was mobbed.

The journalists stepped back and watched the Busby booth come together in a huddle. They did not disturb them. This was their moment.

In Estadio Nou Camp the seconds ticked down as the Bayern Munich players looked overwhelmed. They didn't understand what had happened. Kuffour and Jancker were distraught. This had been their game.

Seven seconds after the game resumed Pierluigi Collina blew the whistle to mark the end of the match and the start of United's celebrations.

"Incredible. I don't think I'll ever see anything like that again." Willie had clapped so hard his hands had a sensation of heat.

Sir Matt's attention was on two scenes; the rolling around of the Babes on the floor and the rolling around of the Manchester United squad and staff on the pitch at the Nou Camp. His hand shook as he brought his pipe to his lips. "They've done us proud. They came back..."

Willie grabbed him in a bear hug, his eyes glistened. "They showed what United are made of. Happy birthday Matt."

Champagne corks flew through the Bar. Shirts danced up above. Fists continued to punch the air. The archangels giggled.

Manchester United Football Club had won the UEFA Champions League Final; they had won the Treble. They won in an unbelievable way; with virtually the last kick of the game.

The Babes picked themselves up, cheeks hurting from smiles that stretched from ear to ear and started to sing.

Happy birthday to you, happy birthday to you, happy birthday dear Boss, happy birthday to you.

An image of Bobby Charlton celebrating at the Nou Camp flashed on the screen that replaced the pitch in the Bar.

Duncan whispered. "Have a great night chief."

CHAPTER NINE

The Omnipotent One *requested* the twenty-five come to the Bar to watch the homecoming parade; no-one else

"What did you do Eddie?" Jimmy was convinced sanctions would be imposed for whatever had transpired between the Babes the evening before.

A wide-eyed Eddie slapped both hands on his chest. "Me? Why me? I didn't do anything!" His mind skipped through the events of the night before and he continued. "Yeah, no, it's not anything I've done."

As captain, Roger decided he would take responsibility for any wrongs that may have occurred after Solskjaer's goal. Roger stood up. A flash of thought communicated between Sir Matt and Roger; Sir Matt smiled and nodded. "Okay son, do what you need to do."

"What did they get up to last night?" Alf checked his handwritten notes but was unable to find anything to merit this *call* from The Omnipotent One and snapped his notebook shut. "I haven't a clue."

Henry opened his mouth to speak but the rainbow orb appeared. Similar to schoolchildren horseplaying in the classroom everyone stopped talking, sat up straight, hands folded in their laps.

Did you enjoy last night?

David held up his palms. "We think so. We're sure we did. But we've been called here so we probably enjoyed ourselves a little bit too much."

Roger stepped in to save the rest from whatever David was falling into. "We did, thank you. And thank you again for everything you did for us last night."

You're welcome. For three hours you will go Down Below to participate in the celebrations.

Silence.

After several seconds Sir Matt stuttered. "We're going down?"

"What?"

"How?"

"I can't believe it!"

"Really?"

"Do we need special clothes?" Eddie received a clip around the head from Jimmy.

"Can we?"

"Can you do that?"

Geoff looked at David and shook his head. "Ermm, The Omnipotent One David."

"Oh, yeah, sorry."

You can stay together or go your separate ways but after three hours you will return. You will not interact with anyone.

Sir Matt glanced around to gauge the opinion of everyone. What he saw made him smile and he said. "Thank you. We'll stay together."

The Omnipotent One transformed the twenty-five men into orbs and they made their journey Down Below.

***

"Where are we going to start?" Mark asked.

Roger looked at Sir Matt and said. "Sale."

There were no arguments. The orbs appeared over the open-top bus as the trophies were taken onto the bus, followed by the squad, backroom staff and then Alex Ferguson.

"Don't get too close Duncan; we don't want you to burst your bubble." Eddie laughed.

The orbs circled all three trophies, swooped into the bus and around the heads of the team.

"Let's get over the supporters and feel what they're experiencing."

Sir Matt nodded his approval of Willie's suggestion and the orbs floated over the supporters shouting their adulation.

They travelled alongside the bus, occasionally switching from left to right, for the whole journey from Sale, along the A56 into the city centre.

When they reached Deansgate several orbs drifted high above the bus, astonished at the sheer number of people that lined the street.

"This will probably never happen again and I'm so happy to be part of it." Tommy had spoken for everyone.

The rest of the journey, towards the Manchester Evening News Arena, was spent in wonderment. Cameras clicked. Flags waved. People shouted their congratulations and love.

The twenty-five floated into the Arena and watched as Alex Ferguson received a hero's welcome carrying the European trophy to the stage.

Behind him were Keane and Schmeichel carrying the FA Cup and the Premier League trophy. The rest of the squad walked and acknowledged the applauding seventeen thousand people who had managed to purchase tickets.

The orbs swooped amongst the crowd. It had been an incredible season; a season that would stay in the hearts of many every United supporter who witnessed it. A season that will never be forgotten.

Some supporters that lined the streets, or were in the Arena, later looked at their photographs and noticed orbs in them.

THE END

Printed in Great Britain
by Amazon

63831157R00102